The Osprey and the Sea Wolf
The Battle of the Atlantic ~ 1942

Mark Scott Smith

Rolling Wave Books
ISBN 978-0-692-13342-2

This book is dedicated to my wife Holly, for innumerable hours spent with me in research, editing and inspiration.

Pilot/Copilot

Bombardier/nose gunner

Flight engineer/navigator

Radio operator/waist gunner

112823

North American B-25 medium bomber

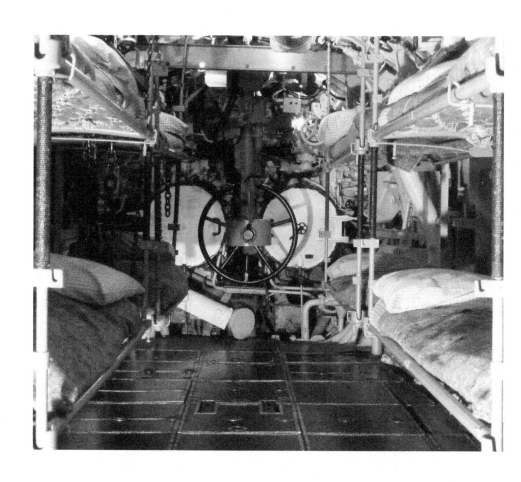

Type IX U-Boat aft crew bunks and torpedo tubes

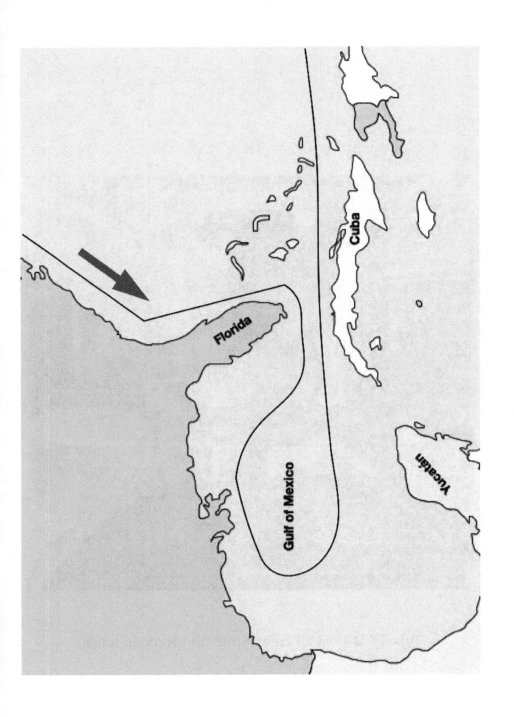

U-Boat patrols 1942

If you know the enemy and know yourself,
you need not fear the results of a hundred battles.
- Sun Tzu, The Art of War

PROLOGUE

Following World War I, fervent isolationism resulted in drastic cuts in America's military funding. Under-manned, under-equipped and inexperienced in modern warfare techniques, America's military was ill-prepared for WWII. In marked contrast, Imperial Japan and Nazi Germany, already at war for several years, had honed extremely effective and experienced war machines.

After the Japanese attack against Pearl Harbor on December 7, 1941, fear of invasion was palpable on the U.S. mainland. As a handful of long-range Japanese submarines prowled the waters from Washington to California, jittery Army Air Force pilots patrolling America's West Coast misidentified tree trunks, derelict vessels or even whales as Japanese submarines.

Soon, however, it became apparent that the major threat was not along the West Coast, but on the Eastern Seaboard where merchant ships carried desperately-needed war supplies for a besieged Great Britain. Shortly after Christmas 1941, long-range German U-Boats were dispatched to the East Coast of North America with instructions to sink any merchant ship they encountered. Over the next year, more than 300 Allied ships and 5000 men were sent to the bottom off the East coast of America, the Gulf of Mexico and the Caribbean Sea.

Chapter One
Bombs Away

With a new submarine attack today on an American freighter in sight of the California coast, the number of such attacks in the Pacific in the last few days rose to at least four.

New York Times
December 23, 1941

40 NAUTICAL MILES OFF THE OREGON COAST
— December 23, 1941

Ramon's headphones crackled and hissed. Then Angelo's voice, higher-pitched than usual, clicked in from the nose of the roaring B-25. "Pilot, bombardier. Did you see that? I'm sure it was a sub! Can you come around again?"

Barreling over the ocean at 200 miles per hour, Ramón caught a glimpse of something dark and narrow through a break in the clouds. An electric sensation surged through his chest as he switched on the intercom and spoke to the stocky, young man on his right. "Copilot, pilot. What do you think?"

The copilot Erik drew his eyebrows together. "Couldn't make it out, Ray."

Ramón tightened his grip on the steering yoke, his mind racing. Since the attack on Pearl, everyone was all nerves. Jap subs were being reported all over the place. This was probably just an unreported derelict, tree trunk or even a whale. But damn. Angelo was an excellent observer and, from the nose bubble, he had the best view. Better give it a shot.

With the thundering roar of twin 1700-horsepower engines muffled to a low-pitched growl by his headphones, Ramón moved his hands and feet in synch with his powerful medium attack bomber the crew had named Sizzling Rita. Executing a series of precise turns, he reversed course and began to sweep the area again.

"Pilot, bombardier," Angelo broke in. "I'm sure I spotted a conning tower."

In narrow sun breaks flashing between billowing clouds, the target was intermittently visible dead ahead. Ramón dropped to 150 feet above the water. Pulse racing now, he looked at Erik who only shook his head. Definitive I.D. wasn't possible. But this was no time for indecision. "Bombardier, pilot. Approaching target. Open bomb bay doors."

The doors sprang open with a jolt that sent a shiver through the cockpit. As Rita tugged a bit off course, trying to point her nose downward, Ramón trimmed the controls with firm but gentle pressure on the steering yoke and rudder pedal. With an eye on the altimeter, he squinted through layers of fog blanketing the target. If it was a Jap he'd be crash diving. This run was the only chance to nail him. "Bombs away."

"Bombs away," Angelo confirmed and released two 300-pound demolition bombs over the hazy, gray silhouette below.

The first bomb splashed short, but the second was right on target. *Whumpf!* A shock wave buffeted the cockpit, flinging the Virgen de Guadalupe medallion looped around the emergency bomb release lever back and forth wildly.

"Hoopty-doo! We pasted her right on the conning tower!" Angelo bellowed.

Erik clicked in. "Pilot, copilot, I'm not so sure it's a sub. You?"

By the time Ramón came around again, fog had completely obscured the target. He climbed to 500 feet and circled for half an hour, scrutinizing occasional cloud breaks like an osprey on the hunt. With no oil slick nor wreckage spotted on the water, Erik reported a possible submarine strike to the Coast Guard and Bomber Command, and Ramón set a course back to McChord Army Air Field in Tacoma.

High above the serpentine Columbia River, Ramón scanned the instrument panel. Everything copacetic. Usual high-frequency vibration of Rita's fuselage. And the familiar odor of avgas mixed with hydraulic fluid, oil, sweat and leather that always pervaded the cockpit.

Although she'd initially challenged him, Ramón loved flying Rita. Once he'd mastered the compensatory moves required to counter her capricious changes in airspeed, altitude, and weight distribution, they danced together like secret lovers.

Over Longview Washington, he turned north between the Olympic and Cascade mountain ranges. The eastern sky above the soaring, snow-capped peaks of Mount Rainier and Mount Adams was a stunning cerulean blue in the fading winter sun. Ramón relaxed his shoulders, but his brow was still quite wrinkled. He couldn't let go of this incident easily. Neither he nor Erik were ever convinced it was a Jap submarine. So why the hell did he drop two bombs? Was it confidence in Angelo? Or was it just his own aggressive nature again? He'd always been quick to act. And maybe that wasn't such a good thing.

A dazzling ray of sunlight burst through a break in the clouds, danced along a wingtip and disappeared. Ramón took a slug of bitter coffee from his thermos and tried to shake the dark mood permeating his mind like icy fog rolling in from the sea. Only a couple of weeks into the war, America was really in the soup. The Japs were steamrolling all over the Pacific. Wake Island. Guam. The Philippines. Back home everyone was on high alert. Boy scouts and grandmothers were being trained to spot enemy aircraft. And vigilant Coast Guardsmen with sinewy German shepherds patrolled the beaches.

Despite all the bugaboo, he knew logistics made an actual Japanese invasion of the mainland unlikely. But one thing was certain. Long-range Jap subs, prowling the coast from Los Angeles to the Strait of Juan de Fuca, had sunk six unescorted merchant ships in the past week.

What were the odds of spotting Jap subs on a six-hour antisubmarine warfare (ASW) patrol down the coast? Peanuts. And for Chrissake! He'd just dropped two bombs on something he could hardly see. Major Anderson would certainly be busting his chops over this one.

Shortly after landing, Rita's crew was summoned to a drafty, corrugated Quonset hut for a special debriefing by Colonel Rushing, the balding wing commander, and their own squadron leader Major Floyd Anderson. Tall and steely-eyed, Major Anderson exuded the aura of the Texas military school

4

graduate he was—strict regulation all the way and not much room for Mexican-American Tejanos. Ramón had trouble with him from the start.

Colonel Rushing ignored Ramón and spoke directly to Major Anderson. "I'm surprised at you, Anderson. Why the hell did you report an attack on a submarine when all you had was a possible encounter?"

Ramón clenched his jaw. This could not end well.

"It was radioed in as a submarine, sir," Major Anderson replied.

Colonel Rushing shuffled some papers on the desk and held up a communications transcript. "Not by this log, Major. 'Possible.' It says possible." He glanced at Ramón. "Is that how you reported it, Lieutenant?"

"Yes, sir," Ramón said, releasing the tension in his jaw.

The remainder of the debriefing was thorough but relatively benign. Given poor visibility and the short window of opportunity to attack a submerging submarine, Colonel Rushing decided the pilot and crew had reacted in a reasonable manner. Nevertheless, despite the bombardier's conviction, he found no evidence to support the sinking of a Japanese submarine. Bomber Command did not ratify the presumptive attack and the matter was closed. Almost.

Later, alone with Ramón in his office, a red-faced Major Anderson, slapped the report down on his desk. "What the hell is this crap, Morales? Trying to make me look like a goddam fool? Jesus. You report a sub attack, then waffle about it."

Ramón remained silent. How many times would he have to take this bullshit from Anglos? He planted his feet wider and gazed into the Major's eyes.

Major Anderson leaned across his desk. "You and that wop bombardier of yours make quite a pair. What'll you come up with next?"

Ramón stiffened, but didn't bite. "The I.D. was uncertain, sir. My bombardier had a better view than I did. I trusted his judgment."

"Enough to drop a couple of bombs on an unknown object? What is wrong with you people?"

Like pent-up steam released from a locomotive's boiler, white heat surged into Ramón's chest and arms. He clenched his fists, then released the muscle tension. You can't win this one.

Major Anderson narrowed his eyes and frowned. "All right. That's all. Dismissed."

Ramón saluted and left the room. Halfway down the corridor, his fist exploded against the corrugated steel wall.

Chapter Two
Heiligabend

In this third war Christmas, we celebrate more spartanly and more modestly than before, but we are protected and guarded against the threats of our enemies...At a later Christmas, we will look back on this Christmas Eve. In the fond light of memory, none of us will wish we had missed it. All the dead of the war will stand as shining heroes before our eyes, those who gave their lives to win a better life for their nation.

Joseph Goebbels
Deutschlandsender Radio Address
December 24, 1941

200 NAUTICAL MILES WEST OF LORIENT, France
— December 24, 1941

On Christmas Eve, *Kapitänleutnant* Rainer Hartmann, a tall, lean man in a warm leather jacket, stood on the bridge of an Untersee Boot in a rolling sea. Cruising at a comfortable twelve knots, the U-023, a type IX U-Boat with the image of a snarling wolf leaping out of the ocean painted on its conning tower, was crossing the Bay of Biscay on a course set for North America. Four lookouts, each systematically scanning a 90-

degree quadrant of the horizon, flanked Rainer and his first watch officer *Oberleutnant zur See* Anton Jäger. Brave, intelligent and resourceful, the stocky Bavarian had been with Rainer on all four of his previous war patrols.

Relishing respite from the foul atmosphere below decks, Rainer filled his lungs with cold ocean air. Crew comfort received a low priority on a long mission. Rationed strictly for drinking, fresh water use was not permitted for bathing, shaving or washing clothes. Although a special saltwater soap was issued, it was rarely used because it left a sticky residue on the skin. Many crewmen doused themselves regularly with 4711 eau de Cologne.

As Jäger and the lookouts scanned the horizon, Rainer trained his Zeiss binoculars on a pale-blue constellation in the North Atlantic sky. The Pleiades. How Anneliese loved that constellation. Only a week ago at the Christkindlmarkt in the snowy, medieval center of Lübeck, his fingers probed inside her mitten for the warmth of her palm. In front of the Lutheran Marienkirche, with the children distracted by dancing marionettes, he swept her into his arms and kissed her fiercely. The taste of almond and honey from the Marzipan angel he'd bought her lingered on his lips.

Rainer lowered the binoculars and exhaled slowly, watching the white vapor dissipate a few centimeters from his face. He missed his family, but it was good to be at sea again. Growing up in the port city of Lübeck, he'd always loved the water. After graduation from the Gymnasium he joined the Kriegsmarine and sailed around the world as a naval cadet. After six years as a junior officer on a battleship and a cruiser, he was selected for submarine training. Now a veteran of four

U-boat patrols in the North Atlantic, he'd survived three depth charge attacks and sunk six Allied merchant ships and a destroyer. But this mission would be different. By all reports, the Amis were unprepared. And that, he knew from experience with the Englander, made all the difference.

Since the fall of France in June 1940, Rainer no longer had to traverse the dangerous waters of the North Sea and English Channel to reach his hunting grounds. The French port of Lorient provided direct access to the North Atlantic during a time when the enemy was unprepared. Hampered by lack of radar, high-frequency direction finders and coordinated tactics, early British ASW efforts were relatively ineffective. From June 1940 to July 1941, 270 Allied merchant vessels were sunk. Although 21 U-boats were lost that year, German submariners called it the happy time—-Die glückliche Zeit. But as British equipment and tactics evolved, the happy time was replaced by a darker reality. The cost of sinking 133 Allied ships over the past six months had been 23 U-boats.

Two weeks after Germany's declaration of war against the United States, *Grossadmiral* Karl Dönitz, known to his men as der Löwe (the lion), launched *Unternehmen Paukenschlag* (Operation Drumbeat). The U-023 and four other long-range U-boats were sailing from their bases on the coast of France with orders to attack any large Allied merchant or warship off the east coast of North America. Rainer was optimistic. If the Amis were truly unprepared, might this become a second happy time?

The navigator *Obersteuermann* Rolf Vogel and Chief Petty Officer *Oberbootsmann* Georg Weber ascended the ladder from the conning tower below to relieve Rainer and Jäger on the bridge. Rainer looked at his watch. 1800 hours. Halfway through the dogwatch and time for dinner. "Let's see if the *Glühwein* is still warm, Jäger."

Midway down the ladder from the bridge into the control room, a clear tenor voice resonated from deep within the submarine.

Es ist ein Ros' entsprungen aus einer Wurzel zart.
(Lo, how a rose e'er blooming, from tender stem hath sprung).

"That's Engel," Jäger said, referring to a young torpedo man from Rostock with an angelic surname.

"Nice voice. He lives up to his name, nicht wahr?" Rainer said, stepping onto the control room floor which rose up to meet him as they rolled over a moderate swell. "Tell me, Jäger. What do you think of the crew's morale?"

Jäger brushed aside a string of sausages hanging from the control room ceiling. "I'm sure the men would rather be home on Christmas eve, *Herr Kaleun*," he said, using the abbreviation for Kapitänleutnant. "Other than that, I think their spirits are high."

"Sehr gut. High-spirited men make good hunters. And there should be many opportunities on this patrol now that *der Löwe* has given us free rein."

"Ja wohl, Herr Kaleun. Unrestricted hunting at last." Jäger stepped aside, allowing Rainer to lead the way through the narrow passage from the control room to the officers' quarters.

Forward of the radio room and Rainer's tiny quarters, the upper berths on either side of the ward room were folded up.

12

A table, covered with white linen, was placed between the lower berths, which served as benches. In the center of the table, four red candles set in a circular *Adventskranz* of pine branches, burned brightly. Rainer savored the refreshing scent of pine needles. Below deck, the odors of diesel fuel, cooking oil, unwashed bodies and cigarette smoke permeated the air, leaving a greasy coat on every surface.

Two officers with glasses of warm, red Glühwein in their hands, stood up from the table. "*Zum wohl*, Herr Kaleun," the dark and balding Lead Engineer Viktor Rademaker said. In the U-Boat service longer than Rainer, Rademaker was responsible for the operation and maintenance of all systems. After three patrols with the man, Rainer knew he could rely on his lead engineer's skill and knowledge. Rademaker knew how to improvise in an emergency.

The other officer, *Leutnant zur See* Gerhard Wolf, was young, blonde and an earnest admirer of the Führer. Responsible for the deck gun and the radio crew, Wolf was on his first combat mission. Although Rainer, like many officers in the Kriegsmarine, had little enthusiasm for Nazi rhetoric, he didn't mind Wolf. He just seemed young and naïve.

Rademaker raised his glass in a toast. "*Frohe Heiligabend*, Herr Kaleun."

"*Frohes Fest,* Herr Kaleun," Wolf said.

Rainer gestured toward the Adventskranz wreath. "Did Sankt Nikolaus bring that, or was it the *Weinachtsmann*?"

"It would be the *Christkind* where I grew up," Rademaker said.

"Of course these are all just Aryan traditions," Wolf said. "Christmas as the winter solstice and the swastika as the sun."

"I guess that's what schoolchildren learn about Christmas these days," Rainer said. "But when my children ask, I tell them it's about the birth of Jesus."

Rademaker raised his glass. "To the Christkind."

Rainer and Jäger clinked their glasses with Rademaker. Wolf merely smiled.

The galley cook laid dishes of pork *schweinebraten*, red cabbage and potato dumpling *knödeln* on the table.

"Mein Gott, Fischer," Rainer said. "A true Christmas feast. I'm proud to have a master chef under my command."

The cook blushed. "Danke schön, Herr Kaleun. I also made Stollen for dessert."

Jäger clapped his hands. "Fruitcake! Bravo, Fisher."

Rainer raised his glass. "To a successful hunt." He smiled. "And frohe Heiligabend."

Chapter Three
Got Your Six

There is better than an even chance for a Japanese air raid on Seattle tonight, Police Chief Herbert D. Kimsey predicted today, demanding that Seattleites celebrate the quietest New Year's Eve in their memory.

Seattle Times
December 31, 1941

McCHORD ARMY AIRFIELD, TACOMA, Washington — December 31, 1941

In the late afternoon, with the winter sun sailing low on the horizon, towering Mount Rainier sparkled like a shaved-ice snow cone. Unusually cold and clear for a Northwest winter day, the temperature had only reached the mid-teens. Ribbons of ruby-red sunlight glinted off the lower reaches of the Puget Sound as Ramón began the descent toward McChord Airfield.

Erik read the landing checklist aloud, pausing for Ramón to assess the appropriate dial or switch on the instrument panel. Antenna? Retracted. Wing de-icers? Off. Heaters? Off. Autopilot? Off. Fuel pressure? Six. Fuel levels? Main 50.

Booster pumps? On. Transfer pumps? Off. Mixture? Full rich. Carburetor heat? Normal. Propellers? 2400 RPM. Landing gear? Down.

While Erik checked with the tower for final landing instructions, Ramón scanned more than thirty toggle switches and gauges arrayed before him like pieces on a semi-circular chess board. With all instruments in the green, he adjusted the power settings on the center pedestal to maintain an airspeed of 150 miles per hour, about right for the initial approach to the field.

"Pilot, copilot," Erik spoke over the intercom. "Tower says there's a west crosswind at ten."

"Roger. Better adjust our landing speed upwards a bit. Want to take her in?"

Erik smiled and assumed control. Checking his distance from the field, altitude, approach speed and angle, he set up the base leg and rolled out of a turn onto his final approach. When fully aligned with the center of the landing strip, he lowered the flaps and dropped Rita's nose, aiming at a point short of the runway.

Ramón checked the airspeed indicator. Whoa! 135 mph. Erik was coming in too fast. Sure, the crosswind required a little more juice, but you still wanted to land as close as possible to the stalling speed of 100 mph. Keeping silent might help Erik learn from his own mistakes. But Jesus. This was way too fast. "You're coming in pretty hot, Erik."

Beads of sweat formed on Erik's forehead as he struggled with the controls that always stiffened with a sudden change in altitude and speed. Adjusting the elevator trim tab, he backed off the throttle just a little too late and Rita raced over the runway threshold at 130 mph.

Thump! The main landing gear hit the concrete with an intense shudder that convulsed the cabin and sent Rita bouncing like a beach ball ten feet into the air. With his sense of time radically slowed, Ramón watched Erik try to regain control over Rita, who, in time-lapsed frames, was floating eerily up and down several feet above the runway.

Trying to plant the landing gear, Erik pulled back mightily on the yoke. Ramón could see by the tension in his arms and face that Erik was using far too much force. He braced himself—a deep stall could mean a nose-first crash. "Forward, Erik!" He shouted. "Ease the yoke forward!"

Erik lightened pressure on the yoke and Rita slowly settled down, allowing the main gear to meet the concrete with a gentle *whump*. Ramón kept silent as Erik used up a lot of runway before Rita's airspeed dissipated enough to turn onto a taxiway.

With a deep sigh, Erik set the brakes and opened the bomb bay doors. After a full-throttle blast to prevent backfiring, he cut the ignition and waited for the propellers to stop turning.

Exhaust fumes, their aroma oddly agreeable to him, lingered in Ramón's nostrils as he watched the left prop spin down. At first a gray whir. Then myriad flashing steel arms, gradually slowing, finally becoming three motionless blades. After six hours of the B-25's notorious engine roar, he welcomed the relative silence of the subtle, high-pitched ringing sound that always remained in his ears.

While the ground crew chocked the wheels, Erik and Ramón ran their final checklist. Parking brakes released. Trim tabs set to zero. Switches and radios all off. Controls locked.

Erik rubbed the back of his neck. "Jesus, Ray. Sorry I screwed up the landing. I just came in too..."

Ramón cut him off with a wave of his hand. "Forget it, buddy. It happens to all of us sometime." He removed a leather glove and lifted the Virgen de Guadalupe medallion off the emergency bomb release lever. Patting it in his palm, he looked obliquely at Erik. "Saved your ass, didn't she?"

Erik cracked a smile. "Maybe so, Ray. Guess she's better than a pair of dice hanging up there."

Ramón clapped Erik on the back as they headed out the escape hatch. "Glad we're both OK with that, amigo."

As Ramón, Erik and Angelo exited up front, the flight engineer/navigator Roy and the radioman/waist gunner Vernon swung down from Rita's rear hatch.

"Had me worried for a minute, Skip. Up there in the nose," the bombardier Angelo said to Ramón with a slow smile spreading across his rugged, swarthy face.

"Sorry Angie," Erik said, shaking his head. "I brought her in. It won't happen again."

Roy and Vernon crowded in and each crew member made a point of touching Erik with a back slap or a nudge. Then, without another word, they walked to the Base Operations Center for debriefing.

Major Anderson and his crew, returning from the northern ASW route, approached as Ramón's crew was entering Base Ops. Everyone was tired. Not much of the usual wisecracking. Just one gibe rang out across the concrete surface.

"Came in a bit hot, eh Morales?" Major Anderson said.

"Yeah, it happens sometimes, Major," Ramón responded without breaking his stride.

Erik started to turn, but Ramón tugged on his sleeve and muttered. "Don't give that bastard any more ammunition."

Inside Base Ops, Erik pulled Ramón aside. "You don't have to cover for me, Ray."

Ramón narrowed his eyes. "Look, Erik. I've got your six."

"I know you've always got my back, Ray. But you shouldn't take the heat for this."

"Listen. It's my ass he's after." Ramón paused, a devilish twinkle in his eye. "And I'm up for the game."

The debriefing for Sizzling Rita's uneventful ASW patrol was swift. Ramón was pleased. He'd have time for a nap before the New Year's Eve party at McChord.

Chapter Four
Violet

The Navy reluctantly closed today its chapter of exploits at Wake Island, which is now assumed lost to the Japanese, by revealing that 378 Marines, assisted by seven members of Naval medical personnel, held off Japanese attacks by sea, air and land for fourteen days before radio silence signaled the end of their vigil.

New York Times
December 24, 1941

McCHORD ARMY AIRFIELD, TACOMA, Washington
— December 31, 1941

Shortly before 10 PM at the McChord Field guard house, Ramón was unable to roll down the frozen driver's window of the 1932 Ford sedan. A sentry, bundled up like a fur trapper in a wool-lined Mackinaw, and armed with an M1 Garand rifle, stepped in front of the car. Acknowledging the guard with a nod of his head, Ramón rotated the silver window crank back and forth until he broke the icy bond between the glass pane and its weather seal.

When he finally rolled down the window, silver clouds of condensed breath and cigarette smoke from his housemates, Erik, Andy and Lloyd streamed over the young sentry like a moonlit river. After careful review of their ID cards with his flashlight, the sentry stepped back with a crisp salute. "Happy New Year, sirs," he said and waved them on through.

The amigos, as the housemates liked to call themselves, had been friends since pilot training in San Antonio. Now, stationed together at McChord Army Airfield on the perimeter of stately Fort Lewis, they lived together in a small lakeside bungalow, a stone's throw from the field. Flying six-hour ASW patrols six days a week with the seventh-day on-call, they had little interaction with the infantrymen stationed at the fort next door. Most of their personal lives centered around the bungalow and whatever nightlife they could find in Tacoma, a grimy port city built on tide flats south of Seattle. The malodorous emissions of the city's paper mills and refineries were known throughout the Puget Sound as the aroma of Tacoma. Entertainment options for the amigos were limited—movies, smoky bars packed with military men, waterfront prostitutes or clean-cut USO girls.

Walking to work at the airfield was no problem, but downtown Tacoma was a bit too far. So, determined to make the best of their winter assignment in the rainy Puget Sound, the amigos pooled their resources and bought a 4-cylinder model B Ford to get them around town.

Ramón shifted into first gear and drove onto the post. Turning down a narrow, dark street, he cruised slowly in second gear past row on row of whitewashed, rectangular buildings and corrugated-steel Quonset huts. Jeez. Why didn't McChord have classy architecture like Fort Lewis? With war clouds looming, did they just slap this all together? What happened to craftsmanship?

Orange light glimmered through frosted windowpanes on the lower floor as the amigos walked toward the entrance of the Officer's Club. Ramón brushed a fingertip across the frozen, emerald-green leaf of one of the drooping rhododendrons lining the sidewalk. Quite smart. Folded inward like someone's tongue about to whistle. This plant knew how to adapt to the frigid night air.

The languid notes of Glenn Miller's *Moonlight Serenade* drifted on a silvery cloud flowing over the transom, cracked open above the entrance. When Ramón opened the door to the club, a blast of warm air, suffused with the odors of alcohol, sweat and cigarettes, washed over his icy cheeks with an oddly-pleasant sensation, like a slice of jalapeño gliding across his tongue. Beneath paper lanterns and crêpe streamers, hanging at odd intervals from the ceiling, Ramón surveyed the packed ballroom floor. Maybe 150 people. Quite a few really, considering all the holiday furloughs granted this week.

"Evening, sirs," a sergeant receptionist said crisply. "Please check your coats and hats at the bottom of the stairway."

Like a herd of spirited, young stallions, the amigos clomped down the steep, winding staircase to the coat racks. Ramón slipped into the men's room, splashed cold water on his face and carefully re-parted his thick, black hair. Straightening the pilot's wings on his lapel, he stepped back, raised an eyebrow and flashed his best Clark Gable smile at the mirror. Not bad. A large whiskey at home had taken the

25

edge off without a sign. Everything jake. Time to join the others in search of their training buddy Frank, the fifth amigo.

As they wove their way through the ballroom, Ramón nodded respectfully at a table of senior officers that included his hostile squadron leader Major Floyd Anderson and his beautiful wife Violet. Boy! Did she add some shine to her surly husband. Deep blue eyes, silky skin and a luscious figure. Tonight in a low-cut evening gown, she was simply a knockout.

He'd first met Violet last summer at an officer's party when, ignored by her husband, she stepped onto the garden patio where Ramón was having a smoke. He offered her a Lucky and they chatted. Although their conversation was brief, the feeling was palpable like the electricity in the air after a sudden, unexpected summer storm. They ran into each other again in the fall on a forest trail around Lake Steilacoom. Surrounded by fallen, dark-red oak leaves, they sat on a moss-covered log and talked for almost an hour. She seemed unhappy and restless. Receptive to his attention. When she left, she kissed him lightly on the cheek.

With a deliberately-casual glance, Ramón walked slowly past Violet's table. Turning her face toward him for a moment, she launched a cascade of lustrous, auburn hair across her bare shoulders. Ramón had to catch his breath. Jeez, what a doll. Walking on, he looked back over his shoulder. Their eyes locked for a tantalizing moment, then quickly turned away. No one seemed to notice their silent connection.

Pearly clouds of smoke floated above the ballroom, curling like wispy phantasms into the yellow beams of light that streamed from the rafters. Ramón moved through the room with a feeling of detachment. He really didn't like big parties. Too many people in one place. Odor of champagne and stale beer everywhere. But seeing Violet made tonight worthwhile. She was really a dreamboat.

Following Lloyd's lead, they soon found their fifth amigo Frank ensconced with his wife Wendy in their usual corner near the bar. Six foot two and 225 pounds, the former All-American quarterback from Michigan State was one of the first to befriend Ramón at Advanced Flight Training school in San Antonio. No grandstander, Frank worked hard and usually opted out of late-night barhopping with the amigos in favor of writing letters to his high school sweetheart. Frank got married immediately after graduation—all the amigos were there.

Corralling a few chairs, they all sat down together. Soon Erik, Lloyd and Frank were talking about football, while Andy and Wendy discussed recent events in the war. Although he smiled and nodded appropriately, Ramón's mind was elsewhere. As the conversation rolled on, he leaned back and quietly allowed the warm wave of camaraderie to co-mingle with the foggy chill in his heart. He closed his eyes briefly. It was good to be surrounded by friends on New Year's Eve. Especially lately, with things not going so well.

Lloyd leaned over. "What's up, Ray? You look a little down in the dumps."

Ramón sat up straight and forced a smile. Although an eager beaver when it came to all the military bullshit, Lloyd was basically a nice guy. "I'm OK, Lloyd. Just thinking."

"Lot to think about, isn't there?" Lloyd said. "Fucking Japs sinking ships right under our nose. Practically daring us to stop them, for Chrissake!"

Ramón frowned and leaned forward. "You're right, buddy. This is nuts. No radar. No depth charges. How the hell are we supposed to catch a sub?"

Lloyd slapped his knee. "I've had it with this horse shit, Ray. I'm itching for some real action."

"You and me both, Lloyd," Ramón said, his voice unexpectedly choking up as the wave of sorrow, he'd been unable to shake in the past week, washed over him again.

Lloyd pulled back. "Hey. You OK, Ray?"

"Yeah. Just got some bad news, is all. An old friend was at Wake Island."

"Oh Christ. I'm sorry, buddy. One of the Marines?"

Ramón nodded. "Angel. We grew up together. He went into the spinach fields when I went on to high school. But we stayed friends. He was always there for me when I needed him."

"Shit, Ray. I'm sorry. I was hoping those guys could hold out. But I guess in the end it was surrender or die, huh?"

"Yeah. And I'll bet Angel chose to die like a Marine."

Andy, a wiry University of Washington graduate from Seattle, stood and raised his glass. "Cheers, amigos!"

They all stood and clinked their glasses together "Cheers!"

"Did you see that Husky basketball score last night?" Andy said. "Trounced NYU 74 to 35. What a humdinger!"

"Jeez. Sounds like they were on fire!" Frank said.

Andy slapped Frank on the back. "Speaking of red hot, tell us. What's up with your recruitment?"

Everyone huddled around Frank.

"Gonna be a Superbomber, Frank?" Lloyd asked.

Frank put his muscular arms around Andy and Lloyd, pulling them close. "Keep it down guys, will you? Nothing's signed in blood yet."

"But?" Erik said, raising an eyebrow.

Frank smiled broadly and lowered his voice. "It looks like I'll be going back and forth between Tacoma and Spokane for work and football."

"Hell, the only work they want out of you is running and passing," Ramón said. "What'll you be doing when you're not playing ball?"

"Teaching pilots how to fly a frigging B-25."

"Not bad," Lloyd said without a smile. "See you in Berlin or Tokyo some day."

"Come on, Lloyd," Ramón said. "You know Frank didn't have to do doodly-squat here with us. Went beyond the call, I'd say."

"Thanks, Ray," Frank said. "But Lloyd's right on the nose. Football's keeping me out of combat. And it's easy to say I wish I were going with you guys."

Lloyd clasped Frank on the shoulder. "You're all right, buddy. Sorry for being an asshole. I'm just jealous. All this flying around in circles, I guess."

Andy pulled a one dollar bill out of his wallet. "Listen up, boys. We'll all be heading off in different directions pretty soon. What say we sign a few greenbacks as short snorters before we get too lit tonight."

Everyone checked their wallets. "I'm tapped out," Lloyd said.

"No problem," Erik said, handing Lloyd a dollar bill. "I've got deep pockets. Just be sure to pony up that beer in Berlin or Tokyo."

All five amigos signed their names to each other's dollar bills for good luck and the short snorter's promise—free drinks from the one who can't show his signed bill the next time they meet.

Ramón stepped back to snuff out his cigarette in the ashtray and froze. From across the room, Violet gazed directly into his eyes, smiled, then turned away. A wave of desire pulsed through his loins. He could almost taste her.

Eyes wide, Lloyd stiffened. "Jesus! Get a load of who's with the old man! It's Jimmy Doolittle."

"Malarkey," Andy said just before he did a double take. "Holy mackerel! It is him."

Their Bombardment Group commander, Lieutenant Colonel Peck, headed straight for them with a short and muscular, middle-aged man. Striding forward with a broad smile, Ramón thought he looked like a friendly torpedo.

"These are a few more of my group," the Colonel said to Major Doolittle. "All B-25 pilots."

Jimmy Doolittle extended a hand to each of them. "Great to meet you boys. I just came from test flying your ship. A bit noisy, but I like the way she handles. Pretty good on a short field, don't you think?"

Lloyd's posture was ramrod straight. "Yes, sir. She's a doozy."

Everyone stood silently, stunned by the opportunity to meet America's most famous airman. World War I veteran, stunt pilot, cross-country racer, engineering Ph.D. from MIT, now back in the Army again, Jimmy Doolittle was every pilot's role model.

As Colonel Peck nudged him toward the next group of pilots, Major Doolittle spoke in a low, conspiratorial tone. "I'll be talking to you boys again real soon. We're working on an interesting B-25 project." Major Doolittle smiled, moving on.

"Boy! What do you think he's up to?" Erik said.

"I don't know, but I'd sure volunteer for any op he's running," Lloyd said.

"Sign me up too!" Ramón said.

Frank sighed. "Have a bash at it, guys. Guess I'll be sitting this one out."

Wendy pressed against Frank's side as the band began String of Pearls. "Come on, baby. Dance with me."

"Let's down some more champagne," Andy said.

Later in the evening, Ramón felt a little tipsy and tired. The party had been OK. Nothing special. Except for an occasional dance with a nurse or female pilot from the Air Transport Auxiliary, he'd spent the evening huddled with his friends, drinking and talking, mostly about sports and the war. Then shortly before midnight, Violet emerged across the dance floor, seeming afloat in the smoky blue light. She paused at the top of the staircase, and looked in his direction before descending. No one followed her down.

Soft light, filtering through the haze above the ballroom floor, cast wispy patterns on couples swaying to Xavier Cugat's *Perfidia*. Ramón worked his way around the perimeter of the room and paused at the top of a staircase winding down to an amber-lit hallway. *To you,* the band's vocalist seemed to sing to him. *My heart cries out Perfidia.* Seeing no one around, he swiftly descended the stairs.

Violet was waiting for him in the shadows between the coat rack and the ladies room. No time to hesitate. He strode directly into her open arms. Before he could make another move, she wrapped her hands around his neck and drew his face down toward hers. Her tongue swept across his lips and probed inside his mouth. Her hands clasped his buttocks and pulled his pelvis tightly against hers. Ramón closed his eyes, throbbing, melting into her body. His hands trailed down the fabric of her gown and lifted the hem of her skirt, then her slip. His fingertips traced widening circles around the tops of her nylons and across the straps of her garter belt.

Thump! With the first heavy footstep at the top of the stairs, Violet sprang out of his arms, darting like a jaguar into the ladies room. Ramón straightened his jacket and walked back upstairs. The band was playing *Auld Lang Syne* as Major Anderson, with a curt nod, clambered down the stairwell in search of his wife.

Back on the dance floor couples embraced, champagne corks popped and a communal 'Happy New Year' cheer filled the room. Frank and Wendy were slow dancing, their eyes closed. Erik and Andy had each found young women to kiss. Lloyd was slumped in the corner, his necktie undone, a glass of champagne in his hand.

Ramón handed Erik the car keys. "I'm walking home."

"Geez, Ray. The party's just starting."

"Have a good time, buddy. I need to clear my head."

Passing through the brightly-lit guard post, Ramón walked on through dark, forested neighborhoods toward the amigo's bungalow on Lake Steilacoom. Silver moonbeams filtered through tall evergreen trees and the scent of pine and fir floated on the icy cold air. Halfway across the wooden bridge over the lake, he stopped, lit a cigarette and leaned his forearms on the railing. The unexpected encounter with Violet had been red hot. Bold and powerful, she'd swept him up like gangbusters. But it wasn't really hunky-dory. Even with a jerk like Anderson, she was still married.

And messing with another man's wife? Dang! That was a mortal sin. Or would be if he still considered himself Catholic. As a child he'd been taught to be faithful in marriage. That is, until one day in his senior year. He took a long drag on his cigarette and stared into the carpet of moonlight spread over the lake.

Football practice ended early that day. Still time to get a ride home from papá at the Mexican school. No one in the teachers lounge. Open the door to the storeroom. Papá and Miss Hernandez, the school secretary, her blouse unbuttoned, brassiere flipped up. Papá's pants at his ankles.

Ramón couldn't shake it. How could he forgive the man who'd betrayed his mother? The father who'd given him so much throughout childhood. But here he was, thinking about sleeping with another man's wife. He should be feeling guilty. But Violet had given him the come on, hadn't she? And damn! Was she hot.

33

Chapter Five
Paukenschlag

We are fighting for a just and clear cause. All the omens for victory are on our side. The peoples on our side are young and healthy and their leadership is determined, whatever the cost, to bring the great struggle for the existence of their nations to a successful conclusion.

Joseph Goebbels
Essay in Das Reich
January 4, 1942

200 NAUTICAL MILES SOUTH OF HALIFAX, Nova Scotia — January 12, 1942

The starboard lookout leaned into the bridge. "Herr Kaleun! Smoke cloud 30 degrees starboard."

Rainer swung his binoculars to starboard and focused the lenses. To the south, a rising gray cloud thinned into wispy strands as it trailed across the crimson sky. He tightened his jaw. The hunt was on! "Set course 210, Jäger. All ahead full. And get Vogel on the bridge."

"Ja wohl, Herr Kaleun," Jäger said, lifting the hinged cover on the voice tube to relay the order below. After fifteen minutes at their top speed of 18 knots, a high funnel and two double masts were visible on the horizon. Salmon-colored rays of the setting sun swept across the bridge in waves of varying intensity as Jäger thumbed through drawings of commercial ships in the *Kriegsmarine* recognition manual. "Looks like a Red Funnel Line freighter, Herr Kaleun. Estimated 10,000 GRT (gross registered tonnage)."

"He's a little more than four nautical miles away, Herr Kaleun," Vogel said. "Running at about nine knots, course 038 with some zigzag."

Rainer turned his eyes upward, calculating. "The surface attack angle should be good in about twelve minutes, Jäger. Assume parallel course. Distance 2000 meters. Sound general quarters."

Soon the U-023, its low silhouette undetected in the darkness, was overtaking the freighter. Rainer ordered a change in course to align the bow torpedoes for a direct shot. Following *U-bootwaffe* protocol for surface attacks, as first watch officer, Jäger assumed targeting duties. At a distance of 2000 meters, Jäger fixed the target through the lenses of the *Uboot-Zieloptik* (UZO). Resembling a pair of binoculars mounted on top of a fire hydrant, the UZO electronically transmitted the bearing, range and target angle to the Vorhaltrechner in the conning tower beneath the bridge. An electromechanical deflection calculator, the Vorhaltrechner then computed the proper angle to launch a torpedo on a collision course with its target.

"Forward torpedo room. Target angle 084," Jäger called into the voice tube. "Enemy speed nine knots. Range 2000 meters. Depth three meters. Fire one. *Los!*" He waited a few seconds. "Fire two. Los!"

Rainer, Jäger and Vogel stared at the face of Jäger's stopwatch. 160 seconds. Nothing. 165 seconds. *Nichts*. Time slowed down. Rainer bit his lip. Had Jäger calculated correctly? Was the torpedo a dud? 177 seconds. A brilliant flash of orange light thrust a column of water high in the air. A hit under the aft mast!

Rainer clenched and released his fist. "Guess he was running a little faster than we thought. I assume you were aiming for the bridge, Jäger."

A second explosion sent a fireball pulsing high in the sky and dense black smoke billowing across the water. "He's broken up amidships," Jäger said.

"All engines stop," Rainer ordered. Drifting at a distance of 500 meters, he surveyed the scene. The flaming stern of the freighter, sheared off from the forward section by the explosion, was rapidly sinking in a pool of steam and smoke. He glanced at Jäger whose face was illuminated by the flames. Neither spoke the obvious—no one in the aft section could have survived. As the bow began sliding beneath the water, several crewmen, their clothing on fire, leapt into the frigid ocean. A handful of survivors in a single lifeboat rowed desperately away.

The heavy odor of burning petroleum flooded Rainer's nostrils as he considered his next move. Standing orders from Grossadmiral Dönitz prohibited any aid to the enemy. Nevertheless, like most U-Boat commanders, Rainer respected the skill and fortitude of men who fought the war at sea. A man in the water was his alter ego. "All ahead slow, Jäger. Come along side the lifeboat."

Rainer cut the engines and called down to the men in the lifeboat in well-accented English. "Where is your captain?"

A seaman with a blackened face and tattered shirt looked up at the bridge."He went down with our ship."

"Where is your ship from?"

"Southampton."

"You have emergency supplies?"

The British seaman shook his head no.

Rainer turned to Jäger. "Give them a compass and some supplies."

Jäger raised an eyebrow.

Rainer stood tall. "There'll be no such entry in the log. Verstanden?"

Jäger nodded. "Ja wohl, Herr Kaleun."

6 NAUTICAL MILES SOUTH OF MONTAUK, Long Island — January 15, 1942

Rainer, Jäger and Vogel stood on the bridge between the lookouts about midnight. The sea was calm and the shore lights of Long Island were clearly visible. Apparently no blackout orders had been issued along the East Coast.

"It's amazing, Herr Kaleun," Vogel said as he focused his binoculars on the Montauk Point lighthouse. "The light is still operating normally. Don't the *Amis* know there's a war on? They've just given me a perfect navigational fix."

Rainer stroked his scraggly two-week beard. The only maps he had were an outdated chart of the Northeast Atlantic coast with little detail regarding navigational lights and markers and the 1939 edition of Knaurs World Atlas. "At 12 knots, I estimate about nine hours to New York. Agreed?" Vogel nodded.

"We should reach it before dawn. Then we'll settle on the bottom until darkness."

"I'm looking forward to tomorrow night," Jäger said. "I've always wanted to see Broadway."

Rainer smiled. "That's an intriguing idea, Jäger. But it might be a bit dangerous sailing all the way into New York Harbor."

"Didn't Prien do just that at Scapa Flow?"

"Ja. Pretty bold sinking a battleship in the middle of the British fleet."

Jäger shrugged. "Why not us then?"

Vogel gave a dry cough. "Scapa Bay was carefully-planned and Prien had extensive knowledge about the harbor. We know essentially nothing about New York Harbor."

"I know there's a fort guarding the entrance and a lot of warships moored there," Rainer said. He leveled his gaze at Jäger. "We're on a hunt, not a suicide mission. Besides, which ships are more likely to be good targets? Those docked and maybe unloaded or those entering and leaving the harbor?"

"Ja, *sicher*, Herr Kaleun. The channel is best."

At 0600 light fog hung over the water and visibility was limited. Rainer called his navigator to the bridge. "What's your best estimate of our location, Vogel?"

"About eight miles off Long Beach, Herr Kaleun. Just south of the main shipping channel into the Port of New York."

"What's the depth here?"

"Fathometer shows 50 meters and steady, Herr Kaleun," Jäger said.

"*Einsteigen!*" Rainer gave the order to clear the bridge in preparation for a dive. "Put her on the bottom, Jäger."

With the U-023 settled in clay and sandstone silt deposited by the Hudson River, Rainer lay on the cot in his tiny quarters, mopping sweat from his brow. He hadn't had much sleep the past few days and this evening he'd have to be alert. He closed his eyes and focused on the pulse thrumming in his ear against the pillow. *Unglaublich.* It was unbelievable to be at the mouth of the Hudson undetected. Where were the patrol boats, the reconnaissance aircraft? Germany would never allow anyone to sail into the Baltic unchallenged. How could the Amis let him get so close? Drifting into sleep, he soon was dreaming.

A light wind off the canal rustled the hem of Anneliese's cotton dress as she stood on a late summer evening in front of their 300-year-old red brick house. On the grassy bank nearby, twelve-year-old Joachim read a Karl May western and eleven-year-old Gisela watched a swan gliding past. Standing in the shadows on the other side of the canal, Rainer called out, but they didn't hear him. Darkness descended. He could scarcely discern their figures anymore. He looked up and realized he was sinking in cold water, a faint light rapidly fading above. He thrust his arms above his head and pulled down in an effort to swim to the surface. But with each stroke the water grew thicker, preventing any upward motion. He continued to sink into darkness.

Rainer was jolted awake by a hand grasping his shoulder. "It's 1700, Herr Kaleun," a seaman said. "Oberleutnant Jäger asked me to wake you."

Rainer sat up on the edge of his cot and dismissed the seaman. Running his fingers through his hair, he reoriented himself. Although he had little belief in omens, the dream was nevertheless disturbing. Every patrol was extremely dangerous. Just this week two U-Boats were sunk in the Mediterranean. But thank God his family was safe. Lübeck was not a significant military target.

Jäger and Vogel, both wearing dark glasses, nodded respectfully as Rainer entered the control room, now illuminated by red light. Rainer leaned into the compartment where the young hydrophone operator from Bremen *Funkmaat* Stein was twisting the dial on the direction finder while listening intently through his headphones. "Are you hearing anything?" Rainer asked.

"Nichts, Herr Kaleun. "

"*Auf periskop!*" Rainer ordered. Scanning the ocean for several minutes through the observation periscope, he spotted no activity. "Take her up, Jäger."

"Secure ventilation. Shut bulkhead flappers," Jäger ordered.

Rainer waited for confirmation that all was secured, then gave the order to surface. "Blow tanks. *Auftauchen!*"

On the surface, Rainer, Jäger, Vogel and four lookouts, dressed in heavy sweaters, oilskins and Sou'westers, opened the hatch and climbed onto the bridge. After breathing the foul air below decks all day, Rainer relished the rush of fresh ocean air, even if it was a bone-chilling -2 degrees Celsius. The fog had cleared and there was little wind. Beneath the dark sky, the shoreline was distinctly silhouetted by the bright lights of greater metropolitan New York City.

Rainer gazed at the skyline, remembering how dazzled he'd been in 1933 when he visited on a transatlantic training cruise. With towering buildings, bustling streets and energetic people, New York was a world-class city. He looked at Jäger and Vogel. "Beautiful sight, nicht wahr, boys? We're enemy sailors right on the edge of one of the greatest cities in the world, completely undetected. Let's see how close we can get. Course 310. All ahead one third."

Cruising toward New York Harbor, a lookout soon reported a loom of light reflecting off the dark western sky 20 degrees to starboard.

Vogel folded his chart. "This doesn't show the navigational markers off Long Island, Herr Kaleun. We might be seeing a lightship or a channel marker."

"Take us there, Jäger," Rainer said.

"Course 330. All ahead one half," Jäger ordered.

With the thrumming roar of twin supercharged, 9-cylinder diesel engines in his ears, Rainer trained his binoculars on the light. What was it? Definitely not a ship and too high for a channel marker.

"Conning tower reports depth 15 meters, Herr Kaleun," Jäger said.

Rainer's shoulders tightened. The depth reports warned of shoaling. Something wasn't right.

"Herr Kaleun!" A lookout shouted. "I see other lights lower down. This light is on the shore!"

"All stop!" Rainer yelled. "Reverse engines. All back full. Report the depth."

The engine roar stopped abruptly. Only the sound of water breaking about the bow continued as the forward movement of the U-023 gradually slowed.

"Eight meters and decreasing," Vogel said.

In the engine room Rademaker leapt into action. He cut the fuel supply to the diesels and blasted compressed air into the engine blocks to slow them down. When the engines stopped, he engaged the reverse cam and set the engines spinning astern with another blast of air before reopening the fuel supply. With a mighty roar, the diesels kicked into reverse, straining to slow the U-023's forward momentum.

Rainer stood on the bridge, staring at the rapidly approaching shore lights. His mouth felt dry. Would Rademaker be able to reverse course before they ran aground? A high-pitched metallic ring rose above the thundering engines as the backing propellers engaged in a mighty battle against the powerful forward movement of the U-023. With a jolt, Rainer was bounced against the fairwater wall as the reverse engines began to gather sternway.

"Starboard stop," Rainer ordered. "Starboard ahead full. Left full rudder." Soon, when he saw they were making slow, but consistent headway, he ordered a twisting maneuver. "Port Stop. Port ahead full. Ease your rudder. Come to course 150."

Back in deeper water, Rainer set a course for the Ambrose Channel, the main shipping route into New York Harbor. When Vogel identified the lightship marking the entrance to the channel, Rainer maneuvered 15 nautical miles south along the shipping lanes. A sea wolf awaiting its prey, the U-023 began circling, dark and close to the surface.

A low mist hung over the water as the last rays of the setting sun faded into the darkening western horizon. Rainer pressed his hands against the UZO and stretched the muscles of his arms and shoulders. *Verdammt!* What impulse had driven him to take such a risk near the largest city in America?

56 NAUTICAL MILES OFF ATLANTIC CITY, New Jersey
— January 16, 1942

At 0730, shortly after sunrise, Rainer and Jäger stood on the bridge drinking strong coffee. Jäger quaffed a large slug from his cup and shuddered. "*Mächtig!* Powerful stuff."

"Would you prefer chicory like in France?" Rainer asked.

"Or at home, last I heard," Jäger said.

A light fog lay over the ocean surface with minimal cloud breaks above. "This won't lift for a while," Rainer said. "Let's keep her on the surface a bit longer. Course 190."

Rainer was eager to reach the prime hunting grounds at Cape Hatteras. On the main shipping route into Hampton Roads, the Cape was only 30 nautical miles from a precipitous drop of the continental shelf. After attacking a merchant ship, he'd only have to travel a short distance to the relative safety of very deep water. Capable of diving 230 meters without pressure damage, the U-023 could escape the effective range of Allied depth charges. In addition, off Cape Hatteras Rainer could seek a layer of cool water to deflect the ultrasonic waves of anti-submarine detection devices (ASDIC) used by destroyers.

Jäger spun around, his binoculars swaying from the strap around his neck. "Aircraft!" He shouted, pointing at a gray twin-engine airplane emerging from a cloud bank on the starboard horizon.

Rainer locked his eyes on the attacker, a medium-sized bomber flying low over the water. "Alarm! Clear the bridge!"

Jäger activated the diving bell. Clang! Clang!

Alarm! Alarm! Crew members shouted throughout the U-023.

Jäger and the lookouts scrambled down the hatch as the enemy airplane roared in just 50 meters above the ocean. As he descended into the conning tower, Rainer swiftly identified the attacker. Two engines. Stubby body. Twin vertical stabilizers. A Hudson A-29. But did he have depth charges? He yanked the hatch closed and secured it moments before two explosions rocked the U-023. Gripping the ladder railing, he slid rapidly down into the control room.

Halfway into the dive, a third explosion knocked Rainer against an instrument panel, drawing blood from the back of his outstretched hand. Then nothing except silence as the U-023 settled to the bottom to remain until nightfall.

Several hours later Rainer, Jäger and Rademaker sat in the wardroom. "Demolition bombs," Rademaker said, lighting his pipe. "It's hard to believe they're still using them against us. If that Hudson had depth charges, we'd probably all be dead."

Rainer traced a finger over the small gash on the back of his hand. "These Amis seem totally unprepared for us. No shoreline blackouts. Navigational markers operating normally. Ship running lights blazing."

"Like the Tommies during the happy time. Nicht wahr?" Jäger said. He offered Rainer a Gauloise and lit it for him. Lacy blue cigarette smoke drifted up into the dim overhead light.

"The Tommies learned from their early mistakes. They're much tougher now," Rademaker said.

"Don't the Allies talk to each other?" Jäger said.

"All military leaders have big egos. Makes it hard to listen," Rademaker said.

"*Schade*," Rainer said. "They could learn a lot from each other."

100 NAUTICAL MILES EAST OF BERMUDA
— January 25, 1942

With all torpedoes expended, the U-023 was heading back to its home port of Lorient. After an early morning watch on the bridge, Rainer returned to his quarters for some rest. The patrol had been extremely successful—nine merchant ships sunk for a total of 57,000 GRT. Yesterday he received a congratulatory radio message from Grossadmiral Dönitz, *Befehlshaber der Unterseeboote (BdU)*.

An den Paukenschläger Hartmann. Bravo! Gut gepaukt. Dönitz. You've beaten the drum well.

Lulled by the steady rumble of diesel engines, Rainer lay on his cot gazing at a photograph of his wife and children. Soon his eyelids were heavy and the photograph dropped from his fingers. Halfway between sleep and wakefulness, images flashed through his mind.

Walking through a winter forest with Anneliese. Clumps of snow nestled in the branches. Sunlight glinting off the powdery, crystalline path. Cold air in his nostrils. Flushed cheeks. Massaging her neck with his fingertips as she soaked in a wooden tub. Her head turned upward to gaze at him, blond hair swirling across her naked shoulders. Taut muscles of her neck silhouetted by flickering candlelight. How beautiful.

Chapter Six
Esmeralda

On the Atlantic Coast, the Navy announced, enemy submarine operations were continuing as far south as Florida, but countermeasures were proving increasingly effective. A Navy spokesman revealed the sinking of one of the marauders by a naval plane that had reported simply: "Sighted sub; sank same."

New York Times
January 30, 1942

EMERALD SPRINGS, Texas
— January 30, 1942

The trip from San Antonio to Ramón's hometown took three hours by Greyhound bus. Erik was gazing out the window when he saw a scaly, gray creature, about three feet long, scampering between the thorny scrub brush and cactus along the road. "What the hell is that?"

Ramón laughed. "Armadillo. Never seen one before? They'll jump straight up in the air if you surprise them. I've creamed a few on the road in my day."

"Are they dangerous?"

"No, but they carry leprosy. You could get it if you eat them."

"Jesus, Ray. I feel like I'm in some other world down here."

Ramón laughed. "Welcome to South Texas, amigo. It's a pretty short layover, but you'll get a taste."

"Any Indians around here, Ray?"

"Not many left in Zavala County. Pretty much wiped out by the whites." Ramón smiled and lowered his voice. "They tried to do the same with Mexicans, but we outnumber them now."

With a blast from its air brakes, the bus pulled into a dusty roadside stop between a gas station and a crumbling café. The air was perfused with exhaust fumes and cooking oil.

"Fifteen minutes!" the driver sang out, opening the door.

A few whites in jeans and cowboy boots piled out of the front seats and headed toward the café. The dozen Mexican Americans sitting around Ramón and Erik were in no hurry. A woman wearing a floral blouse turned her back to the aisle and nursed her baby. Men in farmworkers clothes ambled off the bus and mingled outside, smoking hand-rolled cigarettes. A few went behind the gas station to urinate in the dust. Erik and Ramón, the only men in uniform, were last off the bus.

Erik gestured toward the café. "Cup of coffee?"

Ramón shook his head and pointed to a spot above the café door. "See that? It's not worth the hassle."

Erik cupped a hand over his eyes and squinted at the rusted metal sign: No dogs. No Negroes. No Mexicans. "What the hell?" He swiveled his head toward Ramón, eyes flashing. "That's outrageous. You don't have to take that shit, Ray!"

A painful memory flashed through Ramón's mind. Driving with Frances. Top down at a stoplight. Truckload of gringos hooting and jeering. Hey baby, what you doing with that spic? Eyes straight ahead, fist slammed into the dashboard.

He laid a hand on Erik's tense forearm. "You have to choose your battles, buddy. That's the way it is around here. I've lived with it all my life."

Erik clenched a fist. "Say the word, man. I'm ready to go in there."

Ramón sighed. "We'd just end up in jail is all."

"Jesus H. Christ! I've never heard of such crap."

"That's because you're from Minnesota, Erik. Calm down. You're more upset than I am. Let's get back on the bus."

As they pulled away from the rest stop, Ramón pointed to a large rock lying near a spiny shrub. "See him all coiled up there in the sun over by the mesquite? Big rattler."

Erik stared, shaking his head. "What else you got around here, Ray? Tarantulas? Scorpions?"

Ramón laughed. "Yep. Got 'em all."

"Well it's a hell of a place to grow up. That's all I can say."

"Think our new base in Florida'll be any better?"

"Shit no. Probably alligators and coral snakes all over the place."

Under a fading winter sun, the bus rolled on across the prairie east of the Rio Grande. Erik soon fell asleep, but Ramón sat wide awake, gazing out the window. Thorny shrubs and clumps of bluestem grass, turned brown by winter chill, dotted the landscape. An occasional cactus, mesquite, acacia or mimosa tree rose above the low-lying vegetation. A pair of whitetail deer, startled by the rumbling bus, froze momentarily by the roadside, then raced away. Ramón smiled. Erik was probably right. A hell of a place to live. Still, for the first time in many months, he felt at home. There was raw beauty in the prairie, hard to explain to outsiders, but beauty nonetheless.

A windmill, barn and grazing cattle heralded approaching civilization. Soon they passed several small ranches and entered into irrigated farmland known as the winter garden of Texas. Bermuda onions, flax, sorghum and cotton all thrived in the mild climate. But in his hometown Emerald Springs (known as Esmeralda by Tejanos), spinach was king.

A dusty tractor, bathed in the lilac afterglow of fading sunlight, rumbled along the road into town. Carrying rakes and hoes over their shoulders, a group of dark-skinned farm workers trudged along behind. Ramón nudged Erik and pointed out the window at a colorful statue of a pipe-smoking sailor. "There's our patron saint."

Erik rolled his eyes. "Popeye? Jesus, Ray."

The bus pulled up to a one-story adobe building and a mixed group of Anglos and Tejanos disembarked. Ramón didn't recognize any of them. After six years away in college and the Army Air Force, his hometown now seemed vaguely unfamiliar. He slung his duffel bag across his back and walked with Erik through downtown toward his parents' house.

Four middle-aged, Anglo mechanics, taking in the last rays of sunlight, wiped greasy hands on their overalls and waved to Ramón.

"How's it going, kid?"

"Keep up the good work, Ramón!"

Ramón turned toward them with a smile, saluted and walked on.

"We're proud of you, boy." One of the men yelled after him.

Walking briskly beside Erik, Ramón spoke in a low voice. "Old high school sports fans. They gave me a pass as long as I was scoring for the mighty Pronghorns. But would they buy me a cup of coffee in that café? Don't count on it, buddy. It was hard enough just getting into that damn school."

"What do you mean, Ray?"

Ramón's nostrils flared, his voice more forceful. "OK, Erik. You're Anglo. No problem. I'm Mexican. I have to apply for admission to high school."

Erik shook his head. "That's completely FUBAR, Ray. But don't take it out on me, OK? Remember I'm from Minnesota."

Ramón grunted. "Yeah. I know."

Neither one spoke as they continued past the Wild Horse Café, Sunset Beer Garden, Emerald Springs General Store and a Texaco station.

At the end of the business district, Erik stopped on the edge of the high school athletic field. "This where you went All-State football, Ray?"

Ramón nodded. "Thanks to muscular grunts like you on the line."

Erik laughed. "How'd you do in track?"

"A lot like you, I guess. Minus the shot put. Javelin and 880 were my events."

Erik shifted his duffel bag to the opposite shoulder. "Football and track were OK, but boxing was my best sport."

"Jeez. I guess so. Goddam Golden Gloves."

"Hell. I never got beyond the regionals, Ray."

Ramón kicked a pebble with his boot. "I got a lot out of sports, you know? And I kind of envy Frank."

Erik laughed. "Well that ain't so hard. We just need to be All-Americans."

Near the First Methodist Church, they entered a middle-class neighborhood of small homes and scraggly lawns. Gradually, once past St. Anthony's Church, the neighborhood transitioned into dilapidated homes and outright shacks where a few dark-skinned children played in the street. A small, stout woman holding a baby was perched on a stool in front of a tortillería. Ramón knelt down beside her. "Señora Rodriguez. It's me Ramón."

The woman beamed. "Ramón! *Guapo*. You're so handsome in that uniform." She looked him over. "Are they feeding you OK?"

"I'm fine thanks, Señora. Just here for an overnight on my way to the East Coast." He gestured toward Erik. "This is my copilot Erik. How's your family?"

"*Todo bien*, gracias."

"And Javier?"

She paused, a shadow crossing her face. "You know Javier, Ramón. He's getting by with some part-time work on the highway."

"Hope I get a chance to see him before I leave. Adios, Señora. A pleasure to see you."

"*Adios, hijo. Que te vaya bien.*"

Near the edge of the barrio, they entered a block of modest bungalows with well-kept lawns and gardens. "This is where middle-class Tejanos live," Ramón said. "Shopkeepers or teachers like my father."

"Looks a lot like my old neighborhood," Erik said.

"Really? Is this how small-town cops live in the Midwest?" Ramón stopped in front of a yellow bungalow, unslung his duffel bag and adjusted his uniform. "Here we are."

A low rock wall separated the sidewalk from a small garden with a statue of the Virgen María. A white flag, bordered in red, hung in the front window. In its center was a blue star.

"Some hero live here, Ray?" Erik said.

Ramón shrugged. "I wouldn't argue with that."

Their boots clumped heavily up the wooden stairs to the front porch. Before he could knock, the door flew open and a teenage girl squealing "Moncho!" was in Ramón's arms. He broke her bear hug and scrutinized her at arm's length. In a wool sweater, plaid skirt just below the knees and bobby socks, Antonia was all teenage girl. "Dang! Look at you. You've grown so much."

"Ramón!" A voice rang out. "You're home." Pushing past Antonia, a slender, middle-aged woman in a blue dress with squared shoulders embraced him.

"Mamá." Ramón squeezed her tight, then released an arm to draw in his sister as well. Closing his eyes, he allowed the warm feeling to flow through his entire body. Then his smile faded as a tall, dark man with thick, gray hair emerged from the shadows of the vestibule.

"Hola, Ramón."

Ramón didn't move. "Hola, Papá," he said, extending a hand.

Antonia broke the ice, pulling Ramón along. "Come inside, Moncho. We can't wait to hear what you've been up to." She turned toward Erik with a smile. "Hi. I'm Antonia."

"Oh! I'm sorry to be so rude," Ramón said. "This is my friend Erik. We fly the B-25 together."

Ramón's mother smiled. "Bienvenido. Welcome to our home, Erik."

His father stepped forward and offered a handshake. "Glad to meet you, Erik. Please excuse the Spanish. We've always used it at home."

"That's fine, sir." Erik nodded toward Ramón. "I've had a little practice with your son."

"Are you Ramón's copilot?" Antonia asked.

"Sure am," Erik replied. "Ever since San Antonio."

"Where are you from, Erik?" Ramón's mother asked.

"Minnesota, ma'am."

"Is there snow up there now?" Antonia asked.

"Lots. Ever seen it?"

"No. But it must be beautiful."

"I think so, but you might get a little tired of it after a few months. Particularly when the temperature never gets much above freezing."

"Yow," Antonia said, shaking her head.

A dog howled down the block. "Come on inside," Mrs. Morales said. "It's getting chilly out here."

Ramón looked over the living room. Not much change in a year. The faded sepia photograph of his grandparents over the stone fireplace. His father's reading chair draped with a colorful blanket from Coahuila. The cactus beside the lumpy sofa. The wooden crucifix on the wall. Smelling the sweet

56

aroma of cinnamon milk wafting from the kitchen, he wrinkled his nose and smiled at his mother. "*Atole de arroz?*"

Antonia tugged at his arm. "She's been in the kitchen all day, Moncho. I helped with the tamales. We used Abuela's recipe."

Ramón nudged Erik. "You are in for a treat, my friend. My grandmother was a good cook."

At dinner Ramón was flooded with childhood memories. His father saying grace before the meal: *Gracias a Señor por estos, tus regalos.* His mother bustling in and out of the kitchen. Toni engaging in animated conversation. Only Luís was missing. But of course, also gone were the angry confrontations between his older brother and father.

"Papá always says that prayer before we eat," Antonia explained to Erik. "It means: Thank you, Lord for your gift of food."

"Thanks for the translation," Erik said. "My dad said something similar before we ate." He looked at Mr. Morales. "But it was in German. My paternal grandparents were Lutherans from Schleswig-Holstein."

"Was your mother's family also from Germany?" Mrs. Morales asked.

"No, ma'am. Norway."

Mr. Morales leaned back in his chair and smiled at Erik. "I guess we're all immigrants at some point in time. My wife and I came here from Coahuila in 1917."

"Where's that, sir?" Erik asked.

Antonia chimed in. "Just across the Rio Grande. Been there?"

"No. I've not been much of anywhere besides Minnesota, Washington and here."

"You've never visited family in Germany or Norway?" Mrs. Morales asked.

"Afraid not, ma'am. The only family I know is in Minnesota."

"It must be tough on your parents now that we're at war with Germany," Mr. Morales said.

"And the Nazis are occupying Norway," Ramón added.

"Oh I don't know. We're pretty much all Americans now," Erik said.

Ramón snorted. "Easy for you to say, looking like every other white American. It's a little bit tougher for us brown-skinned folks."

Mrs. Morales leaned back in her chair. "Ramón! Don't be rude."

Erik waved his hands above his plate as if declining a penalty. "Don't worry, ma'am. Your son and I are good friends. We usually level with each other."

"Let's have some tamales," Antonia said. "They've been steaming all day. I can't wait to dig in."

Ramón felt a surge of love for his little sister. Smoothing things over. Just like she always did. "Me too. Let's eat."

Erik took a bite of tamale. "These are delicious, Mrs. Morales. How do you make them?"

"Antonia can tell you. It's an old recipe from my mother-in-law."

"First," Antonia began, "you boil the corn in lime water. Then…" As she continued to describe the lengthy process of preparing tamales, memories of his maternal grandparents' farm in Coahuila rolled through Ramón's mind. His abuelo, a serious man who always expected some useful work from his visiting grandson, taught him about soil, crops, weather and how to ride well. But it was his abuela who taught him how he should live his life. She was the one he turned to during rough times. Like Anglo townies harassing him as a child. The unexpected death of his older brother. Or when his girlfriend got pregnant his senior year. Although his abuela died before he finished college, he still felt her presence every time he touched the Virgen de Guadalupe medallion she'd given him.

Why do you have to cook the cornmeal so long, Abuela? Because only then does it become rico, hijo. Entiendes? Things only become rich if we take the time to do them right. And remember. You're my hijo de oro, my golden boy. There's nothing in this life you can't do as long as you work hard and take time to do things right.

Slices of juicy red grapefruit and a side dish of sautéed squash, peppers and onions over steamed spinach, enhanced the perfect tamales. But it was dessert Ramón was waiting for.

"Ta-da! Your favorite, Moncho," Antonia said as she emerged from the kitchen with a steaming bowl in her hands. "Atole de arroz."

Mrs. Morales leaned toward Erik. "It's just rice pudding made with milk, cinnamon and sugar."

"And it's delicious," Ramón said. "Gracias, Mamá."

"De nada, hijo. Now tell us about your new assignment in Florida."

Ramón pushed back from the table and glanced at Erik. "It looks like pretty much the same as McChord."

59

"Except we'll be looking for U-Boats instead of Japanese submarines," Erik added.

"Why are they called U-Boats?" Antonia asked.

"*Untersee* boats in German," Mr. Morales said. "Under the sea."

"Oh I get it." Antonia said, then gave her father a wry smile. "I mean, I see."

Ramón nudged Erik's arm. "As you can see, Antonia's the quick-witted one in the family."

It was almost midnight when Erik and Ramón settled into his old bedroom for the night. Except for a desk cluttered with his mother's papers and a bookcase filled with volumes of Spanish poetry, the room was unchanged. Various trophies and certificates from Ramón's high school years lined the walls above two bunk beds.

"Whose bed was this?" Erik asked, slipping under the covers as Ramón turned off the light.

"Luís's. We bunked together until I was about thirteen." Ramón was silent for a moment. "Then he died."

"What happened?"

"Motorcycle accident. Luís was a wild one."

"How old was he?"

"Eighteen."

"Geez, that must've been tough. Were you close?"

"Yeah, kind of. He was a real night owl. Always came in late and sat on my bed. I'd pretend to be asleep, but he knew I wasn't. He'd just start talking."

"I had an older brother like that." Erik laughed. "Guess I learned a lot about the real world from him."

"Me too. But it wasn't a good time. He and the old man were always fighting. Sometimes I had to break it up."

Erik hesitated. "I don't mean to be nosy, but what's up with your father? It doesn't seem like you two are getting along that well."

"Yeah, well that's about something else. I'll tell you about it sometime. Let's get a little shut-eye. Tomorrow's another day."

Chapter Seven
Bittersweet

Axis agents in Mexico are systematically propagandizing by word-of-mouth the rumor that when the United States occupies Mexican ports and airfields it will soon afterward occupy Mexico City. Another rumor is that the United States is luring Mexican boys into the American army...

New York Times
January 30, 1942

EMERALD SPRINGS, Texas
— January 30, 1942

Saturday afternoon was sunny and clear as Ramón and Erik walked down Zavala Avenue to Neiman's Drugstore. "Sure they serve Mexicans in this place, Ray?" Erik said with a smile.

"No problem. This was our hangout when I was in high school. Old man Neiman's Jewish and pretty open to everyone."

A bell hanging on the door jangled airily as they entered the drugstore. The familiar welcoming sound, coupled with the aroma of menthol and malt, sent Ramón momentarily back in time. With a warm feeling spreading through his chest, he sauntered across the tiled floor toward the soda fountain. Just as he'd always done.

A smiling, bald man in a white coat leaned across the counter and shook his hand vigorously. "Hi, Ramón. You look swell in that uniform. Staying for long?"

"Thanks, Mr.Neiman. Just passing through and seeing some old pals."

When his friends saw Ramón strolling across the room toward them, they all rose from their booth like players welcoming back their team captain.

"Hola, Ramón!" A dark-complexioned woman in a small, black hat hugged him so tight her feet came off the floor.

"María. *Que tal?*" Ramón said, setting her back down again.

"Hi, Ramón," the pale-blonde Thelma said with a light embrace.

A lanky man with thick eyeglasses gripped his wrist and pumped his hand fiercely. "Looking pretty spiffy in that uniform, Ray."

"What's cooking, Bernard?" Ramón said.

Insisting that Erik sit in the booth, Ramón dragged over a chair for himself. The old friends, who hadn't seen each other in over a year, launched into animated conversation. Throughout the sunny afternoon they sat in the shadows of the drugstore chatting over coffee and ice cream sundaes. Everyone but María smoked.

María was working at the cannery. No boyfriend at present and still living at home. She seemed alright, perhaps a little fatalistic. Thelma had gained some weight, but still looked pretty good. She was working as a typist for the Zavala County Herald. Her boyfriend, a reporter, had just been drafted into the army. Bernard was still teaching science at the high school. In his usual sardonic manner, he joked about being classified 4-F for poor eyesight. His wife had recently given birth to their second child.

"Any news about Angel?" Ramón asked María.

Tears glistened in the corners of María's eyes. "No news from Wake Island since Christmas." She dabbed her eyes with a handkerchief. "He was such a sweet boy."

Shafts of orange light, teeming with oscillating dust motes, swept across the darkening room when the reunion finally broke up. Against token resistance, Ramón paid the four dollar bill and his friends departed. Good luck, Ray. Come back safe, buddy.

Thelma was last to leave. At the door Ramón put a gentle hand on her shoulder and drew her back into the room. Erik politely turned away and began perusing the magazine rack by the counter. Ramón stepped closer to Thelma and spoke in a low voice. "Have you heard anything recently from Frances?"

Thelma stepped back and folded her arms across her chest. "I visited her in Galveston last spring. She's married to a really nice guy."

"That's great. I'm happy for her." Ramón cast his eyes downward. "Sometimes I can't help thinking how it might have been different." He looked up into Thelma's eyes. "With the baby, I mean."

"Let's not start that again, Ray."

"Does she have any kids?"

"This is not a good idea, Ray."

"Come on, Thelma. You were her best friend. You know I loved her."

Thelma stepped back. "Maybe so. But you chickened out when she needed you. Didn't you?"

Ramón drew his shoulders back like a challenged warrior. "What the hell could I do, Thelma? Her parents wouldn't even let me talk to her before they shipped her off."

"Forget it, Ray. She doesn't want anything to do with you now. Just respect that, will you?"

Ramón grasped her hand. "I often wonder if the baby got a good home."

Thelma withdrew her hand. "A bit late for that, isn't it?" Then her face softened. "You don't have to worry. I know for a fact that baby's loved."

Ramón's heart stirred. "How do you know that?"

"I just know, is all." She turned toward the door. "I really have to go now. It was great to see you."

In growing darkness, Ramón plodded along like a weary hunter returning from a fruitless expedition. Erik, adjusted his own pace accordingly, and finally asked. "What was that all about, Ray?"

"Just some unfinished business."

"Want to talk about it?"

Ramón shook his head and picked up the pace. Silently, Erik stayed with him, a few steps behind. After a few minutes, Ramón stopped abruptly and pivoted on his heels. "Okay. Here's what happened. I knocked up my high school girlfriend. Then her parents sent her away and I never saw her again."

Erik scuffed the toe of his boot against the pavement. "Shit, Ray. What was her name?"

"Frances."

Erik raised an eyebrow.

"Yeah. She was Anglo."

"I'll bet her parents weren't too happy about a Mexican boyfriend."

"It was more complicated than that. Her father was a minister."

Erik slapped his forehead. "Not a Baptist, I hope."

"No. Methodist. Always talking about racial harmony and stuff like that." He sighed. "He took a lot of flak because of me, Erik. And in the end I just let him down."

"What happened to the girl?"

"She had the baby and gave it up for adoption. Thelma said she's married now."

"Good for her. High school was a long time ago."

Ramón sighed. "Yeah. A real long time."

As darkness fell the streets were solely illuminated by dim light escaping from the houses along the way. Then the stars came out and the town was bathed in pale-blue light.

"Ever think about the baby?" Erik asked.

"All the time. But it's funny. Thelma said she knew for sure the baby was loved. How the hell could she know that?"

"Beats me, Ray. I thought you couldn't have any contact after you gave up a baby for adoption."

After dinner Ramón and Erik walked with Antonia to the high school where Emerald Springs was playing their arch rival from Uvalde. Antonia wore a bright green sweater and a yellow scarf, the colors of the Mighty Pronghorns.

"So, does your boyfriend start?" Ramón asked.

Antonia smiled. "He's team captain just like you."

"What's his name again?"

Antonia wet her lips. "Howard."

"Hmm, not a Tejano I suppose."

Antonia shook her head. "Nope." She grinned. "Guess I'm a lot like you, Moncho."

Ramón wrapped an arm around her waist. "Hope not."

Antonia waved to a group of her friends sitting in the bleachers."Want to sit with us in the student section?"

"No, I wouldn't want to crimp your style. Have fun. We'll meet you after the game."

"Actually, Moncho." Antonia hesitated. "A few friends..."

Ramón cut her off with a wave of his hand. "No problem. Erik and I'll find our way home." He smiled. "Say hello to Howard for me."

Although several adults in the crowd recognized him, Ramón felt strangely anonymous among these teenagers and their parents. Was it really only six years ago he'd drained a last-second jumper to defeat Uvalde in the semifinals?

"Hola, Ramón!" a familiar voice called out from a group of Tejano men sitting in the top row of the bleachers.

Ramón looked up at a young man dressed in baggy pants, a silver chain and a long coat with padded shoulders. "Another old friend," he said to Erik. "You okay to sit with them?"

Erik shrugged. "As long as they don't mind. But they do look a bit like pachucos, don't you think?"

Ramón laughed. "Just small town wannabes. Don't worry."

68

Smiling, the young man extended his hand to Ramón. *"Qué pasiones, vato?"* He asked in the caló slang popularized by the zoot suit culture.

"I'm doing fine gracias, Javier. Great to see you. This is my friend Erik."

Javier hesitated, then extended his hand. "Hey, any friend of Ramón is a friend of mine." He turned toward the Tejanos sitting next to him. "Ramón and I go way back. *Es de aquellas.* He's one of the best."

The other Tejano men sitting in the row nodded and turned away, leaving Javier and Ramón to their conversation. Like Ramón's other childhood friend Angel, Javier had dropped out of school early. But Ramón kept up with both of them as he moved on to high school. Now Angel was lost or captured on Wake Island and Javier was drifting.

Javier's expression turned solemn. "Did you hear about Angel? It just doesn't jive, man. You know how much he wanted to be a Marine. Makes me want to get even." He took a slug of whiskey from a flask concealed beneath his oversized jacket and offered some to Erik and Ramón. They both declined.

"You know," Javier said. "I was called up, but they gave me a 4F." He laughed ruefully. "Just like in school, no?"

"What was wrong?"

"Something about my heart. They told me I should get it checked out by a specialist."

"Did you go?"

Javier pulled on the flask. "No, I feel fine. Besides, where would I go around here?"

The crowd noise surged as the teams lined up at mid-court for the tipoff. Erik leaned over, raising his voice above the clamor. "Which one's Howard?"

Ramón smiled. "My money's on the brawny forward with blonde hair. Looks a bit like you, Erik."

"Yeah, well maybe back in the old days. I've put on a few pounds since then."

The game was a rout. Uvalde pulled away in the first half and never looked back. The forward they'd pegged as Antonia's boyfriend played pretty well, but fouled out in the last quarter. Ramón recalled playing a few games like that. The after-game party might be a bit subdued.

Ramón gave Javier a fierce farewell handshake. "Take care of yourself, amigo. I'll get some payback for Angel."

Javier's eyes glistened. "*Al rato*, amigo, see you around." He turned and swaggered away with his friends.

On the way back to his parents' house Ramón and Erik said little to each other. Vivid high school memories rolled through Ramón's mind. Barely overtaking the Corrizo Springs runner in the final 200 yards of the mile relay to win the regionals. Dancing with Frances in her taffeta green prom dress. And receiving a full scholarship from Southwest Texas State Teachers College. Despite some sorrow, it was a time when he'd shined.

When they came through the kitchen door, Ramón's mother was kneeling in front of Antonia, gently cleaning her skinned knee with a soapy washcloth. Antonia's cheeks were streaked with dried rivulets of tears that pooled at the corners of her mouth.

"What happened, Toni?" Ramón asked.

"Nothing to worry about, Moncho," Antonia said. "Just a little scratch." She sniffled. "Howard's the one that got hurt."

Ramón's shoulders tightened."What are you talking about? Was there a fight?"

"Just a couple of older guys from town giving Howard a hard time for fouling out and losing the game."

Ramón laid his hand softly on her shoulder. "Anything else, Toni?"

Antonia looked at her mother who silently shook her head. "They said a few things too." Antonia paused and looked down. "Something about dating Spics."

A fiery wave coursed from Ramón's belly into his shoulders. Face flushed and ears pounding, he clenched his fists. "Who was it?"

"Now, Ramón," his mother said. "It won't help to add more trouble."

"Ricky Sherman and another guy I don't know," Antonia said. "I think they'd been drinking. They followed us in the parking lot, saying lots of mean things. When Howard turned around, Ricky hit him hard in the face. I jumped in, but Ricky pushed me away. I fell and skinned my knee."

"That redneck sonofabitch," Ramón said, turning to Erik. "I know where to find him."

"Don't go looking for trouble, Moncho," Antonia said. "He didn't hit me. I just fell down."

In a flash, Ramón pushed past his mother out the door. With Erik following close behind, he strode down the street.

"Where're you going, Ray?"

"Remember the Wild Horse Café?"

"Mind if I join you?"

"Not your fight, Erik."

"That's where you're all wet, Ray. Antonia's a swell kid. No creep should push her around. Remember. I've always got your six, buddy."

Orange light, filtered through the partially-closed blinds of the Wild Horse Café. Someone inside was singing in Western swing style along with Bob Wills and his Texas Playboys. *Deep within my heart lies a melody,* a song of old San Antone. Ramón pushed open the door and stood with Erik at the threshold, surveying the room. A few men in Western shirts, jeans and boots stood at the bar. Several others were playing cards at a corner table.

"Sherman!" Ramón called out, striding toward a husky cowboy standing with one foot on the railing of the bar. "Do you like pushing women around?"

Ricky Sherman turned to face Ramón. "Hey, Charlie," he said over his shoulder to the bartender. "I thought no Spics were allowed in here."

The harmony of the Texas Playboys pierced the stillness of the room. *Lips so sweet and tender like petals falling apart.* Without warning, a scraggly young man in overalls standing beside Sherman grasped Ramón's arm and spun him around. Ramón pulled away just in time to be met by a fierce haymaker to the jaw unleashed by Sherman. With his vision reduced to sparks on a black field, Ramón staggered backward.

"I'll be danged, boys," Sherman said. "The greaser's still standing." Fists raised, he tried to close in on Ramón, but was blocked by Erik. "Don't mess with me, flyboy. This spic's not worth the trouble." He took a swing at Erik.

72

Erik deflected the punch and swung into action with lightning speed. A right to the jaw. A left to the gut. Right to the jaw again. And Sherman was out cold as a mackerel. Sherman's scraggly companion pulled a hunting knife and lunged at Erik. Erik parried the thrust with a forearm and twisted the man's wrist so hard he dropped the knife. Then right left right. To the head. To the belly. To the jaw. Blood streaming from his nose, Sherman's pal crumpled to the floor. No one moved nor said a word as Erik steadied Ramón on his feet and ambled out the door like a wild bear, powerful and invincible.

The next morning, with a swollen jaw and sunrise still a few hours away, Ramón hugged his mother on the doorstep while his father heated up the old Chevy sedan for the trip to the bus station. Only one duffel bag fit in the trunk; the other went in the back seat with Erik. Antonia insisted on squeezing herself between Ramón and her father.

A few travelers, bundled against the cold, stood in front of the bus station as Erik and Ramón unloaded their duffel bags onto the sidewalk.

"Take care of yourself, hijo," Mr. Morales said after a prolonged handshake. "And write."

"Oh, Moncho," Antonia sniffled. "I'll be thinking about you every day." She glanced at Erik. "And you too."

"Thanks for the lift, Papá," Ramón said. "We'll be fine. You can head on home now."

Mr. Morales stood silently for several long moments. Ramón saw sadness in his face, perhaps longing. Should he leave it like this? Why was it so hard to forgive?

Mr. Morales coughed and shifted his feet. *"Pues, buena suerte, hijo.* Let's go Antonia." He opened the door and nudged her in. Ramón watched the car disappear around the corner with Antonia waving out the back window.

The bus arrived on time and the driver stowed their bags in the luggage compartment. Just as Ramón was about to get on board, he heard his name called out from down the street. With coattails flying, Thelma rushed up to him. "I couldn't let you go without knowing," she said, catching her breath.

"Geez, Thelma. What are you talking about?"

"About the baby. Your baby. God help me. Frances will kill me if she ever finds out I told you." She grasped both Ramón 's hands. "She kept the baby."

Ramón stood dumbfounded.

"Everybody on board!" The driver shouted.

"Here. Take this photo," Thelma said, her eyes misting. "And please don't get yourself killed, Ramón."

Erik pulled Ramón on board and the bus rumbled out of Esmeralda. On the open road, with Erik napping, Ramón scrutinized the yellowed photograph Thelma had given him. A small boy stood between Frances and a man in summer uniform. He couldn't make out the rank, but the man looked decent enough. Maybe things had worked out for the best. Who knew what kind of a father he'd have been? But Jesus. He had a son. Absentmindedly, he opened the lunch bag his mother had prepared for them. On top of the tortillas was a sheet of linen paper with his favorite poem by Antonio Machado, written in the graceful pen strokes of his mother's hand.

Las más hondas palabras
del sabio nos enseñan,
lo que silbar del viento cuando sopla,
o el sonar de las aguas cuando ruedan.

The deepest words
of the wise man teach us,
the same as the whistle of the wind when it blows,
or the sound of the water when it is flowing.

Chapter Eight
France occupée

On the seas our U-Boats have put all of Roosevelt's plans to shame. He meant to drive the German U-Boats out of the oceans gradually...And, my fellow countrymen, the number of damages or sinkings by our U-Boats has risen greatly.

Adolf Hitler
Sportpalast Berlin
January 30, 1942

LORIENT, France
— February 9, 1942

A gray seagull, perched on a dockside piling like a wary sentry, fluttered its wings when the Kriegsmarine band struck up a spirited rendition of the national anthem *Deutschland Über Alles*. A light crowd, mostly women and children, some clutching small Nazi flags, pressed against the railing on the street above. Many sang along with the band: We stand as brothers together in protection of Germany above all in the world.

Weary and proud, Rainer strode past his unshaven crew standing at attention along the deck of the U-023. Since

Grossadmiral Karl Dönitz declared that growing a beard on patrol was the sign of a true warrior, no one was worried about appearance on return to port. Stepping on to the creaky gangway, Rainer fixed his gaze on the dock below where, dressed in a long, black leather coat, Grossadmiral Dönitz waited with a group of Kriegsmarine officers.

A kaleidoscope of memories flashed by with each step Rainer took down the ramp. The mill pond in Lübeck where he blithely sailed his toy boat. Heeling in a fierce Baltic wind aboard the training schooner Niobe. A tense North Atlantic patrol with his late mentor, *Korvettenkapitän* Müller. Paddling a canoe with Anneliese along the tranquil river Trave. And now he was about to receive a special reception from the supreme commander of all U-Boat forces.

With one hand gliding along the railing, Rainer steadied his sea legs as he descended the ramp toward Grossadmiral Dönitz. Disregarding the customary Heil Hitlers used by the Wehrmacht, he gave a brisk Kriegsmarine salute. "Kapitänleutnant Hartmann reporting, sir."

Grossadmiral Dönitz returned his salute, then smiled broadly. "*Sehr gut gemacht*, Hartmann." He nodded toward an aide who handed him a silver and red ribbon attached to a black iron Maltese cross with a swastika inscribed in its center. Rainer's pulse rose into his throat. This was unexpected. The *Ritterkreuz* was Germany's highest military award for extreme bravery or outstanding leadership.

Grossadmiral Dönitz raised his voice. "Operation Drumbeat has been a resounding success. On this patrol the U-023 sank nine Allied ships. No U-Boat commander has proven himself more worthy of the Ritterkreuz than Kapitänleutnant Rainer Hartmann."

A loud Hurra erupted from the deck of the U-023. Jäger whirled around, facing the crew. *"Ruhe!"* Despite his stern reprimand for silence, broad smiles spread across their faces. When Jäger faced forward again, he understood. Grossadmiral Dönitz was saluting the crew.

Grossadmiral Dönitz fastened the award around Rainer's neck, stepped back and placed both hands on his shoulders like a proud father. "I wish I had a few more like you, young man. Get a good rest now. I'll be sending you out again in a few weeks."

As soon as the Admiral and his staff left, Jäger dismissed the crew and allowed the waiting civilians to surge on to the dock. Rainer and Jäger forged their way through a throng of sailors eager to begin shore leave with their friends and loved ones and, no doubt, a few French prostitutes who always seemed to know when a submarine was returning to port.

Ascending a steep, concrete staircase, Rainer and Jäger emerged on the street above. The firm cobblestone pavement felt strange beneath Rainer's feet. After six weeks on the rolling ocean, his first few steps were like those of a toddler lurching from his mother's arms. And the air of the port city, unlike the familiar, stagnant odors of the U-023, assaulted his nostrils with a volatile mixture of salt air, oil, smoke, garbage and exhaust fumes. He offered Jäger a Gauloise, lit it and one for himself. "Where are your wife and child?"

Jäger leaned closer, speaking in a low voice. "She's not exactly my wife, Herr Kaleun. I told her not to come here. We're trying to be discreet. Verstehen Sie?"

"Verstanden. French woman, German sailor."

"Exactly. She's waiting for us at the apartment." Jäger paused, then smiled. "I must warn you she's not a good German cook."

Rainer began to respond, but Jäger cut him off with a laugh. "However, she is an excellent French cook."

The late afternoon sky was clear and the temperature was a pleasant 10°C. as they walked through the center of Lorient. Civilian and military traffic flowed along the main boulevard like fallen leaves jostling about in a rushing stream. Although shopkeepers were beginning to shutter their storefronts, sidewalks were bustling with pedestrians. Rainer was intrigued. How different this port city was from Paris where the icy stares of pedestrians bespoke anger and resentment of the German occupation. Here, although many pedestrians avoided eye contact, the sidewalk cafés were filled with exuberant German military personnel and laughing young French women. How serious could the problem Jäger described be?

As usual, Jäger perceived Rainer's thoughts. "I know it looks happy and calm, Herr Kaleun. But the Resistance has roughed up many collaborators. Even killed a few." He shook his head. "Better she stays home, *nicht wahr?*"

The apartment building was in a quiet, somewhat shabby neighborhood. When Rainer smiled at an old woman standing on her balcony, she turned her back and stepped back inside. A young woman pushing a stroller down the sidewalk crossed over the street as they approached. Rainer wasn't certain if it was hostile behavior or just fear. Nevertheless, the building seemed in good repair. Jäger certainly was trying to take good care of his family. He was a good man on land as well as at sea.

Jäger knocked on a door at the top of a long staircase. The door flew open in a flash and a dark-haired, young woman rushed into Jäger's arms. Smothering him with kisses, she embraced him fiercely like a mythic warrior returning from a perilous odyssey. Rainer stepped aside, smiling. She was truly a French beauty. Full figure, nice legs. Good for you, Jäger.

Rainer tried to keep his visit brief, but Jäger and his common-law wife Lea insisted he stay for dinner before beginning his railroad journey to Lübeck. In the end, he was glad he stayed. Saving her rations, Lea had prepared an excellent dinner of steamed mussels with white wine, shallots and thyme and delicious crêpes filled with cheese, egg and ham.

After chatting in pidgin French with Jäger and Lea, viewing their sleeping baby and drinking a couple of bottles of Muscadet, Rainer found his way to the train station. It was late, but one ticket window was still open.

"Where are you heading, Herr Kapitän?" the balding agent asked in perfect German.

Rainer chuckled to himself. Good language skills, but these Frenchmen never can understand naval insignia. "Lübeck. Round-trip, "S'il vous plaît."

"You'll have to change trains in Paris, Herr Kapitän. The next express departs at 0700."

After a few hours dozing on a cold wooden bench, Rainer boarded the train to Paris. With a slight headache and a cotton-dry mouth, he sat by the window in a compartment shared with an elderly French couple and a young man with a cane. After mumbled bon jours, no one spoke further to him. The young man held his cane between his knees and closed his eyes. Perhaps he had been wounded in the invasion? Entranced by the clickety-clack rhythm of the iron wheels rolling over the tracks, Rainer watched the market towns, bleak moors, lakes and forests of Brittany roll by. Crossing into Normandy, he dozed off.

PARIS, France—February 10, 1942

Rainer stepped off the train in Paris to the clamor of rolling carts, blasts of steam and voices echoing off the high-domed ceiling above the tracks. Several *Wehrmacht* military policeman with the brass plate of the *Feldengendarmerie* hanging around their necks, saluted as he walked along the platform into the station. Inside beneath a dark red Nazi banner, a young German soldier checked his rucksack into the transient military baggage area. "Guten Tag, Herr Kapitänleutnant. Traveling far?"

"Lübeck this evening."

"A beautiful city." He saluted. "Enjoy your brief time in Paris, Herr Kapitänleutnant."

On the busy Rue La Fayette Rainer exchanged brisk salutes with the many German military personnel on the sidewalk, but avoided eye contact with most Parisians who either frowned or outright glared at him. How different the city felt now. On several visits with Anneliese before the war, although reserved, Parisians had been cordial. Now he was clearly an enemy soldier in occupied territory. Nevertheless, the occupation of France was a wartime necessity. And it certainly made a great difference for U-Boats. Before the occupation, the only routes from Germany's North Sea ports to the Atlantic Ocean were dangerous passages through the Norwegian Sea or English Channel. Now, from the Keroman U-Boat base in Lorient, the U-023 had direct access to hunting grounds on the open ocean.

Hand-drawn carts, pedicabs and bicycles clattered and clanked amidst honking trucks and automobiles on the busy street. A somber man wearing a red beret stood on the corner playing Edith Piaf on a gramophone with a huge horn-like speaker. *C'etait une histoire d'amour.* His misty eyes scarcely acknowledged the occasional coin tossed in his hat on the sidewalk. It was a love story, Edith Piaf sang. Nothing of it's left now.

Parisians certainly were an interesting lot. Although there was a food shortage, probably made worse by the demands of the Reich, most Parisians were still fashionably dressed, perhaps more so than Berliners. Two attractive young women passed by with yellow stars sewn on their lapels. Rainer sighed and looked away. Why was his government so obsessed with the Jews? Growing up in Lübeck, the few Jews he encountered hardly seemed threatening.

The heady aroma of fresh bread wafted from a boulangerie beside a sidewalk café that seemed equally occupied by Germans in uniform and French civilians. On a large poster across the street, a smiling German soldier, surrounded by young children, held a baby in his arms. The caption read: *Populations abandonnées, faites confiance au soldat allemand!* How pathetic. Where was the nuance, the subtlety? Would Germans trust a French soldier occupying the Fatherland?

After a shave and haircut at a *salon de coiffure*, Rainer sat on a bench along the Seine watching the crowd entering the ornate baroque building that housed the Musée du Louvre. Lighting a cigarette, he gazed vacantly at the bobbing heads of pigeons strutting along the sidewalk. Had it really been thirteen years since he and Anneliese, a few months pregnant, had wandered through the galleries hand-in-hand, full of love and expectation? Although they later visited many great art museums together, the Louvre remained their favorite.

From Lübeck, he an Annelise still enjoyed regular visits to the *Kunsthalle* in nearby Hamburg although the expressionist work of their favorite artist Max Lieberman was no longer exhibited. Rainer stood and crushed his cigarette butt into the pavement with the heel of his boot. How mindless this suppression of Jewish art. Lieberman's death in 1935 wasn't even reported in German newspapers. Now there was even an exhibition of "degenerate art" staged by Dr. Goebbels that expunged modern art deemed to be "un-German, Jewish or Communist" from German museums.

With only a few hours to spend, Rainer was eager to view the works he most admired in the Louvre collection: the Mona Lisa, Venus de Milo, Winged Victory, and Anneliese's favorite, Antonio Canova's ethereal white marble statue of Psyche being revived by Cupid's kiss. But on entry to the Louvre, he learned that none of these works was still in the museum. As war clouds loomed, much of the Louvre's precious art collection had been moved to the countryside, safe from destruction. Disappointed, he made a brief tour of some lesser works and purchased a small porcelain replica of Cupid's kiss to take home to Anneliese.

At a small restaurant near the Pont Neuf Rainer declined a window seat in favor of a table against a back wall where he could watch the entire room. He had to smile. Anneliese often teased him about this behavior. You're always on the alert, she said. Even on shore. He ordered escargot, Coq au Vin and a bottle of dry Alsace Riesling. Although the food was delicious, he didn't linger. He never enjoyed dining out alone. Soon he was on his way to the *Gare de l'Est* to catch the train to Lübeck.

Chapter Nine
Heimat

The races or blood communities are part of the world's natural order. Keeping the blood pure means the preservation of the German people's character...The family is the eternal wellspring of the people. From it the people (das Volk) is constantly renewed.

Walter Tiessler
Nazi pamphlet, 1942

LÜBECK, Germany
— February 15, 1942

In his blue Kriegsmarine dress uniform, Rainer sat with his wife Anneliese, twelve year-old son Joachim, eleven year-old daughter Gisela and his father Gustav Hartmann in their customary seats in the fourth row of the 650 year-old Lutheran Marienkirche. As always since childhood, his eyes turned toward the long, narrow medieval painting stretched across the stone nave wall of the twin-towered gothic church. Completed in the fifteenth century during the plague years, the painting was known as *der Totentanz*, the Dance of Death. Each time he studied it Rainer noticed another detail. Death links his bony arm around the farmer's elbow. A smiling

Death, with a scythe hidden behind his back, greets a young maiden. Boney fingers grasp the doctor's arm. One skeletal hand clutches the Cardinal's robe, the other shoulders a heavy wooden cross. Rainer glanced down at his own hands folded in his lap. Noticing his fingertips were cool, he rubbed them together. *Memento mori.* He must always remember death is never far.

The choir, accompanied by a Baroque instrumental ensemble that included his own mother Elsa playing cello, soared with his favorite Bach cantata *Wachet auf, ruft uns die Stimme.* Awakened at home, far from the menacing dream of war at sea, Rainer closed his eyes and swayed imperceptibly with the music. Over the past few days, as a native son and recipient of the Ritterkreuz, he'd been lauded as a hero by nearly everyone on the street. And each night he'd slept in the arms of his beloved Anneliese. What more could he ask? Encircling Anneliese's fingers with his own, he let the music carry him higher.

Rainer partially opened his eyes and glanced at the Totentanz mural. With a lurid smile, Death danced arm in arm with the knight. An icy wave spread across Rainer's chest. When he closed his eyes again, distressing images flashed through his mind. Soot-black clouds billowing over burning slicks of oil. Ships exploding, burning, sliding beneath the frigid water. Scattered and scorched, men screaming in the darkness. Rainer's fingertips brushed across the Knights Cross around his neck. How many men had died for this?

Anneliese squeezed his hand and whispered in his ear. "*Ist alles in Ordnung, Liebling?*"

Rainer pressed his body against her. "I'm alright," he murmured.

After the service old friends and acquaintances greeted Rainer and his family in the church vestibule. Although nearly everyone commented on his mother's excellent cello performance, the warmest praise was directed at Rainer for receiving the Ritterkreuz in service of the Fatherland.

When the crowd thinned, a smiling young man in a Wehrmacht officer's uniform approached. As he reached to shake the hand of his old school friend, Rainer was startled. "Mein Gott, Horst. "What happened to you?"

Horst held his right hand, twisted within a leather glove, limp at his side and offered Rainer his left. "I was wounded in Smolensk. We never made it to Moscow." He shrugged. "*Aber es macht nichts.*"

"Well, it matters to me, my dear friend. Listen. We need some time together. Martin Ehrlichmann and I are meeting at the Ratskelller this evening. Can you come?"

Horst smiled broadly, revealing his deep dimples and strong jaw. Rainer felt a rush of warm familiarity as their deep friendship was reignited. Beside the distressing hand, not much had changed. Horst was always the most handsome of them all.

"You want me to relive old times with you and the pastor?" Horst said. "Certainly."

It was a clear, crisp winter day. Perfect for the short walk down *Fischstrasse* to *An der Obertrave* and the family home by the river. Anneliese and his parents lagged behind as Rainer strolled with his two children past the medieval city gate known as the *Holstentor.*

Gisela, a slim eleven year-old with braided hair, wore a tan Hitler Youth jacket with a swastika armband and a *Jungmädelbund* (JM) scarf. Contrary to the exhortations of his youth group leader, Joachim chose to wear his *Deutsches Jungvolk* (DJ) uniform only on special occasions. He preferred his black overcoat and a grey woolen suit for family affairs. Tall and rangy, the twelve year-old had many of his father's features: broad shoulders, square jaw, deep blue eyes, thin eyebrows.

"The Wehrmacht has a new exhibit in the Holstentor museum, *Vati*," Joachim said, using the term of endearment for father. "My DJ group visited it last week."

"Did you learn anything useful?" Rainer asked.

Joachim shrugged. "Not much I didn't already know."

"My JM troop went there too," Gisela said. "They have lots of different weapons." She rolled her eyes. "But the only things that interest Joachim are the radios."

"Ja? Is that right?" Rainer smiled approvingly at Joachim. "The radioman's one of the most important members of my crew."

"When I'm fourteen, I can take the Hitler Jugend radio operator's course, Vati." Joachim frowned. "All we do in the DJ now is exercise, march around and listen to lot of boring lectures."

"Is there anything you like in the DJ?" Rainer asked.

"I like shooting at targets."

"He's the best shot in the Lübecker DJ, Vati," Gisela said. "He won the gold medal in the winter competition. They say he'd be a great sharp shooter."

Joachim winced. "That's the last thing I want to be."

Phew. A wave of relief passed through Rainer's heart. "I'm proud that you're a good marksman, but being a radio man sounds much better to me."

"What about you, Schatzi?" Rainer said to his treasured daughter Gisela. "What do you do for fun?"

"School's boring, Vati. But the JM's fun. We go camping and play lots of sports."

"Gisela's their best runner, Vati," Joachim said. "She's always way ahead at the finish line."

Half way down an der Obertrave, they paused in front of a 300 year-old yellow brick building that had belonged to the family for several generations and waited for Anneliese and his parents to catch up.

Rainer inhaled the fresh Baltic air, his thoughts clear and relaxed for the first time in months. The decision to live in Lübeck with his parents instead of buying a separate home for his family seemed to be working well. He was at sea more often than home and the three-story house allowed plenty of room for privacy. With his father frequently away on business and his musician mother often not at home, the family servant Frieda, who lived in a narrow attic room, kept the house clean and prepared meals. This left the overall management of the household to Anneliese, an arrangement that was acceptable to everyone.

Rainer turned the polished brass knob and held the door open until all had stepped inside.

"Smells good, Frieda," Rainer said as the stout housekeeper took his coat. "What are you making for lunch?"

"*Schnüsch mit Hackbällchen*, mein Herr."

Rainer beamed. Frieda's vegetable stew with meatballs was one of his favorites. "Du bist wunderbar, Frieda."

Frieda blushed. "Ach, Herr Hartmann."

"Schon gut, Frieda," Anneliese said. "We'll eat in an hour."

Joachim and Gisela tramped upstairs to their bedrooms and the adults retired to the living room. It was a time Rainer treasured. Honest conversation with his family about what was happening with them and his homeland.

Rainer knelt and stoked the fire. Periodically, a log popped and snapped, showering crimson sparks onto the Baroque floral tile that ringed the hearth. Adding a final log to the fire, he sat down next to Anneliese on a sofa facing his parents. "It sounds like this Nazi Youth activity is taking up a lot of their time," he said. "How are the children doing in school?"

"Oh, the schools. Mein Gott, the schools," his mother said, touching a hand to her temple. "They're not what they used to be, Rainer. Not at all like the Lutheran school you attended."

Rainer raised an eyebrow "We both know there were good and bad things about that, mother."

"Maybe so," his father interjected. "But the emphasis then was on academics. Now, in the *Volksschule*, it's all ideology."

"And some of the things they're teaching, Rainer," Anneliese said. "Some very un-Christian things." She leafed through a stack of papers on a side table. "Look at this homework for example. It's a social studies problem Gisela showed me."

Rainer scanned the homework sheet:

1. Caring for a psychiatrically-ill person costs four marks a day.

2. In the Fatherland there are 300,000 such people in care.

3. What is the total cost of care for these people?

4. How many 1000-Mark marriage loans could be granted to Aryan couples with this money?

Rainer shook his head in disgust. What rubbish were the Nazis feeding his children now? It was good to be back with his family where at least he could talk freely about these matters. "More of that eugenics nonsense," he said. "I thought they put that to rest after all the uproar from the churches a few years ago."

"Nothing stops this regime," his father said. "If there's opposition, they just crush it and continue in silence."

"Of course it's not the type of thing anyone will talk about," his mother added. *"Vorsichtig.* One has to be very careful these days."

Rainer looked at his mother until she looked away. How cautious his parents had become. "How does Gisela react to this?" He asked.

"She's only eleven," his mother said. "I worry she might believe it."

"She does love her JM activities," Anneliese said. "These days the children spend almost as much time with that as with their school work. Lots of singing, dancing, camping and sports."

"And plenty of Nazi ideology, nicht wahr?" Rainer added.

"I do my best to neutralize it, Rainer," Anneliese said. She gestured toward his parents. "We all do."

"Fortunately, she's not the kind of child that reports household conversations to her youth group leaders," his mother said.

Rainer felt a chill run down his spine. "What about Joachim?" He asked.

"He doesn't seem as vulnerable," Anneliese said. "Participation in the DJ is mandatory and he performs well. But I don't think he believes a lot of what he hears."

"Hopefully this war will be over before he's called to service," Rainer's father said.

"Joachim's also going to a Lutheran youth group run by your friend Martin," his mother said. "He doesn't tell us a lot, but it sounds like they get into some interesting ethical discussions."

Like a lookout spotting imminent danger, Rainer felt his heart beat faster and the muscles of his chest tighten. Something seemed to brush against his arm. Was it Death's icy fingertips? Martin could be too outspoken at times. Might his conscience actually threaten Joachim? No. Not likely. He settled back against the sofa, his hand brushing against Anneliese's thigh for reassurance.

At eight PM, wearing a woolen deck cap, black leather jacket and scarf over his grey denim field uniform, Rainer walked to the Rathausplatz central square. On Sunday evening there was little traffic and few pedestrians. Occasionally, a red banner with a black swastika encircled in white hung from a century-old row house along the way. Scattered Nazi flags lined the streets and kiosks at the end of each block were plastered with news reports, patriotic exhortations and condemnation of Jewish traitors.

Although this was the same walk through the historic Hanseatic league city he'd taken since childhood, recent Nazi trappings lent it a sense of unfamiliarity. In wartime, he knew

94

patriotism, resilience and a unified home front were vital. But the Nazi government's attempt to extend its ideology deep into the private lives of ordinary citizens seemed sinister. Rainer loved his family, but he had to admit, he was generally more content at sea.

A stone stairway beneath the Rathaus, with its Baroque façade and five medieval turrets, led to the cave-like *Ratskelller zu Lübeck* restaurant below. Seated at an old wooden table toward the back of the dimly-lit dining room, were Horst in a gray Wehrmacht officer's uniform, and Martin, in the black tunic and round white collar of a Lutheran pastor. Although a few other people were scattered about the room, the table was an excellent choice for private conversation.

Martin rose and strode toward Rainer. Grinning broadly, he seized him by both shoulders. "Wie geht's dir, mein lieber Freund?"

"Guten Abend, Rainer," Horst said, extending his left hand.

Flushed with warm affection for two of his oldest friends, Rainer hung up his jacket and sat down.

"Horst and I are drinking Beck's. What'll you have?" Martin asked.

"A liter of Beck's sounds good."

Martin caught the Fräulein's eye, pointed to his stein and raised his index finger for one more. "Now, Rainer. Tell us how you've been."

After the usual reminiscences and updates of their lives, lubricated by a third round of beer, the conversation became more intense.

Martin exhaled slowly, studying the cigarette held between his fingertips. "I'm afraid my life is becoming a bit more risky these days, meine Freunde." He lowered his voice. "There are just too many things I can't ignore as a Christian pastor."

"What are you talking about?" Rainer asked.

"Speaking out against evil disguised as historical necessity. Euthanasia. Disappearing Jews. Assassination of dissidents."

Rainer, a bit beschwipst from the alcohol, was feeling increasingly disinhibited and a little queasy. "Hör zu, mein Freund. These days you must be very careful what you say."

"Mein lieber Rainer," Martin said, slurring his words slightly. "If I'm truly obedient to God..." He paused for a small burp. "I must stand fast." He leaned back and furrowed his brow. "In a way, I envy you. Although you're in great danger, you don't have time for all this moralizing."

Rainer blew a stream of cigarette smoke into the smoky-red beam of light from the wrought iron lantern above their table. "I don't know, Martin. They keep congratulating me for sinking so many tons of enemy shipping. But I've been doing some calculations." He tapped his index finger clumsily on the fingertips of the opposite hand. "I've probably killed more than 200 men." He leaned back in his chair. "Of course I usually can't see them from a submarine in the dark. But I've had a few too many glimpses of men swimming in an ocean covered with flaming petroleum." He closed his eyes momentarily. "Fire on the water I created."

Everyone was silent for a while. Then Horst spoke. "I saw some terrible things on the Eastern front. One day Wehrmacht soldiers shot a mother and child right in front of me. Another time I just stood around as they burned a house down with maybe a hundred Jews inside. They weren't *Einsatzgruppen*, my friends. They were ordinary Wehrmacht soldiers like me."

Rainer felt the room spinning. He'd heard rumors about ethnic paramilitary and SS Einsatzgruppen death squads murdering Jews and partisans on the Eastern front. But this was the first time he'd heard of ordinary German army units murdering civilians. "Are you sure they were Wehrmacht, Horst?"

"Sadly, Ja. My own unit in fact. But I was spared the special duty. I was wounded before the order came down."

"Mein Gott, Horst," Rainer said. "What would've happened if you'd been healthy?"

Martin shook his head. "I don't know, Rainer. In the Wehrmacht, anyone resisting an order might be shot. But I can't imagine shooting civilians. It's disrespectful of all military honor."

"*Gott sei dank*," Rainer said. "Thank God you were never ordered, mein lieber Freund."

For several long minutes they all remained silent. Rainer tried to clear his head. How much had changed since they were carefree schoolmates. Flying kites in the park, sailboating on the Baltic.

Horst drained his beer and pulled back his chair. "Well, I'd better go. Ilse will start worrying about me. It's been great seeing you again. Take care of yourselves. Both of you."

Rainer grasped Horst's good hand. "What will you do now?"

"I've been assigned to a local transport unit," Horst said, pulling on his jacket. "Don't worry about us. We're not likely to be bombed like Hamburg or Kiel. But you should be careful out there." He patted Rainer on the shoulder. *"Gute Jagd,* mein Freund. I hope your next hunt is as successful as the last."

Rainer sat back down, gave Martin a cigarette and lit one for himself. "I wouldn't believe the Wehrmacht murdered civilians if Horst hadn't actually witnessed it."

Martin leaned close. "There are a lot of things going on here you're unaware of."

"For example?"

"Do you remember Aaron Blumenthal in the Gymnasium?"

"Funny little math genius. Wasn't he?"

"Ja. Blumenthal always had the right answer. He went on to be a successful accountant, but now he's in a labor camp."

"Arbeitslager? Why?"

"Don't you know?" Martin said, shaking his head "All Jews are being systematically eliminated from the Reich."

Rainer felt he might vomit. Too many beers. So many bad things happening in his homeland. But what could he do? It was so much simpler on patrol. Kill or be killed. No time for moral decisions. "I think I've had too much to drink, Martin. Time to go home."

Martin smiled. "Leb' wohl, mein Freund. I'll see you next time you're in Lübeck."

The *Rathausplatz* was completely dark. Although no one thought Lübeck was a significant military target, the usual lights illuminating the medieval spires of the 13th-century building were extinguished. Walking past rows of darkened windows and empty streets, Rainer felt the chill of the night. He longed for Anneliese's touch. To dissolve in her arms in his own warm bed.

TRAVEMÜNDE, Germany
— February 19, 1942

Outside the Bahnhof a light snow was falling. Carrying their single suitcase, Rainer took Anneliese's gloved hand and tested the pavement with the toe of his boot. The snow, about ten centimeters deep, was dry and fluffy. The familiar walk along the Baltic Sea would be easy. In his youth, the *Gasthaus Rosalinde* had been a favorite family summer retreat. Now, with his parents minding Joachim and Gisela, he and Anneliese had two days on their own.

Smoke rose from the chimneys of the hotels and private mansions lining the boardwalk. Along the seawall, a row of wicker enclosures for summertime bathers was layered with snow. Icicles glistened on lampposts and gusts of frigid Baltic wind swirled the top layer of snow along the path. Offshore, a light cruiser, its red and black naval pennant flapping in the wind, was gliding toward the mouth of the Trave river. Rainer felt proud. Unlike the contested Atlantic shore, the Baltic coast was completely controlled by the Kriegsmarine.

After a warm reception by the Gasthaus owners, they settled in to a large 19th-century bedroom with a balcony overlooking the Baltic Sea. An oak bed covered with a down-filled Federdecke and an ornately-tiled ceramic stove in the corner gave the room both warmth and charm.

Annelise drew back the lace curtains and stood gazing at the water. Silently, Rainer pressed his body against her back and began nuzzling her neck with his lips and tongue. With Rainer's swollen phallus pulsing against the cleft beneath her buttocks, Anneliese's breath grew rapid and shallow. She tilted her head back, unbuttoned her cardigan and allowed him to peel it off her arms. Through the soft fabric of her brassiere, his fingertips kneaded the supple flesh of her full nipples until, swollen and erect, they were transformed into the wondrous pillars of flesh his hungry lips desired.

A sunbeam, passing through scattered clouds, illuminated the room for a moment, then flickered along the walls. Anneliese turned, allowing her brassiere to fall to the floor. Mein Gott, she was beautiful. Eyes transfixed on her swaying breasts, Rainer tore off his shirt and swept her into his arms. Her fingers fumbled with the buckle of his belt. Then, with one great tug, his pants were at his knees and his pulsing flesh was in the palm of her hand. Their lips met fiercely, tongues probing each other's mouths. Shuffling backwards in this primal embrace, they fell onto the bed.

Throughout the timeless afternoon, they lay together, caressing, kissing and making languorous love. At sunset, waking from a brief nap, Rainer lay naked beneath the Federdecke, silently watching Anneliese as she sat up in bed, absorbed in a book of poetry by Agnes Miegel. Her bathrobe, relaxed about her neck, exposed one collarbone, rounded beneath ivory skin. Her bare foot was resting against his thigh and her hair fell across her shoulders. Such stillness and beauty.

"*Gut geschlafen, Liebling?*" Anneliese asked.

"Fantastisch." He smiled, then slid out of bed to retrieve a small package from their suitcase. " I have something special for you, meine Liebe."

Anneliese tore open the wrapping and gasped as she saw the small porcelain statue. "Cupid and Psyche!" She threw her arms around his neck. "Ach, Rainer. Du bist wunderbar."

Chapter Ten
Along the First Coast

The-month-old campaign by German submarines off the Atlantic coast of the United States is furnishing rather bitter evidence of the fact that the world war no longer is a matter of distant interest for residents of this country...The U-Boats have sunk at this writing 15 out of 16 large vessels attacked, taking a toll of 113,163 tons, and have created a roll of 438 sailors known dead or missing.

New York Times
February 15, 1942

VILANO BEACH, Florida
— February 15, 1942

A light breeze, carrying the sound of breakers from the beach below, ruffled the curtains of the tiny room in the Flamingo Motel as Ramón traced lacy patterns along Violet's naked hip exposed in the moonlight. Mesmerized by the texture of her silky skin beneath his trailing fingertips, his breath and thoughts became entrained with the rhythm of the Atlantic ocean.

Violet was not only beautiful and alluring; she was fascinating. Witty and erudite, she fully embraced all of the sensual aspects of life. So how did she ever end up with a guy like Major Anderson? Maybe as a handsome young man from Texas A&M, he'd swept her off her feet. And now, after ten years of childless marriage, she was looking for some spice in her life.

STRAC—strictly according to Army regulations. That was Major Anderson all the way. But not Violet. As soon as their squadron arrived in Jacksonville, she'd called him. Now they arranged clandestine encounters when her husband was away. This month, with Major Anderson training in ASW techniques with the RAF in Scotland, they'd slipped away for a weekend at the beach near St. Augustine. Violet pursued their sizzling liaison with no sign of remorse, but Ramón had some reservations. He didn't really like going behind another man's back. But damn! What a bang-up dame. How could he resist?

Ramón glanced at the luminescent hands of his A-11 wristwatch. 0400. He'd need to be on the road in half an hour to make the flight line on time. Slowly, he inched his way out of the covers, trying to slip out of bed without waking her. He made it to the edge of the mattress before the smooth rhythm of her sleeping breath caught and she opened her eyes and sat up in bed. Ramón watched her tantalizing breasts sway in the dim light as she brushed the hair away from her face. Jesus. Was she beautiful.

Gazing at Ramón standing naked by the window, Violet whispered: "Good morning, Adonis."

Ramón knelt by the bedside and took her head in his hands. "You're so dazzling." He kissed her. "You must be Aphrodite."

He stood and began dressing. "Got to get moving. I need to be on the flight line at six thirty."

Violet stretched her arms and yawned. "Well, I might sleep in a bit, then take a walk on the beach. Floyd's not getting back until this afternoon."

"Looking forward to that, are you?"

"Oh stop it. He's not a monster."

"Maybe not to you, but for me..." He paused and smiled. "He's all monster."

Violet laughed. "It's true he does have a thing about Mexicans, even handsome ones. But there's a reason for that."

Ramón stopped buckling his belt. "What do you mean?"

She cocked her head. "Did you know his grandfather was killed by Mexican border raiders."

Ramón dropped his jaw. "Really? When was that?"

"Sometime early in their revolution. He owned a ranch in Glenn Springs. Floyd's parents never stop talking about it. I'm sure they passed on some negative attitudes about Mexicans when he was growing up in Pearsall."

"Pearsall, huh? So he's a small-town guy like me."

"Yep. I guess it takes a big city girl to handle you country boys."

Ramón narrowed his eyes. "Is that what you're doing, handling us both?"

Violet held up her hand. "Come on. I'm just teasing you. What I mean is I'm married to the guy and that's that." She paused. "But you're something special in my life. Understand?"

He gazed deeply into her eyes. "And you're pure dynamite to me. Do you know that?"

Outside the motel, Ramón pushed a low hanging palm frond away from his face and stepped onto the concrete parking lot. The brisk ocean breeze rustled his pant legs but failed to penetrate his leather jacket. He looked up at the motel's sign. With the letters g and o burnt out, the neon message sent out to sea read: Flamin Motel. Stupid bastards. With housewives along the coast cooking by candlelight, how can so many businesses ignore the black-out request? Christ. Our merchant ships were being silhouetted against the shore like rubber ducks in a shooting gallery.

Gliding his fingertips along the shiny paint of Violet's red Cabriolet, he walked to his low-slung 1930 Harley-Davidson motorcycle. With a rag from his canvas backpack, he wiped dew from the leather seat and twin headlights. He opened the gas line, primed the choke and keyed the ignition. After a few vigorous kick starts, the engine roared to life, vibrating the leather seat and rear fender with its growling, staccato rhythm. He put on his goggles, zipped up his jacket and climbed on the motorcycle. Advancing the throttle while slowly engaging the clutch, he pulled out onto the coastal road that led to Route 1, the Dixie Highway.

A diaphanous cobweb of silver fog hung low in the salt grass along the roadside heading north to Neptune Beach. With little traffic, Ramón cranked the Harley. Despite the recent reduction in speed limit, it was unlikely any speed traps were active at such an early hour. Soon he was cruising at his top speed of 60 miles per hour through a starlit landscape of sandy pines, tall grasses and saw palmetto.

Erik was waiting outside The Breakers, one of many Jacksonville hotels requisitioned to house the burgeoning military community. Just a block from a small amusement park on the beach, Erik and Ramón felt lucky to share a small room with a peekaboo view of the ocean.

"Heard the news?" Erik asked as he hopped on the motorcycle.

Ramón shook his head. "Too busy. What's new?"

Erik frowned. "Singapore's fallen to the Japs."

"Shit." Ramón lifted his goggles and spat on the pavement. "So much for the impregnable fortress of the Far East."

"Forget about the Japs. We've got more than we can handle with these frigging U-Boats," Erik said. "I heard we lost another tanker yesterday off Savannah."

"Guess the boys out of Chatham went sub hunting then. Any luck?" Erik's glum response was lost in the roar of the engine as Ramón pulled away from the curb.

The early morning route to Imeson Army Air Field was clear and they passed through the checkpoint in plenty of time for the 0610 pre-mission briefing.

At 6 PM, after an uneventful, six-hour ASW patrol along the coast, Erik and Ramón met Erik's former college roommate at the Lighthouse Bar and Grill. Adam Peterson wasn't the Midwesterner Ramón expected. Unlike the tall and brawny Erik, Adam was thin and wiry like a spider monkey. When he stood to greet them, an officer's hat, with an eagle perching atop a shield and two crossed anchors, fell from his lap to the floor. Above his left shirt pocket was a half eagle and on his collar, brass Ensign bars.

With a broad grin, Adam stepped forward, grasped Erik's hand and slapped him on the back. "Sonofabitch! Imagine us both ending up here."

"Glad you called," Erik said. "It's been a long time." He turned to Ramón. "Adam and I go way back, Ray. Roommates since freshman year at Carleton. He saved my ass a few times." He tapped Adam on the shoulder. "But I never thought he'd end up being a poopie bag sailor."

Adam laughed as he shook Ramón's hand. "Actually, we prefer to call ourselves LTA pilots," he said, raising an eyebrow at Erik.

"LTA?" Ramón said.

"Lighter than air. Blimps to you guys." Adam gestured for them to sit down. "I'm drinking Schlitz. What'll you have?"

Erik chuckled. "Adam's from Milwaukee. He always sticks to the home brew."

"Schlitz is fine with me," Ramón said. "Let's order a pitcher and get some deep-fried gator tails."

Eyes wide, Adam touched his throat. "You serious?"

"Now don't get jazzed, Adam. It tastes like chicken," Erik said.

"And it's great with hot sauce," Ramón added.

Adam placed a Lucky Strike between his lips and offered the pack around. "You've certainly gone native, Erik." He struck a match and lit everyone's cigarette. "You guys spend a lot of time hanging out in bars?"

Erik frowned. "Hardly. We fly six hours a day, six days a week and on the seventh, we're on alert all night." He groaned. "And pretty soon that free seventh day will be taken up with some bombing practice. Once our squadron leader gets back from his RAF course."

Adam shook his head."That's not so bad. We're in the air about sixteen hours a day."

"Sunk any U-Boats with that gas bag of yours?" Ramón asked.

"Well, early in the game we thought we had one, but it was never confirmed."

"Are you kidding?" Ramón said. "Join the club. We had a questionable hit on a Jap sub back in December."

Adam looked at Erik, who nodded. "He's right. We've taken a lot of crap for that one."

Ramón shrugged. "Erik was pretty uncommitted. I made the call, but in retrospect, I think it was probably just a big tree or maybe a whale."

"Shit. Back then we knew nothing about the hunt, right?"

"Nada," Ramón said.

"It's still like a needle in the haystack, don't you think?" Erik said. "Mighty big ocean out there."

"What brings you to Jacksonville?" Ramón asked.

"Just an overnight at the Naval Air Station. I'm on a test run from Lakehurst down the coast with some new equipment."

Ramón leaned forward. "What kind of equipment?"

Adam lowered his voice. "Well, of course this is top secret." He paused and smiled. "Though I'm sure the Krauts know all about it."

"Anything new sounds good to us," Ramón said. "Hell. We just got depth charges last week. Other than that, we've got zip."

"No radar. No nothing," Erik said. "We just fly in circles out there."

"Yeah," Ramón said. "Then the goddam U-Boats sink ships right under our nose at night."

"How the hell do you see anything at night?" Adam asked.

"Good question," Erik said.

"If a ship's been hit, we go out with the Navy," Ramón said. "Sub chasers and destroyers cruise around and we drop flares if we see something."

Adam shook his head. "So most of the time you're just out there relying on visual contact?"

"That's about the size of it," Ramón said.

Adam leaned in close and lowered his voice. "Well, that's the nice thing about the blimp I'm on now. We've got radar and a magnetic anomaly detection (MAD) device."

"Really? How're they working out?" Erik asked.

"Radar's good for detecting a large ship at 15 miles and a periscope at five. Then, if they dive, the MAD device is good for about 400 feet."

"Wow! That sounds pretty nifty," Ramón said.

"Yeah. If we're right on top of them," Adam said. "But subs are a lot smaller than ships. And I'll be damned if they don't go underwater." He pulled on his cigarette. "Radar picks up big ships a hell of a lot better than subs and the MAD device often gets false signals from the ocean floor."

"Well shit," Ramón said. "Are you guys going to be any more use to us than the Hooligan Navy cruising around out there in their pleasure boats?"

"He's talking about the Cruising Club of America," Erik explained to Adam. "Maybe they're good for morale, but they don't make much difference against U-Boats."

"Look. I don't mean to sound so pessimistic," Adam said. "From time to time, everything works just great. And that's when we call you guys in for the kill."

"I'll drink to that," Ramón said, raising his glass.

Chapter Eleven
Lighter Than Air

Blimps, "gas bags of the skies," may be one of the effective answers to the continuing German submarine operations along our coasts... Along the American coast, where they are not exposed to attack by enemy aircraft, an attack to which they are extremely vulnerable, blimps are a relatively cheap but highly effective form of patrol.

New York Times
February 13, 1942

50 MILES EAST OF JACKSONVILLE, Florida
-— March 15, 1942

At a distance of three miles from a submarine cruising on the surface in the early morning sun, Ramón banked into a shallow turn and began a steep descent toward his practice target. Below, a light blinked on and off from the submarine's conning tower.

"Pilot, copilot. He's ready." Erik said.

"Roger, pilot. Executing attack."

A mile away, the submarine began to dive. Like an osprey, Sizzling Rita leveled off 50 feet above the water and roared toward her prey at 230 mph.

With the bomb site useless at this altitude, Ramón had to rely on his bombardier Angelo to estimate the range of the diving submarine and time the release of three non-explosive bombs, spaced 40 feet apart. When the practice bombs struck the water, a spotting charge of black smoke would be released. Circling above, the squadron leader Major Anderson waited to observe the distance between a water slug discharged from the submarine's torpedo tube and the columns of smoke released by Ramón's spotting charges.

An hour later, back at Imeson Field, Major Anderson reviewed the day's practice bombing. "Not bad, Morales. Your range and line errors have improved significantly. And you were pretty much on target. Unfortunately..." He shook his head. "The sub was already over twenty seconds into its dive. You know the drill. The probability of an effective hit was less than five percent."

In the late afternoon, wearing swim trunks, Erik and Ramón read the Jacksonville Journal on the veranda of Hattie's Beach Bar and Grill. Ramón crumpled the newspaper and looked out at the ocean. The war news was pretty grim— we might just lose this fucking war. Our Navy got pretty banged up last month in the Java Sea. MacArthur hightailed out of Corregidor. And Rommel was rolling across Libya. Here on the East Coast, seven ships were sunk in the last week. Everyone was on edge. Although our boys had begun arriving in England, Americans had yet to dust a single Nazi.

"Y'all have some more coffee, boys?" The weather-beaten waitress with gnarled hands asked. "Better enjoy it while you can. They say the ration books are coming out in May."

Ramón drained his cup and gave it to her for a refill. "You don't think they'll put coffee on there, do you darling? Hard to survive without it."

Erik looked up from the sports page. "Did you see this, Ray? They're letting two colored boys try out for the White Sox. One of them was a football star at UCLA."

"Really? What's his name?"

Erik scanned the newspaper article. "Jackie Robinson."

"Well, I doubt much'll come of it. But good for him."

"Damn, Ray. Before you know it, they'll be letting Mexicans play."

"Listen, buddy. There's a few of us in the Majors already." Ramón cocked his head to one side. "Did you know Ted Williams' mother's Mexican?"

"The slugger? You kidding? What's next, Japs on first base?"

"Maybe so. Guess there're plenty of Krauts in the big leagues already."

Erik laughed. "Yep. Hard to tell us good guys from the Nazis, isn't it?"

Ramón threw his towel at Erik. "Go for a quick swim?"

"I don't know, Ray. Last time I hit that water I couldn't find my balls for a week."

Ramón stood and started walking toward the beach. "Come on. The air's seventy five and the water's probably at least sixty degrees. What more could you ask for?"

At twilight, a sea breeze rippled the flags along the landing strip as Erik and Ramón walked toward the officers club at Imeson Army Air Field. There wasn't much activity except in

Sizzling Rita's hangar where the ground crew was grooming their B-25 for possible action on tonight's alert duty.

Vernon, the skinny radio operator/waist gunner from Oklahoma was standing on the cabin rooftop adjusting the antenna.

"Any problems, Sergeant?" Ramón called out.

"Nothing big, sir. I'll have everything shipshape soon."

"Shipshape?" Erik said. "Boy, you've been breathing this salt air too long."

"Thanks, Sergeant," Ramón said. "Hope we all get a good sleep tonight."

On a Sunday evening, few tables were occupied at the officer's mess. Ramón loaded his tray with a Bunyanesque meal of pot roast, mashed potatoes, gravy, green beans, bread, butter, a tall glass of milk and an orange. "Shall we sit down with that guy?" He said, gesturing toward a Royal Air Force officer sitting alone. Erik nodded.

"May we join you, sir?" Ramón asked, recalling that three bars on the officer's epaulets indicated a Squadron Leader, the equivalent of a U.S. Army Major.

"Certainly, Yanks," the RAF officer said with a warm smile. "I'd be delighted." He extended his hand. "Duncan Richardson's the name. Pull up a chair."

Ramón liked the few Brits he'd met so far. They were friendly and often had a wry sense of humor. Now, with the Royal Navy's converted corvettes joining ASW patrols off the coast, British sailors were not rare in Jacksonville. But this was the first RAF officer he'd met. "What brings you to Imeson, sir?"

"Just trying to pass on a few tips from our experience with the U-Boats in the North Atlantic."

"That should be helpful, sir," Erik said.

"Tchah," Richardson said with a hint of annoyance. "I'm not sure anyone's really listening. And your Army and Navy don't exactly see eye to eye."

"We know what you mean, sir," Erik said. "The Navy wants control of the sea. But they don't have enough aircraft, so they need us to help out."

"And they want overall command," Ramón added.

"Precisely." The lanky Squadron leader smiled and ran his fingers through his graying, auburn hair. "It's a bloody cockup, lads. General Arnold agrees with the idea of a coastal command, but Admiral King's not on board. He's also against convoys along the coast, the only thing we've found to be effective against the Jerries." He drained his glass with a slight shake of his head. "A bit dodgy this cold beer. Don't you think? So what are you lads up to tonight?"

"On alert," Ramón said. "Not much happening at the moment. But we'd sure like to hear some of those tips you were talking about."

"Nice to hear someone's interested," Richardson said. "We've been at this for a while you know."

"We're all ears, sir," Erik said.

Richardson smiled. "Convoys are the main thing. But I don't suppose you pilots can do much about that. The hunter-killer tactics your command favors are fine, but first, you have to protect the transports. Hopefully, our trawlers will demonstrate that. Unescorted tankers along your coast are tempting targets for U-Boats."

Ramón's sigh was deep. "Don't we know that!"

"Once it's perfected," Richardson continued. "Airborne radar's going to be a big addition to high-frequency and magnetic anomaly detection. Afraid it has a bit of limited range now though."

Ramón glanced at Erik. Just what Adam's blimp was testing.

"We don't have any radar yet, sir. And Army-Navy operations are…"

"Pretty crappy," Erik interjected.

Richardson shrugged. "That's why you need a unified coastal command like we have. Of course, it took us a while to overcome traditional rivalries. But huge shipping losses have a way of forcing the issue. Wouldn't you say?"

"Thanks for the tips, sir," Ramón said, pushing back his chair. "A bit frustrating though. Doesn't seem like there's much we can do differently right now."

The squadron leader placed a hand on Ramón's forearm as he rose to leave. "Perhaps I can give you chaps one useful piece of advice." Erik and Ramón leaned in like football players huddling around their quarterback. "Stick with it longer."

"Sir?" Erik said.

"You chaps drop a few depth charges, circle around for a while and leave the scene within a few hours. Am I right?" Erik and Ramón nodded. "Our crews stay around much longer. A day or two if necessary. Jerry needs fresh air and battery charging. He's got to come up sometime."

Shortly after midnight, Bam! Bam! Bam! Ramón was wrested from deep, dreamless sleep by pounding like a sledgehammer on a steel door. "Alert, sirs!" An airman called out. "Report to the ready room."

"We're on our way!" Ramón shouted as he threw off the covers and jumped out of bed before he was fully awake. Fumbling in the dark, a stream of excitement surged through his body, clearing the fog of sleep and focusing his mind. Erik snapped on the overhead light and they both dressed quickly. Moonlight filtering through a cloud bank cast flickering shadows against the wall as they clambered down the stairwell to Base Ops.

A musty odor of mold and cigarette smoke pervaded the air in the ready room where the major on duty wasted no time. "A blimp has picked up a U-Boat on radar," he said, handing Ramón a yellow sheet of paper with a decoded Morse message from the naval air station.

031542 2350 hrs.
TO: USAAF JAX
From: NAS JAX
At 2345 NZNO2 blimp sighted U-Boat on attack course six nautical miles south of unescorted northbound freighter. Lat 31 deg 3 min 29 sec N. Long 80 deg 16 min 25 sec W. Navy PBY and Coast Guard cutter dispatched. Request assistance.

The major pointed to a red pin already placed on the wall map of the Atlantic coast. "It's about 48 nautical miles off the coast, 72 from here. The blimp has orders to continue tracking but avoid engagement. Good hunting, boys."

Erik turned toward Ramón as they jogged across the runway toward Sizzling Rita. "NZNO2. That's Adam, Ray. Guess all that fancy equipment's paying off."

Ramón picked up the pace. "Let's hope so. About time we catch one of those Kraut bastards."

The ground crew had already completed preflight inspection and Sizzling Rita was soon soaring above cloud banks that billowed like ashen snowfields in the moonlight. Occasional breaks revealed the dark surface of the ocean below. Ramón squinted into the murky darkness beneath the clouds. It was going to be difficult to see anything tonight. But with guidance from Adam's blimp, and a fortuitous break in the clouds, they might have a chance to catch a U-Boat on the surface. He consciously relaxed his shoulders and adjusted his radio headset.

"Navigator, pilot," Ramón said over the intercom.

"Roger, nav," Roy answered.

"Destination latitude 31 degrees, 3 minutes, 29 seconds north. Longitude 80 degrees, 16 minutes, 25 seconds west," Ramón said. "Estimated speed, two three zero, altitude three thousand."

"Radio, pilot," Ramón said. "How soon can we establish VHF voice contact?"

"Roger, radio. Estimate ten minutes."

"Pilot, bombardier. Pretty cloudy, Skipper. Can't see much."

"Pilot, navigator. Flight plan complete. Estimated time of arrival 0048."

Eyes fixed on his instrument panel, Ramón reviewed his plan of action. Once VHF communication was established with the blimp, he'd drop to 500 feet. Despite the moonlight, the dense cloud cover would make spotting a low-lying vessel on the ocean very difficult. Hopefully, the blimp would be able to guide him to the target.

"Pilot, radio. Received a Morse message from NZNO2: U-Boat attack imminent. Preparing to engage."

Ramón's stomach felt queasy. This was bonkers. The blimp was no match for a U-Boat. The only armaments they had on board were a Browning machine gun and a few depth charges. The U-Boats had powerful antiaircraft weapons, including two large flak guns and the same cannon that was used against tanks. They'd already shot down a number of RAF aircraft in this war. And airplanes were a hell of a lot faster than blimps.

"Pilot, navigator. ETA thirteen minutes."

"Radio, pilot. Can we establish VHF voice contact yet?"

"Roger, radio. Calling now."

The second hand inched around the face of Ramón's watch at a glacial pace. Damn fools. They're sitting ducks up there.

"Pilot, radio. VHF contact established."

"Patch them through, Vern."

The blimp's signal was weak and distorted by static, but Ramón recognized Adam's voice. "9100. This is NZNO2. Over."

Ramón switched channels to the intercom. "Copilot, pilot. You better take this."

Erik spoke into the microphone. "NZNO2 this is 9100. Is that you, Adam? Over."

"9100, NZNO2. Roger that." Adam laughed, his voice fading in and out through static interference. "Glad you could make it…" Crackle. Sizzzzz. Static briefly overwhelmed the signal. "U-Boat's clearly within attack range of the freighter. Don't think they've spotted us…" Sizzzzz. "Descending through the clouds. Over."

Erik leaned forward and spoke slowly. "NZNO2, 9100. Maintain contact, but do not engage target. Repeat. Do not engage. Our ETA is less than ten minutes. Over."

"9100, NZNO2. Negative. Can't wait…" Crackle. Sizzzzz. "Attack imminent. Heading down. Over."

"NZNO2, 9100. Over." For the next few minutes, Erik repeatedly tried to raise the blimp with no response.

Then Adam's voice abruptly returned on the VHF channel. "9100, NZNO2. Over."

"NZNO2, 9100. Go ahead," Erik responded.

"9100, NZNO2. We have visual contact. Dropping down to initiate attack at 200 feet. We'll open up with the Browning and drop depth charges as we pass over them."

There was a long pause in the transmission punctuated by static. Then Adam's voice returned with an urgent tone. "Looks like they've spotted us! Tracers coming in and…" *Krumppff! Ping. Klank!* The sounds of a muffled explosion followed by tearing metal was transmitted through Adam's microphone. "Cannon fire. Direct hit to port engine. On fire!" The radio went silent.

"NZNO2, 9100. Over." Erik repeated multiple times with no response. Ramón gripped the steering yoke and dropped to 500 feet above the darkened ocean. Nothing on the horizon and no communication with the blimp. Christ. Why couldn't they have waited? He narrowed his eyes and focused all his concentration on the water's surface.

Several minutes later the last transmission from Adam came in. The signal was surprisingly strong. "9100, NZNO2. Multiple hits to the balloon. Engine on fire. Losing altitude fast. Go Knights! Erik."

"NZN02, 9100. Over." Erik tried repeatedly to raise the blimp, but there was no further response. Ramón circled the area several times, then placed a gentle hand on Erik's shoulder. "We need to let it go, Erik. They're down."

Cigarette smoke mingled with dust particles scintillating in the morning light above their table in the Officer's Club. Since their return to base at 0400, Erik and Ramón had received no news of the downed blimp. The freighter, spared a U-Boat attack by the blimp's intervention, was unaware of the incident until contacted by the Coast Guard. PBYs and cruisers had searched the area all night without luck.

"Go Knights? What did Adam mean by that?" Ramón asked.

"School mascot," Erik said. "I played ball and Adam was captain of the cheerleading team."

"Sonofabitch. He went down cheering you on."

"Yeah. Imagine that." Erik's voice was quavering.

"You said he saved your ass a few times. What'd he do?"

Erik bit his lip and stared out the window. "Helped me cram all night for a class I was failing. Backed up a few alibis. Got me home when I was plastered."

"Sounds like a good friend."

"The best."

"Well, let's not give up hope yet. There's still no confirmation."

An anxious looking airman approached their table. "The major said you would want to know, sirs. A PBY found remnants of the blimp's balloon."

"Survivors?" Ramón asked.

The airman looked down at the floor. "None found, sir."

Chapter Twelve
Before Your Very Eyes

The normal large German submarine has a cruising radius of about 10,000 or 11,000 miles. It can remain away from its home base for periods ranging from 60 to 90 days, depending upon the amount of time at which it must cruise at high speed, abnormally exhausting its fuel reserves. It can carry from twelve to twenty torpedoes and from 100 to 150 shells for the five-inch gun generally carried on its deck for use against unarmed ships.

New York Times
March 8, 1942

SAINT AUGUSTINE, Florida
— March 28, 1942

A young Seminole man in a gray shirt with black stripes was circling a large alligator. The alligator, following his every movement with narrow, vertical pupils, swept the dusty pit with its great reptilian tail. The man stripped off his shirt (revealing deep scars across his muscular chest and arms) and sprinted behind the alligator's tail. Tossing his shirt over the creature's head, he sprang like a Florida bobcat onto its back and wrapped his legs beneath its hind feet. He pushed down over the alligator's eyes with one hand and slid the other beneath its jaw. The great reptile thrashed as the man pulled its head upward to a 90-degree angle, but was unable to open its jaws or perform its notorious death roll. The young man raised an arm in victory and the crowd at the St. Augustine Alligator Farm broke into applause.

Violet pressed her lips against Ramón's neck. The subtle aroma of jasmine and cedar wafted into his nostrils. In a white cotton, knee-length dress that accentuated her lithe figure, she looked more beautiful than ever. "That was exciting," she said. "Did you see those big scars?"

Ramón smiled. "Looks like he must've lost a few of his earlier matches."

Violet squeezed his arm with both hands. "Still. He was magnificent, wasn't he?"

"He's good alright. Even if the gator's jaw muscles are weak opening up, it can still bite down with a whole lot of pressure. And that body and tail?"

"Powerful." She widened her eyes. "That was real wrestling."

"Got to hand it to these guys," Ramón said. "After getting kicked off their own land, they sure figured how to make a buck or two off tourists."

The temperature was in the high seventies and the sky was clear. Dressed in slacks and a Hawaiian shirt, Ramón was an anonymous tourist visiting America's oldest city on a Saturday afternoon. No use chancing recognition in uniform. Arm in arm, he and Violet headed for his Harley in the parking lot.

Back on the Atlantic Coast Highway, they left Anastasia Island and crossed over the Mantanzas River on a long stone bridge guarded by growling, white marble lions. They parked halfway up the Avenida Menendez and walked the rest of the way along the bay to the imposing Castillo de San Marcos. On the grounds of the old fortress they rested on a bench between a pair of colonial Spanish cannons. Violet drew a fingertip softly across his cheek. "Does this feel like your heritage?"

Ramón shrugged. "Hard to say. The Mexican revolution was all about getting free from Spain, wasn't it? What about you? Do you feel connected to England?"

"Well, my grandparents were Cody and Edwards. Probably Irish and English." She wrinkled her forehead. "Yeah. I guess I do feel a bit connected." She snuggled against him and whispered. "But you have a bit of Indian blood in you, right?" She squeezed his hand "Maybe that's why you're so handsome."

Ramón laughed. "I'm glad you go for us mixed bloods. Although I'm a little ambivalent, I do think the history of the conquistadors is fascinating. They actually tried to build a new Spain over here." He frowned. "Unfortunately, some of my Indian ancestors ended up on the short end of that stick."

Violet sighed. "And I guess it's not much better in Texas, is it?"

Ramón guffawed. "That's an understatement. Remember that husband of yours?"

Violet pulled back. "I thought we agreed not to talk about Floyd today."

Ramón took her hand. "You're right. I'm sorry." He paused, looking out over the bay. "It's interesting. Maybe it's because I'm in the Army, but I have yet to be challenged by any racists here."

"What do you mean?"

"See all those water fountains? White and colored? How am I supposed to take that? Am I white?"

"Hmmm. I'm not sure about that." She laughed. "You could be Italian." She shook her head vigorously. "No, probably not a good idea with the war going on. Maybe some other dark, white person?"

Ramón laughed. "You're something else. Let's go see the old town."

They walked through the stone gates of the city to St. George Street and spent the next hour meandering past 17th-century buildings, tourist shops and restaurants. As they passed by a newspaper stand, Ramón glanced at the headlines: *Japan Heavily Bombs Bataan*. Images of Angel going down on Wake Island flashed through his mind. He stopped for a moment and looked at Violet. "Those poor bastards on Bataan can't hold out much longer."

Silently, Violet took his hand, kissed it and resumed walking.

Past the cathedral, they came upon a grove of oak trees with an open-air pavilion beneath a small cupola. Violet stopped and sighed. "Funny about this place. Although they call it the public market now, it was actually where they sold slaves."

Ramón studied the old building. "Jesus. A slave market. I don't know. Think they've gotten much past that now?"

Turning up a side street, they walked in silence. Ramón had mixed emotions. The old colonial city was truly beautiful.

But beneath its charm he sensed a dark undercurrent of injustice and racism. Not so different from where he'd grown up really. But here the hatred was directed against Negroes instead of Mexicans. Anglo Texans weren't fond of Negroes either, but the slave trade had not extended much into the upper Rio Grande Valley where he grew up. Near the border with Mexico, Anglo racism was directed mostly against Indians and Mexicans. Here in Florida he was seeing extreme forms of racism, but somehow he remained outside of it.

"Getting hungry? I am," Violet said.

"How about that place?" Ramón said, gesturing across the street toward an old Spanish style building with pastel blue siding and a sign that read Mango Bar and Grill. As they entered the restaurant, he glanced at a Coca-Cola sign in the window and tightened his jaw. Ice cold Coca-Cola. White customers only.

The setting sun cast a canopy of orange light over palm trees lining the Atlantic Coast Highway as they rode back to Neptune Beach. On the ocean side of the highway, waves crashed and receded along the sand. With Violet's arms wrapped around his waist, and the roar of the Harley in his ears, Ramón enjoyed the ocean air rushing over his face and streaming through his hair. Leaning his body from side to side through the curves on the highway like a graceful surfer, he flowed with the rhythm of his powerful motorcycle.

Shortly after sunset, Ramón and Violet cruised past the gaily-lit boardwalk at Neptune Beach. Hundreds of uniformed young men, many with women on their arms, bought beer, snacks and souvenirs before clambering aboard an amusement park ride or trying their hand at a game of chance or skill. Ramón felt vaguely uneasy. What were the odds someone might recognize them together? He glanced at Violet. Her relaxed expression showed no sign of concern about their risky behavior. Maybe that's what made this dangerous affair so tantalizing.

On the way to the Breakers Hotel from the parking lot, Violet stopped and looked back at the amusement park. "Want to go on the Ferris wheel tonight?" She asked, pointing to a huge wheel, wreathed in colored lights, spinning high above the beach to the ebullient rhythm of a driving, steam calliope.

He gave her hand a squeeze. "Sounds pretty romantic to me. But how about a little rest first? Erik's out for the evening."

She wet her lips with her tongue. "A little rest sounds great."

Ramón nodded at the young man reading a magazine at the reception desk, and hurried upstairs with Violet. Visitors of the opposite sex were technically prohibited in rooms requisitioned by the army, but enforcement was slack. Tomorrow he'd be sure to give the receptionist a pack of cigarettes for his discretion.

The room Ramón shared with Erik was just big enough to hold two beds, a dresser and a chair. A hotel sign across the street cast pale blue fluorescent light into the dark room and a soft ocean breeze streamed through a cracked-open window.

As Ramón reached for the light switch, Violet grasped his hand. "Let's leave them off. I like blue." She took off her shoes and sat on the bed.

"How about a beer?" Ramón asked. "Afraid all I've got is JAX." He opened the cooler and saw the ice was melted. "And maybe it's a little warm."

"Warm JAX is fine," Violet said, placing a cigarette between her lips. "Give a girl a light?"

Ramón plucked the cigarette from her lips and swept her off the bed into his arms. She opened her mouth to his tongue and pressed herself against him. A wave of ecstasy pulsed through his loins, swelling his cock against her pelvis. His fingers combed through her thick, auburn hair, trailed down her neck and shoulders, and drew furrows in the space between the ribs across her back. Violet pushed gently against his chest, opening a narrow space between them. Feverishly, their hands began unfastening each other's buttons, buckles and clasps. Stepping away from the pile of clothes at their feet, Violet lay back on the bed. With his forearms planted on the mattress, Ramón lowered himself slowly, bit by bit, onto her delectable, warm body. With a soft breeze from the open window wafting across his sweating back, he slid gently in and out, deeper and deeper, between the moist, muscular lips of her secret body.

Later that evening, Violet snuggled against Ramón as a burly man secured the metal bar across their laps and signaled the operator to resume the ascent of the Ferris wheel. Their car lurched, then swung back and forth each time it stopped as more passengers were loaded below. Lively barrel organ music and the aroma of cotton candy and axle grease gradually waned as, fully loaded, the Ferris wheel began to spin, carrying them smoothly upward. The raucous crowd along the boardwalk below became a distant blur and the stars over the ocean sparkled in a moonless sky.

Violet rested her hand on Ramón's thigh. Wrapping an arm around her shoulder, he looked out over the ocean. At 0600 he'd have to be on the line again, but right now there was nothing he had to worry about.

Shortly after they reached the apogee of the Ferris wheel's revolution, a brilliant white light flashed above the ocean's horizon. "What the hell was that?" Ramón exclaimed. "It didn't look like lightning."

Violet opened her mouth to speak, but Ramón raised a hand. "Wait." He began to count. At one thousand and ten, a deep rumbling sound reached their ears. "Holy smoke! It's an attack about two miles out!"

As the Ferris wheel continued its downward arc, Ramón and Violet, shocked into silence along with the crowd on the boardwalk, stared incredulously out to sea. On the horizon was the unmistakable outline of a tanker enveloped in flames. Then a fiery-red ball rocketed into the sky, followed by the sound of another explosion.

As the Ferris wheel approached the unloading platform, Ramón turned to Violet. "Can you get home by yourself? I've got to get to the base."

Chapter Thirteen
The Second Happy Time

The submarine menace on our Atlantic seaboard has not yet been successfully met. The U-boat toll of nearly half a hundred vessels in less than three months cannot be offset by any complacent estimate that this represents only a small part of our coastal shipping... Eventually most of the marauders can be driven out to sea by a combined sea and air patrol which will leave safer channels near shore for marine traffic.

New York Times
March 23, 1942

10 NAUTICAL MILES OFF JACKSONVILLE, Florida
— March 28, 1942

"Herr Kaleun!" The starboard lookout called out in the darkness. "Lights, bearing 190, horizon."

Rainer and Jäger swept their binoculars to starboard and focused the lenses. Ten nautical miles south, red and green lights flickered near the coast.

"If he's a tanker, he's probably doing about twelve knots," Jäger said.

"Ahead one half. Course 240," Rainer said.

With the low silhouette of its conning tower, the U-023 was capable of maneuvering unseen, like a shadowy, lone wolf closing in on its prey. When the northbound tanker, a dark behemoth silhouetted against the blazing shore lights of Jacksonville, came fully into view, Rainer turned north and idled the engines, waiting. "Mein Gott!" He whispered as, a mile to port, a huge ship with a wine-red hull and towering, white bridge, steamed past. "He must be over 150 meters long." Ordering full speed ahead, Rainer soon had the U-023 in position for an attack three nautical miles off the amusement park at Neptune Beach.

Jäger assumed targeting duties. "Forward torpedo room," he called into the voice tube. "Target angle 118. Enemy speed eleven knots. Distance 1800 meters. Depth three meters. Fire one. Los!" He waited a few seconds. "Fire two. Los!"

Rainer squinted through his binoculars as Jäger timed the run. At 170 seconds. *Wham! Whoosh!* A powerful explosion amidships hurled a great ball of fire high into the air.

"Perfekt, Jäger!" Rainer exclaimed, shifting his weight like a counterpuncher as he waited for the second strike. Wham! Another explosion tore away a section of the tanker's bridge. A thick cloud of intense black smoke billowed into the air. "Engines one third. Bearing 250," Rainer ordered. "We'll use gunnery off his port side."

"But Herr Kaleun," Jäger said. "That will silhouette us against the flames."

Rainer gestured toward the Ferris wheel lights on the shore. "Do you want to fire our guns toward tourists? Bring her around."

A great flame rising from the center of the fractured tanker, lit up the ocean like a giant torch as the U-023 closed in for the kill. At 300 meters, clouds of smoke, laden with soot, drifted over the ocean. His nostrils awash with the acrid odor of burning petroleum, Rainer scanned the scene with binoculars. Three lifeboats were full of survivors; a fourth was aflame. About forty men were in the water. Many were burned, their oil-streaked faces black as cormorants, as they clung to debris. Others thrashed about in open water, struggling to stay afloat. Some drifted facedown, lifeless.

When Rainer cut his engines 250 meters from the flaming tanker, the cries of survivors rang out across the water. Help! Over here! As he squinted into the flames, a familiar burning sensation arose in Rainer's throat. After eight submarine patrols, he still experienced this feeling each time he was confronted with the carnage of a successful attack. Tightening his jaw, he gave orders for the *Fängschuss*, coup de grâce. "Battle stations. Gun action!"

A three-man deck gun crew, commanded by Leutnant Wolf, readied the powerful 10.5 cm deck cannon and loaded it with 25-kilogram shells. Cannoneers on the bridge and machine gunners on the Wintergarten platform behind the bridge took their positions—ready to fire. Frightened survivors in a nearby lifeboat jumped into the water. Rainer held up a hand. "Don't fire on any men in the water! Deck gun, direct fire at the bridge and superstructures. Begin with ten rounds of incendiary shells. Machine guns, fire at the stern. Ready to fire."

"Halt!" Wolf cried out as he angrily tore the forgotten muzzle protector from the deck gun. *"Fertig!"* Wolf shouted up to the bridge. "Ready, Herr Kaleun."

"Ready to fire," Rainer repeated, looking down at Wolf and the face of each man in the deck cannon crew. Scheisse. Only weeks ago, a U-Boat crewman in the Caribbean was killed by a barrel explosion because someone forgot to remove the muzzle protector. He raised a hand. "Feuer!"

Salvos from the large deck gun flooded the tanker's engine room and set the bridge and remaining oil tanks afire. Four merchant seamen, clinging to a railing astern, fell into the sea after a burst of machine gun fire.

"Cease firing!" Rainer ordered. "Secure the deck gun. Clear the deck."

Survivors in lifeboats, or clinging to debris in the water, stared up at the bridge of the U-023 looming less than 50 meters away. Careful not to return their gaze, Rainer removed his cap, ran his fingers through his hair and looked toward the shore.

A Ferris wheel, merrily ablaze with multi-colored lights, turned against the horizon. For a brief moment, a childhood memory was reignited. One hand clutching his mother's arm, he waved to his father below as the Ferris wheel rose above the beach at Travemünde. What if he hadn't circled around the burning ship for the Fangschüss? What would a child see when a 105-millimeter cannon shell tore through the fragile aluminum and wood of his Ferris wheel car?

He replaced his cap and tugged it down over his forehead. "Ja gut, Jäger. New course. Bearing 100. Careful for survivors in the water. Slow until we're clear, then full speed ahead."

Twenty miles east of the burning tanker, the light from billowing red clouds on the horizon was barely visible in a moonless sky. Rainer stood on the bridge of the U-023 rinsing the raw smells of battle from his nostrils with the cool ocean breeze. It had been a clean kill of a monster tanker carrying tons of oil to be used in a war against his homeland. But the images of merchant seamen blown sky-high, set afire or dashed, screaming into the sea were not easily washed away. Nevertheless, it was time to return to the hunt. "New course, Jäger. Bearing 015."

"Ja wohl, Herr Kaleun. Bearing 015. We still have two eels to fire."

At 0200 a northbound freighter was sighted hugging the coast. Rainer was beginning attack preparations, when a lookout noticed a suspicious shadow about a mile to starboard. Barely visible in the darkness, Rainer and Jäger tried to identify the object with their binoculars.

"It doesn't look like a freighter," Rainer said.

"It's not moving, Herr Kaleun."

"Or it's moving at dead slow speed," Rainer said.

Pop. Swoosh. A brilliant white flare burst 100 meters astern and drifted slowly down, illuminating a broad swath of the ocean around the U-023. Rainer hastily scanned the sky. Two twin-engine bombers, circling 500 meters above, were exchanging light signals with the suspicious shadow to starboard, now clearly a destroyer.

"Alarm! Alarm! Clear the bridge!" Rainer shouted.

Jäger rang the diving bell. *Clang! Clang!*

Jäger, the second watch officer, the gunner and the lookouts scrambled down the hatch. With the bow of the diving U-023 awash, Rainer glanced swiftly at the approaching airplane before descending into the submarine. Vroomm! A B-25, it's nose painted with a reclining négligée-clad woman, roared over the deck. *Bratatatat. Ping. Zzip.* Sparks flew as machine gun bullets ricocheted off the deck and fairwater of the bridge. *Voompf!* A demolition bomb exploded 50 meters astern with a great geyser of water.

Rainer secured the hatch and clambered down into the control room and checked the depth gauge. 30 meters. Not bad for a crash dive. Screee. With a jolt, their rapid descent was halted as the hull began plowing into mud at a depth of 50 meters. Rainer ordered a halt to the dive. "Zero bubble. Make your depth 45 meters. Slow ahead. Course 120. We have to get into deeper water."

The U-023 crept along with its electric motors just above the ocean floor. Rainer stood silently with his motionless crew, his eyes fixed on the sound man Funkmaat Stein who was listening intently through his headphones for the slicing sound of approaching propellers. Five minutes passed. Stein shook his head. Nichts. Rainer relaxed his tense shoulders. Maybe they'd make it to deeper water before being detected.

Several moments later, Stein raised a hand. The noise of an approaching destroyer's screws were growing louder. "*Stillschweigen*," Rainer whispered. "Silence. Lay her on the bottom."

Soon the destroyer was running right above them. Stein thrust a hand in the air. "*Wasserbomben!*"

Wham! Swoosh! A muffled roar above them was followed immediately by a violent shock wave, twisting and heaving the U-Boat. Several crew members tumbled to the deck; others gripped whatever they could. Shhweee. Water whizzed around the hull. Then five more explosions and convulsions in rapid succession.

Pow! Shusshh! Several pipes burst, spraying pressurized water across the control room. *Zzzt!* Light fixtures sparked and bulbs flickered off and on. Clipboards, cups and broken equipment clattered across the deck. The hull creaked and groaned. *Eeee*—an eerie harmonic sound coursed through the pipes along the bulkheads.

Then, abruptly as it began, the cacophonous clamor ceased. The only sounds remaining were intermittent pops and creaks of the hull and random air bubbles escaping into the ocean. Funkmaat Stein reported the destroyer's propeller sounds were becoming more distant, but Rainer guessed he would return soon enough. He pushed back his hat and wiped his damp forehead with his fingertips. Expecting sweat or water from burst pipes, he was startled to see a thick layer of bright red blood dripping from his hand. Then he remembered. He'd struck his head against the periscope with the first depth charge. There was no time for first aid now. He found a small towel and held it against his forehead as Jäger and the engineer Rademaker gave him the damage report.

"No hull leaks reported, Herr Kaleun," Jäger said. "But control is unable to move the rudder and stern planes."

"Why?"

"The positioning screws are jammed, Herr Kaleun," Rademaker said.

"Verdammt! Can you fix it, Rademaker?"

Rademaker nodded, his lips forming a half smile "Ja. I can fix it, Herr Kaleun."

"Gut. What else?"

"A small air leak of undetermined source, Herr Kaleun."

Rainer cocked his head. "Undetermined?"

"It's probably one of the ballast tank blow valves," Rademaker said. "I'll find it."

Rainer nodded. "Is that all?"

"Battery voltage is very low," Jäger said.

Rainer swallowed hard, suppressing the desperate sensation surging upward from his chest like the last breath of a drowning man. "I don't think we can survive a second attack. Break out the Dräger breathing equipment and prepare to destroy all secret documents."

"Screw noises increasing, Herr Kaleun," Funkmaat Stein called out.

Thrum thrum thrum. A dull, rhythmic sound grew in intensity and soon was immediately overhead. Rainer dropped the bloody towel and grasped an overhead pipe with both hands, his knuckles turning white. He glanced at Jäger who was gripping the barrel of the periscope. The stocky Bavarian's feet were spread wide, but his face showed no expression. There was no tin can submariner's fright in this man. Always steady and reliable.

Rainer held his breath. The next depth charge attack could prove fatal. Ten seconds. His pulse pounded in his ears like pistons at attack speed. Anneliese, hold me tight. Twenty seconds. Nothing. God, forgive my sins. Thirty seconds. His breath rushed out. The sound of the screws was fading away. He tilted his head toward Jäger whose eyes were wide in disbelief.

144

Rainer was dumbfounded. Why hadn't the destroyer attacked again? And where was the familiar ping? Didn't they have sonar? Why didn't they drop more depth charges over the same area as their first run? They must have spotted the air bubbles. He'd ordered distribution of underwater escape gear and was about to destroy all secret documents. Was machen sie denn? These Amis don't seem to know what they're doing.

The destroyer cruised back and forth over the submerged U-023, but dropped no more depth charges. Gradually, its route became less exact, missing their position entirely. Finally, the sound of propellers faded, then vanished. Rainer glanced about at his crew and held a finger to his lips. Stillschweigen. Perhaps the destroyer was lying in wait nearby. Best to hold their position for another hour.

During the next hour of tense silence, Rainer became more aware of his own body. His heartbeat, breath, sweat mingling with the dried blood on his forehead, tightness in his shoulders. He checked his watch-0500, two hours before dawn. "Tell Rademaker to get to work," he said to Jäger.

At 0600 Rademaker reported. "The rudder and planes are now operative, Herr Kaleun."

"Gut. Time to move. Pump the regulating tanks to sea and get us off the bottom, Jäger. When we're rising, go ahead one third."

With electric motors engaged, the U-023 began to rise, accompanied by a persistent vibratory noise. Ratta tatta tatta. Rainer clenched a fist and rolled his eyes upward. "Was ist denn los, Rademaker?"

"We must have damaged the propellers when we bottomed, Herr Kaleun. Let's see what happens at higher turns," Rademaker said.

"Auf periskop!" Rainer ordered. Surveying the dark ocean above, he saw no enemy ships. "Auftauchen!"

"Herr Kaleun," a seaman called out. "We're unable to blow starboard tanks five and seven with high-pressure air."

"Verdammt! The venting valves must've been damaged," Rainer said. "But I think we'll swim well enough on tanks five and seven. Nicht wahr, Rademaker?"

"Ja wohl, Herr Kaleun. We'll get by if the sea's calm. Poppet vents can work themselves out as they cycle."

Rainer gave a tight-lipped smile. "Maybe so. But without those tanks, it might be a wet ride on the bridge."

Back on the surface, idling in the dark, rolling sea with the starboard deck low in the water, ocean spray swept across the bridge. With salty rivulets streaming across their faces, Rainer, Jäger and the lookouts scanned the area. There was no sign of the enemy nearby. An occasional flare, bursting high on the western horizon, drifted slowly down like a burning ember ejected from a crackling campfire. "What a fool," Rainer said. "Just one depth charge run."

Rademaker appeared on the bridge with an update. "The dive planes and rudder are slightly bent, Herr Kaleun. Only half the batteries are functioning. One diesel isn't running yet and both propellers are banging loudly at slow speed."

"What do you recommend?" Rainer said.

Rademaker gave a curt nod. "We'll have the other diesel up and running soon, Herr Kaleun. Vibration parted the fuel line, but we can easily fix that. And despite the noise, the propellers are still functional."

"The venting valves?"

"I recommend we just get underway, Herr Kaleun. They often readjust themselves once we're moving."

"Batteries?"

"We're checking bussing and switches in the battery well. I think they'll be fully functional soon."

Rainer turned to Jäger. "Course 060. We'll run half speed until dawn. Then rest on the bottom during daylight."

The last rays of sunset were fading in the west when the U-023 surfaced on a calm sea. Standing on the bridge with Jäger, Rainer drew in a deep breath of fresh ocean air. What a relief after twelve hours of intense heat and the noxious smells of men, oil and smoke. Soon the batteries would be fully charged, oxygen replenished and necessary repairs made for the two-week trip back across the Atlantic to their base at Lorient France.

"Not bad, Herr Kaleun," Jäger said. "Seven ships and a blimp in one month. Der Löwe should be roaring, nicht wahr?"

"Ja, I'm sure Dönitz will welcome us in Lorient. But it's Lübeck I'm looking forward to. That is if the old lion gives me enough leave to get there."

A smile spread across Jäger's face like a sunbeam emerging from a cloud bank. "Lorient will be just fine for me, Herr Kaleun."

Rainer chuckled. "Will that French girl still be waiting for you?"

"Along with my daughter."

"Ja, gut, Jäger. I like a family man."

Rademaker proved good as his word, and the U-023 was underway before midnight. Rainer retired to his tiny cabin, drew the curtains and put his favorite Deutsche Grammophon disc on his wind-up record player. Soaring with Bach's St. Matthew Passion, he closed his eyes. Tomorrow was Palm Sunday. How he wished he could be there in full uniform, walking down the aisle of the Marienkirche with his parents and family. Just before the last notes of the ethereal contralto aria Erbarme dich, mein Gott, he fell into a deep sleep.

At 0600 Rainer awoke from a disturbing dream, kicking at a huge shark ascending from below as he struggled to stay afloat in an ocean blanketed with fog. Wiping sweat from his brow, he sat on the edge of his cot and slowly reoriented himself to waking reality. He'd slept little in the past few days. It was natural to feel exhausted and on edge. But forget the darkness. This was a time for joy. He was heading home.

In the control room. Jäger stood stiffly with a radio dispatch in his hand. "You better take a look at this, Herr Kaleun," he said, handing Rainer a yellow sheet of transcribed Morse code.

Rainer scanned the message: *29 March. RAF night attack on Lübeck. Heavy losses. Further details pending.*

What? Rainer steadied himself against the bulkhead. Silently, Jäger stepped close, shielding him from the astonished crewmen in the control room. Rainer's eyes darted back and forth. His breath caught in his chest. His family lived in the center of the city. Anneliese. The children. His parents. Mein Gott. Mein Gott. Why? Lübeck wasn't a high priority target like nearby Hamburg or Kiel. He turned toward the ladder leading to the bridge. "I need fresh air, Jäger."

"Ja, Herr Kaleun. Air is good."

Chapter Fourteen
Totentanz

With the recent British raid over Hitler country, the old Lübeck has had to suffer. That is my home town...Did Germany believe that it would never have to pay for the misdeeds which its leap into barbarism enabled it to commit?

Thomas Mann
Deutsche Hörer BBC Broadcast
April 1942

LÜBECK, Germany
— April 11, 1942

Due to ongoing repair of track damaged during the March 28 RAF raid, the train from Hamburg stopped short of Lübeck's *Bahnhof*. The first thing Rainer noticed as he shouldered his rucksack and began walking toward the medieval *Innenstadt*, was a peculiar odor, perhaps a blend of creosote and an odd acrid, but sweet smell like leather seared over an open flame. Once-familiar buildings were now dusty piles of concrete, twisted rebar and the skeletal remains of scorched walls, shattered by the firebombing. It was hard to imagine. The last time he'd walked from the Bahnhof to the city center, graceful Baroque-style buildings, dusted with freshly-fallen snow, had lined the avenue.

Since receiving the terrible news from Grossadmiral Dönitz upon his arrival at Lorient several days ago, Rainer had been stumbling through each day like a lost explorer in a boundless wilderness. Anneliese, Gisela, his parents. All gone. Joachim was the only one to survive the RAF firebombing of his hometown on the night before Palm Sunday. Horst had telegrammed assurance he was looking after him. The train ride back home had been a blur of alcohol, intermittent sleep and gazing mindlessly at the landscape through clouds of cigarette smoke.

As he approached the Puppenbrücke bridge, the tension he was holding in his shoulders like an overwound clock abated slightly. The eight statues lining the bridge were relatively intact. Halfway across, he stopped near the statue of Mercury. Undamaged by the bombing, the naked young god faced the medieval Holstentor city gate, bending slightly to lift a large parcel at his feet. Rainer's nostrils flared as he suppressed the tears welling up in his eyes. Anneliese always found Mercury amusing. The god of commerce and communication, she said, welcomed travelers to Lübeck with his bare bottom. Other citizens of this Hanseatic League port on the Baltic Sea claimed Mercury's intention was to exhibit contempt for northern raiders who contemplated attacking their city. Rainer looked up at the cloudless sky. Mercury's alternate task, he recalled, was guiding souls to the underworld.

Across the Puppenbrücke, on a narrow island in the Trave river, the turreted twin towers of the Holstentor gate still leaned in, at their usual quirky angles, sandwiching the medieval three-story arch between them. Rainer sighed, shaking his head. Miraculously, no bombs had disrupted their delicate balance. He glanced at the inscription above the arched passage leading to the Innenstadt. Concordia domi foris pax—harmony at home, peace abroad.

Rainer crossed a second bridge over the river and turned south onto An der Obertrave as he'd done countless times since childhood. He slowed his pace, then came to a halt, his jaw going slack. The street was no longer recognizable. The odors of burnt wood, crumbling plaster and raw dirt filled the air. Where rows of gabled townhouses once faced the grassy river bank, now flattened lots, littered with piles of debris, lay between an occasional intact building.

Using familiar landmarks along the river bank, he trudged dolefully down the block. He sat on a stone bench and looked across the narrow, cobblestone street at an empty lot, layered with ashes and pieces of burned timber, that was once his family home. Powerful waves of anguish coursed through his chest, into his arms, his fists. A whirlpool of astonishment, anger and dismay swirled through his head. He closed his eyes and tried to visualize the house, but could bring no clear image to mind.

Did his family awaken when the bombs fell? Did it happen in a flash or were their last moments filled with pain? Goddamn those Tommies. This wasn't incidental damage from a raid on an industrial or military target. This was ruthless murder of civilians. He recalled his parents condemning the 1937 raid on Guernica. The Condor Legion volunteers were barbarians, his father said. Our Luftwaffe would never deliberately target civilians, his mother added.

Mein Gott. Is this what this war will be? The one who kills the most women and children will win?

Gradually, Rainer's rage ebbed, his heart beat slowing to the rhythm of deep despair. Unglaublich. This was a nightmare from which he couldn't awake. Time stood still. Finally. Was it an hour? He dragged himself to his feet and continued walking toward the Innenstadt.

Sleepwalking down Holstenstrasse toward the Rathaus square, another wave of sadness engulfed him. He stepped into a darkened doorway, partially blocked with piles of fallen stone, and pressed both hands against his forehead, squeezing his eyes tightly closed.

Anneliese, silhouetted against the lace curtains at Travemünde, turned her face toward him as the last rays of the setting sun shimmered, then exploded into the room with a burst of orange-red light.

"Ist alles in Ordnung, mein Herr?" asked a helmeted young woman dressed in an olive drab civil defense Luftschutz uniform. Rainer opened his eyes and shook his head. "Ja, danke. Just a little dust in my eyes."

He straightened his braided white Kriegsmarine hat and continued walking. At the Rathaus square dusty children, perched on piles of fallen bricks, watched civilians, soldiers and civil defense workers clear rubble with picks and shovels. Nearby, an old woman sat on a charred wooden bench staring blankly at passersby. As Rainer stepped off the curb around a fallen slab of concrete, a horn blast from a dump truck, whining in low gear, jolted him back into alertness.

Everything had changed. Accustomed to strategic bombing raids by the RAF on nearby Hamburg and Kiel over the past year, most Lübeckers had assumed their city was not a significant military target. The recent nine-month Blitz of London and other British cities and the retaliatory response of the RAF against Germany had failed to alter the course of the war. Over the past year, the frequency of air raids had actually decreased. Now the British were re-opening that chapter in the air war with deliberate firebombing designed to terrorize the civilian population and decrease morale.

Behind the gutted Rathaus, the twin towers of the Marienkirche, severely damaged but still proud, towered above piles of rubble, broken walls and shattered glass. When he approached the church yard's twisted wrought iron gate, half blown off its hinges, Rainer hesitated. In late afternoon, there was no rush to reach Wehrmacht headquarters. Horst and Joachim would certainly be occupied until the end of the day. He had time to visit the church that held so many memories. Stepping around fallen masonry and fractured gravestones, he ducked under a rope stretched across the entrance and entered the rubble-strewn center aisle of the sanctuary.

A teenager in a Hitler Youth uniform scurried across the courtyard and saluted. "Heil Hitler!"

Rainer turned and touched the brim of his officer's hat.

"You're can't go in there, sir. There's danger of falling debris," the youth said.

With a steady gaze fixed on the boy, Rainer pulled on a pair of leather gloves. "I'll take my chances, young man," he said in a firm, but not unkind tone. The startled boy stepped back in deference to a superior officer.

Sweeping shards of concrete and broken glass aside with his boots, Rainer made his way down the aisle to the fourth row where he sat in his usual family pew. A light breeze whistled through shattered stained-glass panes above the sanctuary and a gray pigeon with brilliant green stripes around its neck fluttered upward through dust-filled streams of light.

Beside the demolished 15th-century organ, two huge iron bells, fallen from the belfry, lay on the stone floor, fractured and partially-melted like chunks of raven-black lava blasted from a volcano. Rainer scrutinized the charred Totentanz mural hanging along the wall. Although most of it had been incinerated, one panel, scorched by the flames, stood out— with a whimsically-macabre smile, a skeletal Death grasped the wrist of a man in full armor. Recalling the touch of Anneliese's warm fingertips against his wrist, he closed his eyes and observed the mysterious dark clusters and wavy patterns that swam across the field of brilliant orange light penetrating his eyelids.

The sky had dimmed to a chalky mauve when a large hand gently shook Rainer's shoulder, causing him to open his eyes. A policeman in the green uniform of the Ordnungspolizei stood patiently in the aisle. "Entschuldigung, mein Herr. But you must leave this area," the policeman said in a kindly, deferential manner.

"Of course," Rainer said. "Sorry to break the rules. I just wanted to sit in the church one last time." He sighed. "It reminds me of the family I just lost."

The policemen seemed distraught. "Such a loss, sir. I'm so sorry to bother you."

Rainer stood and grasped the policeman's hand. "Please take good care of our city, Kamerad." The policeman straightened, clicked his heels together and saluted. "Ja wohl, Herr Kapitänleutnant. My pleasure." Rainer returned the salute and walked out of the Marienkirche toward Wehrmacht headquarters.

Housed in an old building in an undamaged sector of the Innenstadt, the army headquarters was a hive of activity. Beneath a large swastika banner hung from brick gables on the building's medieval façade, military personnel, motorcycles and trucks hummed about the entrance. A sentry directed Rainer toward Horst's office on the second floor. At the top of a winding, marble stairway he saw Horst through the glass panel of his office door.

When Horst noticed Rainer, he turned abruptly from a group of aides and strode into the hallway to greet his old friend. "Ach. Mein lieber Rainer." He grasped Rainer's arms with both hands and squeezed. "Such a sad time. I'm so sorry."

With a fleeting pang of sorrow, Rainer noticed the partial grasp of Horst's gloved right hand. "Danke, Horst. It's so good to see you again. But you must be extremely busy. I can wait."

Horst brushed his objections aside and dismissed his team."Sit down, Rainer. Don't worry. Joachim's all right. He's out with his DJ troop helping clear away debris. He'll meet us here at the end of his shift."

"How is he, Horst?"

"Joachim works all day with the DJ team, comes home, eats dinner and goes to bed. He doesn't talk much, Rainer. I think he's still in shock."

Rainer stared at the floor. "So am I, Horst. I thought my family was safe here." He looked up, his eyes watering. "I mean I'm the one that's supposed to be at risk, nicht wahr?"

With a silent nod, Horst closed his eyes briefly in affirmation.

"Do you know what happened to Joachim?" Rainer asked.

"Not really. I picked him up at the aid station a few hours after the bombing. He had a burn on his hand, that's healing well now, but otherwise he was uninjured. Somehow, he escaped the house before it burned to the ground. Either he doesn't remember, or just doesn't want to talk about it. Ilse and I have stopped asking him." Horst hesitated. "I'm afraid he saw some terrible things, Rainer. The DJ boys were helping us right from the start. Sometimes we pulled people out of the rubble alive. More often than not, we dug out bodies. Or parts of them. It was a terrible scene."

"And from my house?" Rainer asked, his voice rising slightly.

Horst shook his head. "Nothing but ashes, mein Freund. A lot of people are simply gone. Nothing to bury. There'll be a memorial service tomorrow at the Rathaus Square."

Rainer rose abruptly and turned toward the door. "Ja, gut. I'll go with Joachim tomorrow. You should get back to work, Horst. I'll return at five."

For an hour, Rainer wandered aimlessly about the Innenstadt. Childhood memories came rushing back. Even during the lean years after the Great War, growing up in a wealthy family in this prosperous port city had given him great privilege. Anneliese and his children had been an additional blessing.

Now, all the familiar places—the merchant district, Rathaus and most of the churches lay in ruins. The wooden model ships at the Schiffergesellschaft restaurant where he'd eaten so many Sunday dinners with his parents were now just ashes. The puppet theater where he'd listened to funny children's stories at Christmas time—gone. Café Niederegger with its Marzipan treats and hot chocolate after a family outing—only a pile of rubble. A searing sensation arose in his chest: after the demolition bombs blew the rooftops away, the incendiaries had come to scorch his heart.

When he returned to Wehrmacht headquarters, Joachim and Horst were waiting for him at the entrance. In coveralls, a swastika armband and Wehrmacht-style helmet, his 12-year-old son seemed older than Rainer remembered. His face was drawn and somber, his eyes somehow distant. Rainer embraced him fiercely, then held him at arm's length. "Wie gehts dir? In Ordnung?"

Joachim's face yielded little emotion. "I'm all right, Vati. Just a little tired."

"Let's go home," Horst said, his voice inflected with tepid cheer. "Ilse will have supper ready."

With minimal responses from Joachim, Rainer was uncertain what to say; and most of the twenty-minute walk to Horst's home was spent in silence. As they approached Kanalstrasse in the northern part of the city, Rainer detected only scattered evidence of the bombing. Apparently, the main target had been a 300 meter-wide corridor in the Innenstadt.

In a white lace apron over her green print dress, Ilse greeted Rainer at the door with a tender smile and a kiss on his cheek. For a moment, the silky brush of her braided hair across his neck ignited a sensuality he hadn't experienced in months. "Wilkommen, lieber Rainer," she said with a warm smile.

As he crossed the threshold into the house, the aroma of steaming vegetables and a cheerful tune on the radio suffused the air. Sing ein Lied, wenn du mal traurig bist. Sing a song when you're sad. The irony was not lost on Rainer.

Ilse looked pained. "Ach. Entschuldigung," she said, switching off the radio. "Just a silly program I listen to while cooking."

"It's called the request concert for the Wehrmacht," Horst said. "Too bad you Kriegsmarine boys don't have one."

Rainer could only muster a thin smile in response to Horst's attempt to lighten the atmosphere. But he was grateful to be once again among true friends in a home with a genuine feminine touch.

When they sat down for dinner, everyone closed their eyes as Horst said a blessing. "Komm, Herr Jesu. Be our Guest and bless these gifts bestowed by Thee." The stew, which contained a small amount of rationed beef, was mostly fat, cabbage, carrots, celery and parsley. "I'm sorry, but meat is scarce and I couldn't find any potatoes," Ilse said. "With all the volunteers in town, there's hardly enough to go around."

"Volunteer relief workers have come from all over," Horst said to Rainer.

"As far as Hamburg and Kiel," Ilse added. "But they're starting to leave now that we're mostly back on our feet again." She smiled at Joachim. "Thanks to all the work that people like you have done."

Joachim barely nodded.

"What happened to the munitions factory or the Heinkel aircraft plant?" Rainer asked.

"Minimal damage to both," Horst said. "The Dräger Company was hit pretty hard, but they're fully operational now."

"Glad to hear it," Rainer said. "We came a bit close to needing their breathing apparatus this last time around."

Joachim dropped his spoon and looked up from his plate. Rainer glanced at Horst. Scheisse. Why did he let that slip out? "Nothing to worry about," he added quickly. "We were fine."

After dinner, Joachim excused himself and went to bed. When her work in the kitchen was done, Ilse also retired, leaving Rainer and Horst alone in the candlelit parlor. Rainer took out a pack of Gauloises, lit two and handed one to Horst. "I can't tell you how much your looking after Joachim means to me. Of course, I'll be sending you some money each month."

Horst shook his head. "Don't worry about it. You can always count on us." He opened a bottle of Korn Schnapps and poured two glasses. "How about a Herrengedeck?" he said, referring to the potent combination of beer and schnapps.

Rainer shrugged. *"Warum nicht?"*

Horst went into the kitchen and returned with four bottles of beer. Sitting down in an armchair next to his old friend, he raised his schnapps glass and clinked it against Rainer's. "Zum Wohl!"

"Zum Wohl!" Rainer replied, draining his glass, then quaffing a beer chaser.

Horst poured two more glasses of schnapps. "It's hard to know what to say. I'm sure you're feeling overwhelmed."

Rainer gazed at the ceiling, trying to gather his thoughts. "Overwhelmed? I don't know, Horst. It's like I'm in a dream. Hard to believe it's real."

Horst dragged on his cigarette while Rainer downed a second glass of schnapps. They sat in silence by the flickering candlelight for several long minutes.

"Tell me about the attack," Rainer said.

Horst sighed and poured more schnapps. Rainer's cheeks felt warm. He was beginning to feel a bit light-headed.

"They came in three waves a little before midnight," Horst said. "Lancasters and Sterlings. More than 200 of them. The first wave dropped flares, marking the target. They just floated down, Rainer. Like a fireworks display. An awful sort of beauty really. Then came the demolition bombs followed by countless incendiaries."

Horst paused, knitting his brows together, his voice now thickened. "The incendiaries sounded like heavy rain coming down." He leaned forward. "Herrgott! We weren't ready for them, Rainer. Half a dozen flak batteries. That's all we had. We shot one Lancaster down, maybe two."

Horst downed his schnapps and clumsily opened another beer. Rainer was silent. "On the ground in the Innenstadt it was chaos," Horst continued. "Explosions. Collapsing buildings. Fire everywhere. Water mains were destroyed by the bombs. Hoses trying to draw water from the canals froze. But somehow, our firefighters got it under control by the next morning." He splashed some beer on his shirt and wiped it away with the back of his hand. "Then came my job," he said, his voice trailing off as he dropped his chin to his chest and slumped into his chair.

Rainer leaned in close. "Tell me about your job, mein Freund," he said softly.

Horst straightened up, lit a fresh cigarette and pulled on his beer. "We dug in the rubble looking for survivors. And there were some at first. But over the next couple of days, all we found were bodies. More than 300 of them. Many were shriveled and blackened. Some blown apart. In the cellars, asphyxiated or poisoned by carbon monoxide, they often looked like they were sleeping." Horst squeezed his eyes shut, shaking his head back and forth " I still see their faces, Rainer. I saw a lot of horrible things on the Eastern front. But, mein Gott! This is our hometown."

Tears streamed down Rainer's cheeks. "Do you think my family suffered, Horst?"

Horst shook his head. "No. I think a demolition bomb killed them all instantly. The fire came afterward."

Rainer ran his fingertips through his hair. "Gott sei dank." At least they didn't burn to death.

Horst stood up, grasping the back of the chair for balance. "There's something else I need to tell you, Rainer."

Rainer looked up. What more could there be?

"Martin's been taken by the Gestapo."

Rainer's head was spinning. "What? Why would they arrest a pastor?"

"*Wehrkraftzersetzung*. They charged him with undermining the war effort. He's being held in Hamburg."

"Those Gestapo thugs have Martin?" Rainer slammed his fist on the table. "Our world's falling apart, Horst."

Horst reached for a book on the shelf and knocked several to the floor. When he leaned over to pick them up, he lost his balance and grabbed Rainer's leg to steady himself. "Here it is." He thumbed through the pages of a poetry book, stopping at at a stanza from Rilke. "The eighth Duino elegy." Horst read slowly, occasionally slurring a word.

We are, above all, eternal spectators
looking upon, never from,
the place itself. We are the
essence of it. We construct it.
It falls apart. We reconstruct it
and fall apart ourselves.

On Sunday morning, with a light rain pattering against their umbrellas, Rainer, Joachim, Horst and Ilse joined a crowd of several thousand people gathered in the Rathaus Square. Beneath two topless Corinthian columns, their floral heads, shattered by the bombs, a small Baroque ensemble played a flowing melancholic piece that pierced Rainer's heart. The last time he'd heard Albinoni's *Adagio,* he was watching his mother, eyes half closed, head and shoulders swaying, as she bowed the cello in the chamber orchestra of Lübeck. Rainer's nose was getting stuffy; his eyes began to water. At first, he fought it, then he let it rise. With tears flowing freely down his cheeks, the music surged throughout his body.

The *Gauleiter* and *Burgermeister* each gave short speeches denouncing "British murderers" and praising "citizen soldiers" who'd died in the bombing. Then a Catholic bishop and an elderly Lutheran pastor stood before the crowd.

Bowing his head, the pastor spoke first. "Vater unser… those who die still live in Your presence. Their lives change but do not end."

The bishop then read from Wisdom 3:1-9. "The souls of the righteous are in the hand of God, and no torment will ever touch them."

Unlike the stirring music, Rainer found the eulogies empty. Had the hand of God returned his family to dust? Was there really an afterlife? He glanced at Joachim. The boy stood tall, no emotion evident on his face. What did he believe? More important, what was he feeling?

The rain stopped on the way back to Horst's. On an impulse, Rainer turned to Joachim. "I want to walk by the old house again. Will you come with me?"

Joachim shrugged. "There's nothing there, Vati. But I'll walk with you if you want."

When they reached the flattened lot that had once been their home, Rainer put an arm around Joachim's shoulder and pulled him close. "I feel like I'm in a dream," he whispered.

"Me too, Vati. And I can't get out."

Rainer leaned down, his face close to Joachim's. "Tell me what happened, son. I need to know."

With a sob, Joachim pressed into Rainer's chest and spoke haltingly. "I was in bed studying for my confirmation. It was very cold, Vati. But the moon was bright. I heard the sirens, but I didn't pay attention. Everyone knew the planes always went to Hamburg or Kiel. So I went to sleep."

Joachim stopped talking. Rainer stroked his back, waiting patiently.

"An hour later," Joachim continued, "a loud explosion woke me up. My room was filled with smoke. I went into the hallway and tried to open Gisela's door." His voice rose. "The doorknob was red-hot. I ran at the door with my shoulder, but it didn't budge. Then Gisela screamed. *Hilfe!* I couldn't help her, Vati. Flames were shooting out of the doorframe. I ran to the staircase. The other side of the hallway was gone. Just open air. Flames spread everywhere. I ran down the stairs and out the door. When I turned back for a moment, half the house was gone. Then another explosion and everything was on fire." He pushed himself away from Rainer's chest and looked into his eyes. 'There was nothing I could do, Vati. Nothing."

Rainer, embracing his son with all his strength, threw his head back and howled like a wounded wolf. "Uhhwhooo!" Sobbing, they both sank to their knees in the ashes of their former life.

Chapter Fifteen
I'll Be Seeing You

Americans are congenital optimists, extroverts and non-fatalists...
The disasters of the first four months of war are an unpleasant
surprise. We are still blinking from the shock of discovering that the
home front is literally "everywhere in the world." We are worried
and confused and dismayed by the size of the conflict, but no
American has the slightest doubt that we are going to win it. The
thought of defeat simply does not enter the American imagination.

New York Times
April 4, 1942

VILANO BEACH, Florida
— April 4, 1942

Before Ramón could shed his beach robe, Violet had raced
over the sand and plunged into the 65° water. With powerful,
gliding strokes, she was soon well out into the ocean. Ramón
hesitated, looking down at his feet, buried in the cool morning
sand, then sprinted to the surf and belly flopped into the
water. With heavy strokes, he muscled his way out to Violet
who was now backstroking gracefully in the rolling ocean.
When she felt his touch upon her leg, she turned to face him.

Like two hummingbirds hovering beside a delectably-flowering fuchsia, they swept their arms back and forth through the water to stay afloat. As Ramón reached out to touch her cheek, a rogue wave of sadness lapped upward from his chest, across the tideline of his neck, etching his brow with unanticipated sorrow. Jeez, he sure was going to miss her.

On the way back in, when their feet reached the sandy bottom again, Ramón swept her into his arms and kissed her with great force. His fingertips trailed over the goosebumps on her arms, across her erect nipples beneath the swimsuit and around her buttocks, pulling her pelvis tightly against his. He pressed his lips against her ear. "I have loved every moment with you."

Their last night in the Flamingo Motel had been filled with passion, tears and sorrow. But no regrets. They knew this day was coming. They just hadn't expected it so soon. On her husband's recommendation, Ramón was being sent to Mérida to train Mexican pilots. Was it because he was skilled in ASW techniques and proficient in Spanish? Or did Major Anderson suspect something? Either way, the guilt steaming deep within Ramón's conscience was about to be released through the escape valve of an assignment to Mexico.

But along with relief came a sense of great loss. Violet had been a magical lodestone, drawing the white-hot heat of his virile, young body into her irresistible field. A beautiful woman, she swam like a dolphin, delighted in the erotic poems of Pablo Neruda, and made love like a jaguar in heat. But they'd never really talked of love. And she'd been clear from the start that she was staying with her husband. Ramón felt lucky. An older woman had taken him higher than he'd ever been before and he was very grateful.

On a bright afternoon with no clouds in the sky, Ramón motorcycled from his Neptune Beach apartment to the Jacksonville Public library. With a few hours to bone up on Mérida before meeting with the wing commander, he asked a curly-headed librarian for assistance. After perusing the newspaper archives and travel books she suggested, he began to see the overall picture. In the last decade, the Mexican government had swung left, then right again. The current conservative government of Manuel Ávila Camacho had spurned Axis attempts at alliance, and was playing ball with the USA. In exchange for oil and minerals, U.S. capital was surging into Mexico like a mountain stream after a heavy rainstorm. And Mexican armed forces were being supplied with U.S. weapons and trainers like Ramón himself.

Despite his heritage, Ramón really didn't know Mexico well. He'd only been to his grandparents just over the border in Coahuila and on one family vacation to Mexico City. Yucatán, with its tropical fruits, spices and mysterious Mayans, was sounding very exotic to a small-town Tejano from Southwest Texas.

Cruising on his Harley with the warm wind streaming over his face, Ramón was filled with anticipation of his new assignment to Mérida Yucatán. Sure, it would be hot as hell, but the old Spanish colonial city with narrow streets and broad plazas sounded intriguing. Known as the *ciudad blanca* for its limestone buildings (or perhaps its light-skinned

171

citizens), Mérida was a cultural capital in the Mayan heartland.

At Imeson Field, the wing commander, Lieutenant Colonel Brennan, a stocky, middle-aged man who parted his thinning hair low over his right ear, wasted no time with small talk. "We've lost 150 merchant ships along the coast this year, Morales. And now the U-Boats are moving into the Gulf and Caribbean. Navy planes sank two of them off Canada in March, and a destroyer got one yesterday off Cape Hatteras. But dammit, Lieutenant." He pounded a fist on his desktop, jouncing his telephone receiver off its base. "The Army Air Force has yet to score a single fucking kill!"

Ramón remained silent as the Colonel continued. "Neither the Army nor the Navy was ready for this type of warfare. The Navy claims command and control over all maritime airborne operations but doesn't have enough aircraft to carry out the job. Bomber Command sees our primary responsibility as land targets and resents our being pressed into ASW duty under Navy control. Old rivalries, poor communication and uncoordinated efforts all add up to one big *snafu*."

Situation normal, all fucked up. Ramón admired the Colonel's candor. But things were sounding pretty bleak. "Most of our aircraft still have no radar, sir. Will we be getting it soon?"

Colonel Brennan frowned in disgust. "They say it's coming, but don't hold your breath, Lieutenant. Right now we have to do the best with what we have. I admit it's a tough problem, particularly at night."

Tough problem? Images of Adam's blimp going down in flames and the tanker exploding off Jacksonville Beach flashed through Ramón's mind. In the darkness, U-Boats could surface and sink any unescorted ship they wanted, for chrissake. And with coastal businesses still refusing to turn off their lights, merchant ships silhouetted against the shore were prime targets.

The colonel leaned back in his chair. "How much do you know about our relationship with Mexico these days, Lieutenant?"

Ramón was glad he'd gone to the library. "Not much, sir. But I guess it's a bit tricky."

Colonel Brennan guffawed. "To say the least. We've got a century of mistrust, son." He shrugged. "Probably justified though. We did take over a big chunk of their territory." He smiled. "But I'm sure you're used to hearing that as a Mexican raised in Texas."

Not sure how to take that familiar comment, Ramón kept his eyes unfocused and jaw slack in the impassive expression that often served him well. "Yes, sir."

"Here's my take in a nutshell, Lieutenant. When the Mexicans nationalized the oil refineries, we were up in arms. But with this war, we're inclined to let that go. Mutual trade's good for both countries." He leaned forward, leveling his gaze at Ramón. "But a military alliance, as you say, is a bit more tricky. Though they've been neutral so far, Mexico's starting to realize they're better off with us than with the Krauts." He paused. "Follow me so far?"

"Yes, sir. What about the opposition?"

"Excellent question, Morales. The pro-fascist *Sinarquistas* have about half a million members. And, on the other end of the spectrum, you've got the Mexican Communist party." He waved his hand. "That's all beside the point. We're supplying Mexico with arms and munitions now. We're lend-leasing them aircraft and negotiating for a new military airstrip at Cozumél." He raised a fingertip in caution. "But they're adamant about one thing. No American troops on the ground!"

"How does that affect my assignment, sir?"

"You'll be a Pan-American Airlines employee developing commercial airfields in Mérida and Cozumél. Do you catch my drift?"

"Yes, sir. No army uniform. No engaging the enemy. What about our aircraft, sir?"

"All markings will be painted over."

Ramón flinched. Dang! What about the nose art on Rita? Forget it. This was not likely to be negotiable.

Colonel Brennan continued. "Commensurate with your new duties, you are being promoted to the rank of captain. Congratulations."

For an instant, Ramón widened his eyes, then stood ramrod straight. "Thank you, sir."

"Don't thank me. You'll need at least that rank to get any respect with this job. To start, you'll have four Mexican pilots who've completed B-25 training in Brownsville. They're supposed to be an elite bunch, fluent in English." He chuckled. "But just in case, how's your Spanish?"

"I'm fluent. But my crew isn't. What role will they have, sir?"

"Each will fly separately in the Mexican bombers to instruct their counterparts in our ASW techniques. My adjutant will go over the training plans with you in detail."

The colonel lowered his voice. "There's one more thing. Someone I want you to meet."

"Now, sir?"

"Actually, he prefers to meet elsewhere." The Colonel narrowed his eyes. "You are not to discuss this with anyone else. Do you understand?"

"Yes, sir."

"He goes by the name Manuel. He'll meet you at ten tonight near the wharf at Neptune Beach. Don't wear your uniform. Any questions?"

"How will I know him, sir?"

"Don't worry. Manuel already knows you. Good luck, Captain Morales."

After dark Ramón walked south along the tideline of Neptune Beach past rows of bungalows spaced ever wider apart until he came to a dark stretch of beach, remote from human activity. Sculpting a headrest in the sand with his foot, he lay down under the stars. Gentle waves lapped against the shore and a full moon cast a shimmering golden highway across the ocean.

Far out to sea a shooting star arced across the sky and vanished. As he looked up at the moon, a line from Billie Holiday came to mind.

I'll Be looking at the moon, but I'll be thinking of you.

Maybe it was the right time to end it, but he was really going to miss Violet. What a dame! It was bad business seeing her behind her husband's back. But that seemed to be what she really wanted. Besides making passionate love, she liked to drink and talk about history, books and movies late into the night. How much he'd learned from her. How much he was going to miss her.

Walking back north, Ramón arrived at the deserted wharf shortly before ten PM and cocked an ear. Thwitt Cheww. The soft notes of a bitonal whistle rose just above the lapping of the waves against the barnacle-encrusted pillars. Then a flash and a glowing cigarette tip beneath the wooden walkway. "Aqui," came a whisper.

Walking from the moonlit sand to the shadows beneath the wharf, Ramón found himself face-to-face with a slender man of olive complexion, dressed Havana-style in pleated trousers and a white Guayabera shirt. "Manuel?" He asked.

Manuel stepped out of the shadows, moonlight washing across his thick mustache and pock-marked cheeks. A narrow scar arced like a scimitar from his jawline to the vermillion border of his left lip. "I need you to recognize me," he said. "We'll meet in Mérida from time to time."

Ramón wasn't going to forget that face. "Are you Army intelligence?"

"No. FBI," Manuel said. "We're tracking Nazi *Abwehr* agents in Mexico."

"Where do I come in?"

"The Abwehr is everywhere in Yucatán. And some are in the military. Military cargo and merchant shipping schedules are routinely radioed to U-Boat headquarters in Hamburg."

Ramón shifted his weight like a reluctant pugilist sizing up an unfamiliar opponent. "You want me to be a spy?"

Manuel chuckled. "No. Relax. You just need to report any suspicious activity."

"How do I contact you if something comes up?"

Manuel tossed his cigarette on the sand and crushed it with his heel. "I'll be in the Plaza Grande of Mérida every Wednesday night at eleven. To avoid suspicion, make a habit of going there on a few other nights of the week as well."

"Where? Plazas can be pretty big."

"I'll be sitting in one of the double, s-shaped chairs. You'll know what I mean when you see one. Some call them courting benches."

Loud voices rang out down the beach. A group of teenagers singing an off-key version of Chattanooga Choo Choo were approaching the wharf. Manuel turned to leave. "Tell no one about this meeting. *Buen viaje.* I'll see you in Mérida."

Before Ramón could respond, Manuel vanished like a mysterious figure that had been sketched in the sand between incoming waves.

Chapter Sixteen
Mérida

To meet the increasing requirements of inter American transportation resulting from the changeover of hemisphere industry to a war basis and to accommodate traffic that cannot proceed by sea, Pan-American-Grace Airways yesterday announced further increases in the company schedules.

New York Times
April 13, 1942

MÉRIDA, Yucatán
— April 15, 1942

Ramón was having a hard time pegging Diego. Although engaged in the ASW training program, he didn't mix much with the other pilots. And he always left immediately at the end of the day. The other three *Fuerza Aérea Mexicana* pilots usually hung around, had a few drinks with the Yanquis and talked a bit about themselves. Not Diego. He went out on the town alone. The next morning he hardly said buenos dias.

But Diego was a good pilot. In the first week of training, he excelled all others in the class. His ability to estimate distance over water was so good that his range errors never exceeded

100 feet. Not many pilots could do that. Handsome and subtly condescending like a casual aristocrat, he was at the top of the class. Although competent in English, Diego always spoke Spanish with Ramón.

"Co-piloto, piloto. *Comienzo el ataque*," Diego's voice crackled over the intercom as he began the practice run.

Ramón was sitting next to Diego in the copilot seat of a B-25 bomber, recently lend-leased by the U.S. to the Mexican Air Force. The last two approaches had been dry runs. This time the bombardier would drop a three-pound practice bomb on empty oil drums lashed together on a narrow raft to simulate the hull of a submarine. A gray minesweeper was towing the target at eight knots, the average speed of a diving submarine. Once the practice bomb hit the target or the water, a firing pin would ignite a flare, releasing a column of thick black smoke.

A mile from the target, Diego descended to 50 feet above the water. "Bombardero, piloto. *Listo?*"

Ramón recalled the RAF axiom Major Anderson had passed on. There are two ways to miss a U-Boat: aim right and drop wrong or aim wrong and drop right. Line and range errors they were called. Most pilots underestimated distances over water by about 30 percent. But a few, like Diego, were able to unlearn this human misperception and estimate the distance with the pinpoint accuracy of an all-star quarterback on third and long.

Diego's run was near perfect and his bombardier released the practice bomb at precisely the right moment. A smoky black cloud billowed up from the ocean within the lethal radius where a depth charge would rupture a submarine's pressure hull. After landing at Mérida Airport, Diego was first to debark the airplane. Barely acknowledging Ramón's praise, he hurried off just as Ramiro's B-25 crew, with Erik as the copilot, ambled past. Mexican and American crews, respectively dressed in olive-green Fuerza Aérea and black Pan American Airways uniforms, intermingled as they headed back over the concrete runway to the Pan Am building.

"Forget it," Ramiro said to Ramón. "Diego's a snob. And not just with you, amigo."

Ramón smiled. Right from the start, Ramiro had been the seasoned alpha male of the pack, shepherding him through the uncertainties and pitfalls of camaraderie and machismo among Fuerza Aérea pilots. Without his enthusiastic participation in the training program, it would've been harder to gain acceptance of the other Mexican pilots. Now, with the exception of Diego, Ramón felt he was in the groove with all of them.

The sleepy airport cantina was almost empty when the two crews took over the marble-topped tables to smoke and share a drink before calling it a day. Everyone ordered Jaguar Yucateca, a popular amber ale produced by a local brewer of German descent.

"Have you ever seen the *danzón*, amigo?" Ramiro asked. Ramón shook his head. "Then you have to go with me tomorrow night," Ramiro said. "It's in the Plaza Grande at dusk. I'm sure you'll find it fascinating."

Shortly after sunset the next day Ramón sat with Ramiro in a sidewalk café beside the Plaza Grande. A six-man danzón ensemble made up of guitar, guitarrón, trumpet, flute, violin and drum, was assembling beneath a colonial archway wrapped in purple bougainvillea. In the center of the square, men in white linen suits and Panama hats mingled with women in ankle-length white dresses embroidered with colorful designs inspired by the Yucatec Maya. Many of the women wore exotic flowers, bursting like colorful birds from their lustrous coal-black hair.

When the musicians began to play a complex, stately introduction, the dance partners aligned themselves silently in the square. Ramiro offered Ramón an explanation. *"Mira,* amigo. They'll play an introduction, then a promenade known as a paseo. Then they'll repeat the same sequence and follow it with a certain melody. Watch the dancers. They won't move until precisely the moment when the band plays the final paseo marked by a distinctive drum beat."

Ramón watched in fascination as the dancers glided about the plaza in a slow rhythmic style evocative of courtship. Every time the introduction and paseo were repeated the dancers stopped, chatted with others, then started again at the end of the last paseo.

As the dancers circled around the plaza, Ramón's gaze was drawn to one particular couple. The middle-aged man was handsome with European features. The woman, much younger, was startlingly beautiful. Olive skin, thick eyebrows, full lips, high cheekbones and a marvelous figure. Ramón's chest flooded with a tantalizingly-warm ache. He turned to Ramiro. "What a beautiful woman."

"I know her," Ramiro said. "Should I introduce you?"

Ramón's eyes sparkled like sunlight atop an unexpected wave. "Would you?"

When the final set of the danzón was completed, Ramiro and Ramón strolled across the plaza to the table where the striking couple sat. The woman remained seated as the man rose and shook hands with Ramiro.

"Buenos noches, Señor Neumann," Ramiro said. "Allow me to introduce you to my American friend Ramón Morales."

Señor Neumann shook Ramón's hand firmly. "A pleasure to meet you," he said in English. "This is my daughter Isabel."

"*Mucho gusto*, señor," Ramón said in perfect Spanish, inflected with a slight Norteño accent. He bowed toward Isabel. "*Encontado*, Señorita."

Señor Neumann's laugh expressed delight. "*Lo siento*, señor. As an American, I improperly assumed you wouldn't speak our language."

Ramón shrugged. "No importa, señor. I was raised in a Spanish-speaking family." He smiled. "But my English isn't bad either."

"Bueno. Prefiero Español," Señor Neumann said. They continued the conversation in Spanish.

Sitting across from Isabel, Ramón realized she was even more choice up close than he'd imagined from afar. Thick black hair braided with red flowers, dark almond-shaped eyes and a subtly-aquiline nose.

"What are you doing in Mérida, Señor Morales?" Isabel asked in Spanish with a smile that Ramón found both cordial and beguiling.

"I work for the Pan American Airport Corporation, Señorita," Ramón said, struggling to keep his eyes off her dynamite body. "We're making some improvements on the airfields in Mérida and Cozumél."

"I see," Isabel said with a slight-raise of an eyebrow. "Will you be here long?"

"Unfortunately, no. Just a couple of months."

"But enough time to enjoy our beautiful city," Ramiro said. "I thought the danzón would be a good start."

Ramón smiled broadly. "I've never seen anything so elegant."

"My daughter and I have been danzón partners since she was a child," Señor Neumann said. "Although it originated in Cuba, it's quite popular here along the Gulf."

"Especially in Veracruz," Isabel said. "I go there often on business."

"What business is that, Señorita?" Ramón asked, his eyes narrowing on her face with genuine interest.

"I'm sales manager for my father's brewery."

Ramiro laughed. "I believe you've already been introduced to Jaguar Yucateca, Ramón." He turned to Señor Neumann. "That's what we drink at the airfield cantina."

Over the next hour, Ramón found himself increasingly drawn toward Isabel and her father. Speaking Spanish with the short pauses and distinct intonation of Yucatán, they exuded warmth and genuine interest in his family and youth in Southwest Texas. No questions were asked about his job at the airfield—most Mexicans assumed Pan American employees were part of the American war effort. Like deferential courtiers in on the ruse, Isabel and her father politely avoided the topic.

"Are you native to Yucatán, Señor Neumann?" Ramón asked.

"Sí. My father was a brewmaster who emigrated from Munich to the German colony of Santa Elena," Señor Neumann said. "When my mother died my father moved to Mérida and opened the brewery."

"And that's where I was born," Isabel said. "My mother is Mayan. She leaves the danzón to my father and me."

"Have you lived in Mérida all your life, señorita?" Ramón asked.

"Sí. Except for a few years at a German high school in Mexico City and universities in Madrid and Munich."

"And now she works for her father, traveling around the Gulf in a BMW sports car," Ramiro added.

Isabel smiled. "*Es una buena vida.* Mérida to Tampico. Every month."

Señor Neumann took out his pocket watch. "I'm sorry," he said rising from his chair. "We have a dinner engagement. It's been a pleasure to meet you, Señor Morales."

"Que le vaya bién," Isabel said cheerfully. "I hope things go well for you here."

"*Igualmente,*" Ramón said with a smile he hoped was subtly beguiling.

"Quite a beautiful woman, no?" Ramiro said when the Neumann's were gone. "I've known her since she was a little girl."

"Is she involved with anyone?" Ramón asked.

"No one I know of. She had a lover when she studied in Madrid. But he died in 1936 during the tumult just before the civil war. I don't think she's ever recovered."

Ramiro ordered two more beers. "Want to try some traditional cuisine?" Ramón nodded. "Bueno. I'll order some cochinita pibil. It's pork, onion and fruit cooked in banana leaves. I think you'll like it."

The meal was delicious. And the woman he'd just met was beautiful. Ramiro was hitting home runs. "Tell me about growing up here in Mérida," Ramón asked.

"I'm the oldest son of the military commander of Yucatán. I grew up in Mérida, then attended the Heroico Colegio Militar."

Ramón was impressed. The Heroico Colegio Militar in Mexico City was like West Point for the U.S.

Ramiro ordered two more beers and continued his story. "After flight school in Guadalajara, I was in Texas for B-25 training. And now I'm assigned here for antisubmarine warfare duty." He laughed. "Perhaps my father had some influence on my assignment back home."

Ramón took a long pull on his beer, then leaned back in his chair in frustration. "Tell me, Ramiro. Why I'm having so much trouble with Diego? Is it about social class?"

"No, amigo. It's not just class. You must understand. Mexicans distrust Yanquis. It's only been 30 years since you occupied Veracruz. Most of us are ambivalent about helping you in this war."

Yanqui? Ramón was taken aback by the appellation. It was certainly a bum rap for a Tejano, but he decided to let it go. "Don't you see Germany and Japan as threats?" he asked.

"For England and America. Not so much for us."

Ramón's fist tightened. "I don't get it, Ramiro. I mean, if we lose, it's only a matter of time before they go after you."

Ramiro seemed unruffled. "Perhaps. But before Pearl Harbor, we did a lot of business with both those countries.

They've promised even more after they win the war." He shrugged. "And at the moment, amigo." He tilted his head to one side. "It looks like they are winning."

Ramón stiffened, his voice rising. "Do you really believe that?"

"Mira, amigo. I'm just telling you what a lot of people here think. It's too soon to know which side is winning." Ramiro sat up straight and put a hand on Ramón's shoulder. "I'm glad you're here training us how to attack submarines. And I'm glad you're my friend."

No pedestrians were on the street when Ramón walked the few blocks from the Plaza Grande to his hotel, La Misión de Fray Antonio. Within the stone walls of the former Franciscan mission, it was quiet as a graveyard at midnight. Soft lights beneath 500-year-old archways filtered through the branches of plumeria trees lining the courtyard and the intoxicating fragrance of their flowers scented the warm evening air. A rushing sound from an old stone fountain, ringed with miniature cherubim, wafted across the courtyard. Then the faint red glow of a cigarette rose and fell in the shadows. At a wrought iron table, flanked by towering, potted palms, sat Erik.

"How was your night?" Erik asked.

"Red hot, buddy." Ramón sat down and lit a cigarette. "Ramiro introduced me to the most beautiful woman I've ever seen. And get this. Her father's the beer baron that makes frigging Jaguar Yucateca."

"A Kraut, eh?" Erik said with a smile.

Ramón frowned. "Aren't you?"

"Sure I am. It's just that around here, shall we say, there's a little more support for the Fatherland."

Ramón laughed. "I always knew you were a Nazi at heart, Erik. Actually, Isabel's half German, half Mayan."

Erik waved a hand. "Ah. That does sound exotic."

"She's beautiful, college-educated and drives a BMW. What more can I say?"

"Can't wait to meet her."

"How was your date tonight?"

"Linda's a nice girl. Someone I can talk with. No hablo mucho Español, you know."

"Yeah, but your Deutsch might come in useful someday."

"When we capture a U-Boat, right?" Erik reached into his pocket and pulled out a crumpled envelope. "I got a letter today from Lloyd filling me in on our McChord amigos."

"What'd he say?"

Erik unfolded the letter in a beam of silver light passing through the dense plumeria leaves. "This was dated a couple of weeks ago. He says he's leaving Florida with Doolittle's group for more training out in California. Looks like Andrew's going to North Africa and Frank's Superbomber football team is shaping up to be a winner this year."

Ramón stood up, stretching his shoulders and back. "Sounds good. We're all still alive anyway."

Erik pushed back his chair with a yawn. "Amen to that, buddy. Let's get some shut eye."

Chapter Seventeen
Wienerlied

MEXICO CITY- Cracking down on axis undercover agents, the federal police have arrested thirteen Japanese found operating a secret radio station near the United States border at Chihuahua City, tracked down three others who fled to the nearby mountains and rounded up 30 Germans and Italians here, including the alleged Gestapo head for Mexico.

New York Times
April 1, 1942

MÉRIDA, Yucatán
— April 18, 1942

The temperature at eight PM on Saturday evening was still 95° when Erik and Ramón stepped out of Ramiro's cream-colored Oldsmobile Special sedan in front of the Teatro Mérida. Dozens of men in Panama hats and white tropical suits, accompanied by women in flowing evening gowns, were ascending the marble entrance stairway. The white limestone building, constructed in neoclassical style with illuminated Corinthian columns circling its second story, filled the entire block like a colossal, Reuleaux-shaped layer cake.

Ramón removed his Panama hat, wiped sweat from his brow, and glanced at Erik who seemed to be sweating more than he was. No use blowing a fuse about it. Neither Ramiro nor any of the locals seemed to share their problem. Besides being acclimated to the heat, the tropical linen and cotton clothing worn by native Yucatecos beat American summer fabric hands down.

Erik seemed to have read his mind. "At least we've got the right hats, Ray," he said with a grin.

Ramiro, looking like a bang-up prince in his summer uniform, emerged from a side street where he'd parked the sedan and joined them at the foot of the steps. "Listos, amigos?"

"We feel a little underdressed, Ramiro," Ramón said in Spanish.

"*Tranquilo,* amigo," Ramiro said. He turned toward Erik and spoke in English. "Don't worry about clothes. Everybody knows you're gringos."

Erik laughed. "Well, maybe next time we should wear our Pan Am uniforms."

The circular concert hall was lined with five balconies containing box seats. A huge chandelier with long, lacy arms of crystal hung from the domed ceiling like a luminous spider. Above the stage, a rounded arch, resting on slender marble columns, was etched with leaves and scrolls. Ramiro led the way up a winding redwood staircase to the third level and opened the curtain to one of the boxes. "Buenos noches," he said in a pleasant, melodious voice.

Isabel and her parents rose from their box seats to welcome their guests.

"Allow me to introduce Mr. Erik Meyer," Ramiro said.

"Mucho gusto, Señor Meyer," Isabel's father said, shaking Erik's hand. "And permit me to introduce my wife Kisa Neumann."

Isabel's mother Kisa wore a long white gown embroidered with colorful Yucatec designs. With silver-streaked hair, dark skin and a high forehead, she was poised and distinctly Mayan. In contrast to her mother, Isabel's light blue gown was stylishly-modern with shoulder pads, a belted waist and pleated fabric that accentuated her shapely hips. Ramón traced his thumb back and forth across his fingertips, assuaging the subtle, tingling sensation that arose with the intense desire to touch her. She was simply stunning.

The men all shook hands and Ramiro kissed Isabel and her mother on the cheek. Not sure of the protocol for strangers, Erik glanced at Ramón. Ramiro was an old family friend. But how do you greet a woman you've just met? They both settled on an abbreviated bow of the head and neck.

"Please join us," Señor Neumann said, gesturing toward chairs behind him. "The concert's about to begin."

After the Viennese orchestra, consisting of an accordion, bass, clarinet, guitar, piano and violin, had taken their places, an announcer mounted the stage. Wienerlieder, he said, were cabaret songs known for their self-referential humor and satire. Sung in a Viennese dialect, they were sometimes carefree and often melancholic. This evening, the renowned Austrian singer Baron Werner von Essendorf had come to Mérida after successful runs in New York and Mexico City.

The tall, blonde Baron, dressed in a black tuxedo, strode onto the stage and stood in front of the piano, erect as a towering oak tree until the audience applause abated. Then, with a deep bow, and a pronounced German accent, he boomed out "Buenos noches señoras y señores." The audience exploded with cheers and applause.

As it turned out, buenos noches was the only Spanish the Baron spoke the entire evening. But it didn't matter. The audience loved him. Even Ramón, who was expecting the familiar oom-pa-pa of German-American music, was astonished when the Baron began to sing. His clear tenor voice had an operatic quality that soared throughout the concert hall like an eagle in a clear, blue sky. Ignoring the Wienerlieder translations in their programs, the audience was mesmerized by the Baron's extraordinary voice.

"This guy's really good," Ramón whispered to Erik. "Are you getting the German?"

Erik shook his head. "Hardly a word. The Viennese dialect is beyond my simple German."

After the performance, Señor Neumann invited them to a reception in honor of the Baron at his home on the Paseo de Montejo. Outside the theater, Ramiro asked them if they'd ever strolled on that fashionable boulevard. "No? Then I suggest we leave our car here. It's only about 20 minutes on foot."

At 10:30 the air was considerably cooler, but still sultry, as they walked north through the city streets. With typical American informality, Ramón and Erik slung their jackets over their shoulders. Ramón glanced at Ramiro, walking along beside him, uniform fully buttoned. Get a load of this guy. Not a drop of sweat. Just a native Méridiano enjoying a relatively cool evening.

194

A few blocks past a Spanish colonial church illuminated by spotlights, they were on the Paseo de Montejo, a broad boulevard lined with shade trees, their sturdy trunks painted white. Many of the graceful limestone mansions along the boulevard reflected the popular beaux-arts architectural style that flourished during the boom of the henequen industry in the 19th-century. Ramiro stopped in front of a white, two-story building surrounded by a black wrought iron fence. "Aquí estamos. This is the Neumann house."

A street lamp with three glass globes cast dim light on the walls, rendering the white limestone a silvery-grey color. In the manicured front yard tall royal palms flanked a large tree with fern-like leaves and scarlet bell-shaped flowers.

"What kind of tree is that?" Erik asked.

"*Arbol de fuego*," Ramiro said. "It means the tree of fire."

At the front gate, Ramiro tugged on a henequen cord, woven as tightly as the braid of a Mayan girl, that was attached to a colonial-era brass bell. A sharp, metallic ring rose, softened and faded into the muggy, evening air. Shortly, a wiry woman in colorful, Mayan dress, came scurrying to open the gate. "Buenos noches, Mayor Valdez," she said to Ramiro in the soft, shushing tones of Yucatec Mayan-accented Spanish. Turning toward Erik and Ramón, she nodded respectfully. "Bienvenidos, señores."

"Que tal, Xelha?" Ramiro asked, wrapping an arm around her shoulders.

"Muy bien gracias, Mayor," Xelha replied with the broad smile of someone who'd known and loved him for many years.

Slivers of light glinted off Xelha's silver-streaked, raven hair as she led them through an archway, past a darkened courtyard garden. The soft, rushing sound of water flowing from a fountain surrounded by palms and shrubs, dampened the impact of their footsteps on the black and white tiles.

"Xelha's been with the Neumanns since I was a boy," Ramiro said. "She has a special place here," he said, patting his heart. "En mi corazón."

At the end of the passageway, orange light flowed between the tall wooden panels of an open doorway. "Por favor," Xelha said, stepping aside as they entered a room that seemed to be an echo of the past. Holy cow! With ochre walls, a mosaic tiled floor and colonial furniture, it seemed like Nueva España all over again.

"Bienvenidos," Señor Neumann said, turning toward Ramón from his conversation with a bald, portly man in a three-piece suit and a Roman Catholic priest. "Allow me to introduce you to my friends."

Ramón quickly scanned the room. Isabel was sitting with her mother Kisa, the Wienerlieder singer, Baron von Essendorf and an older Mayan woman he hadn't met.

The women remained seated as the men stood while Señor Neumann made introductions. "Permit me to introduce my mother-in-law Nicté Canul," he said, gesturing toward the older Mayan woman.

Erik and Ramón bowed. "Encontado," Ramón said.

"The Baron von Essendorf."

Ramón shook the Baron's hand with earnest enthusiasm. "I really enjoyed your concert tonight, sir."

"*Ihre Musik war ausgezeichnet, mein Herr,*" Erik said."

The Baron grinned. "*Ach! Sie sprechen Deutsch!*"

"*Nur ein wenig,*" Erik said with a sheepish grin.

"Not a problem, sir," the Baron said in excellent English. "I've spent the last year performing in America."

"Are you actually from Vienna, Baron?" Ramón asked.

"I was, sir," the Baron sighed. "But after the Anschluss with Germany, there were some difficulties and I thought it best to leave."

Señor Neumann interrupted. "This is our longtime family advisor Padre Guzmán," he said, introducing the priest with hazel-green eyes. Then he gestured toward the portly man. "And my good friend Carlos Alvarado."

"Señor Alvarado is the editor of our local newspaper, La Revista del Sureste," Ramiro said.

Ramón's shoulders tightened. He'd read Alvarado's editorial in last Sunday's edition. It seemed fairly supportive of the Axis powers. He'd have to be doubly careful around this guy. But before Señor Alvarado could engage him in conversation, Isabel rose and took his arm, leading him across the room to meet her grandmother Nicté.

A graying, Mayan woman with narrow creases radiating from the corners of her eyes like rivulets of dried tears, Abuela Nicté spoke sophisticated Spanish, albeit inflected with a throaty accent Ramón hadn't heard before.

"Isabel tells me you're from southwest Texas," Abuela Nicté said. "What kind of Indians live there?"

Ramón sighed. "Lo siento, Señora. They're all gone now. Killed or chased away by the Anglos."

Abuela Nicté's smile was sorrowful. "Doesn't that seem to happen everywhere?" She looked deeply into Ramón's eyes. "Do you have some Indian blood in you, señor?"

Ramón grinned. He liked Abuela Nicté. "Most Mexicans do, señora. We're all mestizos."

Abuela Nicté chuckled. "Well of course you are."

"My grandmother's proud to be pure Mayan," Isabel said.

"*Una cultura muy impresiónante*," Ramón said to Abuela Nicté.

Across the room, Erik seemed to be holding his own in a German conversation with Señor Neumann and the Baron. Now was the time to make a move on Isabel. Ramón turned, and was about to engage her in conversation when—damn! Her mother Kisa was bringing the newspaper man Alvarado across the room.

"Do you have any good Pan American stories for Señor Alvarado?" Kisa asked.

"Nothing very exciting," Ramón said. "We're just making improvements at the airfield."

"Pan American added several new routes recently, didn't they?" Señor Alvarado said, probing Ramón's face for unspoken information.

Ramón nodded pleasantly. He wasn't going to let this bozo smoke anything out of him. "We do our best to serve the region, señor."

"*Felicitaciones.* I see your Navy finally sank a U-Boat last week. It sounds like the destroyer was using British radar equipment. You don't have that on your airplanes yet, do you?"

"That sounds like a question for the military, señor. I'm certainly no expert," Ramón said, ignoring Alvarado's-raised eyebrows.

"I've heard some Mexican Air Force pilots are sharing the Pan American airfield," Alvarado said.

As Ramón was wrestling with the appropriate response to that question, Isabel interrupted. "Would you like to see the garden?"

"I'd love to," Ramón said, extending his hand to Alvarado. "Encontado. A pleasure to meet you, señor."

In the shadows by the fountain, the evening air carried the spicy-sweet aroma of citrus. "Gracias for rescuing me from that interrogation," Ramón said.

"De nada. I wasn't sure what he was going to ask you next." Isabel smiled. "But you Pan American men must be used to those kind of questions by now."

Ramón laughed. "I like your sense of humor. And I really appreciate your taking care of me."

"No hay problema. Even my Abuela Nicté likes you."

"I like her very much. Are you close?"

"Ever since I was a baby."

"I had an abuela like that," Ramón said. "Sometimes I still talk to her at night."

"Then we already have something in common," Isabel said.

Gazing at the narrow groove in the middle of Isabel's full, upper lip, Ramón felt the glowing coals of desire flare up deep within his loins. How he'd love to kiss that spot, press his body against hers. But hold the horses. It was much too early in the relationship. "Maybe we'll find other things in common as well," he said. "Can I see you again, señorita?"

She touched his cheek. "Please call me Isabel."

Shouts from inside suddenly shattered the silent enchantment of the garden. Ramón dropped a shoulder and whirled about, his fists instinctively tightened.

Isabel turned toward the house. "We'd better go in."

In the living room, a group of uniformed policemen surrounded the sputtering, red-faced Baron who was protesting loudly in German.

"How can you arrest him, Captain?" Señor Neumann said to a middle-aged man in a dark suit. "He's an Austrian citizen and a refugee from the Nazis. There must be some mistake."

The police captain shook his head. "Lo siento, Señor Neumann. There's no mistake. My orders are to expedite this man's deportation from the country."

Ramon fixed his gaze on a man in a Panama suit standing behind the uniformed officers. Narrowing his eyes, he scrutinized the man's face. Jesus! The scar left no doubt. It was Manuel, the FBI agent he'd last seen in the shadows beneath the wharf at Neptune Beach. With a quick glance at Ramón, Manuel made no sign of recognition. Ramón looked away.

On Wednesday evening at 11 PM Ramón met with Manuel in a darkened corner on the Plaza Grande. "What was that all about with the Baron?" Ramón asked.

"Mexico's been getting a lot of pressure from the State Department to expel known Axis agents pronto." Manuel dragged on his cigarette and exhaled slowly. "Well, they certainly had the goods on the Baron in the states. But I wish they'd waited a bit here. We could have seen what contacts he was going to make."

"Do you suspect anyone else who was at Neumann's?"

"Alvarado's an open right-wing journalist and the priest has made remarks supportive of Franco's regime. But we have no evidence that either of them is involved with the German spy ring operating here."

"Anything else I should know?"

"FCC long-range direction finders in the U.S. have detected a clandestine radio station somewhere within the Gulf region that's transmitting to Germany. We're going to try to pinpoint it with Navy ships and some land-based mobile units."

"Any tips for my meeting in Veracruz this Friday?"

"Cárdenas is a straight shooter. President Camacho was smart to make the ex-president Secretary of Defense. He wants equipment and training from us, but he's very wary of any American military presence here. I'm not sure what to tell you about Colonel Rodriguez, the Gulf region Air Force commander. He's a bit of an enigma. His wealthy parents have contributed to Franco's Falange movement here and he had some brief Luftwaffe training before the war. Other than that we have nothing on him." Manuel took one last drag on his cigarette and crushed it beneath his heel. "*Nos vemos*," he said over his shoulder as he strode away.

Chapter Eighteen
Veracruz

Four months and ten days after "the date that will live in infamy" the armed forces of the United States carried the war to Japan's mainland. The news yesterday of a sudden and dramatic attack on the major cities of Nippon came from the Tokyo radio. It interrupted broadcasts describing the flowering of the cherry trees, a Spring festival that summons the folk of Nippon to parks and countryside for "blossom viewing."

New York Times
April 19, 1942

HEROICA VERACRUZ, Veracruz
— April 23, 1942

Shortly before his breakfast meeting with Lieutenant General Krueger, Ramón sat in a wicker chair on the patio of the Gran Hotel Diligencias and perused the morning edition of El Universal. Worried about his old training buddy Lloyd, he was eager for more news about the Tokyo raid. Lloyd's last letter suggested Doolittle was preparing his team for short field takeoffs. Although FDR quipped yesterday that the bombers flew from a secret base in Shangri-La, they must've been launched from an aircraft carrier. With a lot of practice, a B-25 could possibly take off from a carrier deck, but it sure as hell couldn't land on one.

Japanese radio claimed two U.S. planes were damaged in the attack, one disappearing in a trail of smoke over the island nation and the other at sea. This morning El Universal reported an American bomber crew made a forced landing in the Far East Khabarovsk region. Since the Russians were not at war with Japan, the crew had been interned. Where did Lloyd end up? Hopefully not in the drink or a Russian prison. Washington probably wouldn't say much for a while. There was nothing to do but wait for more news.

At 0700 an American soldier in full uniform stopped Ramón as he entered the grand dining room. Five stripes on his sleeve indicated first sergeant, a very high-ranking enlisted man—probably an aide to the general.

"Captain Morales?" The first sergeant asked, uncertain whether or not to salute since Ramón was wearing civilian clothes. Ramón nodded.

"Follow me, sir," the first sergeant said as he led Ramón to a private dining room where General Krueger and an army colonel were eating breakfast.

A lean man with a hawkish nose and three silver stars on the epaulets of his khaki shirt looked up from the table. "Welcome, Captain Morales," the general said. "Pull up a chair. This is Colonel Neal, my chief of staff for the Southern Defense Command." He turned toward a rugged looking, middle-aged man with a silver eagle pinned to the right leaf of his khaki shirt collar and crossed muskets on the left. "Morales is training Mexican pilots up in Mérida, Bill. He might help us a bit with the political etiquette down here as well as the language."

"I'm not sure about the etiquette, General," Ramón said. "But I've been speaking the language all my life."

General Krueger nodded without a smile. In his 60s, his manner was brusque and exacting. Colonel Neal, however, seemed more engaging. "Quite the uniform you have there, Captain," he said, glancing at Ramón's Guayabera shirt and pleated slacks.

Ramón felt a twinge in his belly. Should he have worn his Pan-American uniform? "Sir, I..."

Colonel Neal laughed. "Just pulling your leg, Captain. I'm well aware of the restrictions you work under."

A waiter poured Ramón a cup of coffee and offered a menu which Ramón declined. *"Quisiera chilaquiles con frijoles y dos huevos estrellados, por favor,"* he said, ordering a traditional Yucatec breakfast of tortillas, salsa, beans and fried eggs.

Colonel Neal gave General Krueger an appreciative wink. "Sounds like he'll do fine as our translator, sir."

The general ignored the remark. "There are a couple of things I want you to know about General Cárdenas," he said to Ramón. He glanced at Colonel Neal. "Or should I address him as Mr. Secretary or President Cárdenas? At any rate, he's an old revolutionary known for honesty and political acumen. As the last president before Camacho, he leaned pretty far to the left. Although Camacho's swinging a bit more in our direction, Cárdenas still isn't welcoming us with open arms. So be on your toes, Captain. I don't want to miss any nuances in our conversation." General Krueger took a final swig of coffee and stood, motioning Ramón to remain seated. "Finish your breakfast, Captain. See you in the meeting room at 0800."

The wood-paneled meeting room had a large circular table and glass-paneled doors opening onto a small balcony. The American team arrived fifteen minutes early, the Mexicans ten minutes late. Standing at General Krueger's side, Ramón noticed he seemed irritated. "It's not necessarily a slight, sir," he whispered. "Meetings down here don't often start on time." The General frowned.

Soon, the Mexican Secretary of Defense Lázaro Cárdenas arrived with the Air Force commander of the Gulf Region, Colonel Rodriguez. After brief introductions, the two teams sat across from one another. Ramón sat to the left of General Krueger. Colonel Neal was on his right. At opposite ends of the table sat American and Mexican enlisted men with notepads.

Secretary Cárdenas, a short, swarthy man, was eloquent and polite. "Although we're not at war with the Axis powers, we understand your need for a stopover point for flights to Panama and the Caribbean. Our government, therefore, is giving your proposal to upgrade the airfield at Cozumél serious consideration."

General Krueger sat immobile, his facial expression blank.

"There remain, however, some details that must be examined," Cárdenas continued, halting briefly after each phrase for Ramón's translation. "First, all construction work must be done by Mexican contractors."

"Under the supervision of Pan-American Airways?" General Krueger asked through the interpreter Ramón.

"Yes. That's acceptable," Cárdenas responded crisply. "Second, the Mexican military will retain full control of the airfield."

After the translation, General Krueger leaned back in his chair and crossed his arms. "How can we run operations without our support and maintenance teams?"

Cárdenas leaned forward. "I understand your concerns, General. We'll allow a small number of your maintenance men to be stationed at the field." He unfolded a copy of the proposed construction plans and pointed to several unidentified buildings. "But first. What are these?"

"Those are barracks, sir," Major Neal said.

"*Cuartel del ejército*," Ramón translated.

Cárdenas glanced obliquely at Colonel Rodriguez, then at General Krueger. "Those are relatively large buildings, sir. I must reiterate. Other than a maintenance crew, Mexico will not allow American soldiers to be stationed on the ground in our country."

General Krueger's gaze was penetrating. "As you well know, General Cárdenas, it takes more than a few maintenance men to run an airfield."

Secretary Cárdenas folded the construction plans. "It's been a pleasure meeting you, General. As I said, this proposal is under review. But I'm sure we can work out the details." He rose, shook hands and left the room with his team.

General Krueger strolled out to the balcony and lit a cigarette. Ramón and Colonel Neal followed. "No troops on the ground," the general said. "The old warrior doesn't mince words, does he? Hell. I'm not surprised. Our occupation of Veracruz was not that long ago."

"General Cárdenas is only one man, sir" Colonel Neal said. "I think President Camacho will still come through."

General Krueger, pinched his thumb and forefinger together. "A declaration of war by Mexico is only this far away. We'll see what happens then."

Isabel arrived in the hotel lobby in mid-afternoon after making her business rounds at the harbor. In a broad-brimmed hat, white summer outfit and a leather bag slung over her shoulder, she looked elegantly professional—an excellent representative for Jaguar Yucateca beer. "Hola, Ramón," she said, as he kissed her cheek. "Ready to see the countryside?"

Exiting the hotel onto the palm tree-lined Plaza de Armas, they passed a dark, unmarked sedan at curbside. As his first sergeant held the door, General Krueger climbed into the back seat. Neither Ramón nor the first sergeant made eye contact.

"I wonder what the American army's doing here," Isabel said.

"Beats me," Ramón said, taking her hand. "How was work this morning?"

Isabel half-raised an eyebrow, then moved on. "It was busy. I checked on a shipment of barley and hops from Galveston, had breakfast with the harbormaster and met with our distributor at his warehouse. What about your Pan Am meeting?"

"Oh. Just going over a lot of details about upgrading our airfields. Nothing's settled yet."

"It sounds like you're finishing up repairs at Mérida. What's next? Cozumél?"

A subtle tingling coursed through Ramón's arms and chest as if he'd brushed his fingertips across an exposed wire from a faulty light switch. "What makes you say Cozumél?"

Isabel shrugged. "When we first met, you mentioned it."

"Oh. Right. I'd forgotten." He relaxed with a prolonged, silent expiration. "Not much happening there right now."

"Bueno. Let's forget about work. *Tío* Julio isn't expecting us in Coatepec until evening. We can take our time."

"Tío? Is he your father's brother?"

Isabel laughed. "No. Actually, he's just an old family friend who went to school with my father in Mexico City. I've called him Tío since I was a little girl."

Heading north on the coastal road, with the top down and a roaring BMW 328 engine, conversation was almost impossible. A scarf tied firmly around Isabel's head allowed only a few strands of her long black hair to flap in the wind as she deftly maneuvered through the curves. It was a familiar feeling for Ramón—like flying Sizzling Rita except Isabel was the pilot, in full control of this powerful roadster.

Half an hour out of Veracruz, the engine surged, then decelerated as Isabel downshifted and turned off the highway onto a dirt road that meandered through grassland dotted with shrubs and palm groves. Cruising steadily in second gear, she navigated the furrows and grooves of the dusty road until they came to a stop by a sand dune above the sparkling, emerald-green Gulf of Mexico.

Below, a narrow beach of glistening, white sand arced half a mile between massive rock formations that dove into the water. In the shallows, large boulders, that looked sedimentary to Ramón, lay stacked or isolated in the gently rolling surf. With only a slight wind and the temperature about 80, it was a dream day for the beach. Ramón removed his shoes and socks, rolled up his pant legs and stepped out of the car. The warm sand grated gently against the soles of his feet and coursed between his toes in a pleasant, grainy caress.

Isabel took off her shoes and slung her leather bag over her shoulder." Let's walk to the top of the dune." She patted the bag. "I've got a Leica in here with a rangefinder and telephoto lens. I like taking pictures of this beautiful coastline."

Ramón was impressed. "A Leica? You must be a serious photographer."

Isabel laughed. "Maybe you should wait until you've seen my prints." She turned and started climbing the dune, each footstep rapidly filling with sand. Ramón followed, his gaze fixed on the firm, heart-shaped buttocks shifting beneath her white linen skirt.

On top of the dune, Isabel took photos north and south with her telephoto lens, then replaced it with a 50-millimeter lens from her leather bag. "Now let's get a few shots of you." She snapped several photos, pausing to adjust the camera's exposure and shutter speed between each shot.

"You really are a professional," Ramón said. "Where did you learn this?"

"I took some photography courses when I was studying in Europe."

"In Madrid?"

"No Munich."

"How'd you end up there?"

"When the Spanish civil war broke out in 1936, I left the university in Madrid. I finished my degree in Munich in 1938."

"Que suerte! You were lucky to get out of both countries before war broke out."

Isabel's expression darkened. "Luck may have had something to do with it," she said, putting her camera gear away. "But mostly I just tried to stay awake."

Ramón looked down at his hands. "I'm sorry. I didn't mean to upset you."

"It's all right. There were many good times there." She hesitated. "As well as sad times."

"Sad?"

Isabel bit her upper lip and creased her forehead. "I was young and intoxicated with the spirit of democracy. We marched with students in the streets, sang anthems and waved the Republican banner." Her voice faltered and her eyes became cloudy as she lapsed into silence.

Ramón waited for a few moments. "What happened?"

"It wasn't just democracy I loved." She spoke haltingly. "There was a man. One of my teachers actually. We marched together." She paused and took a deep breath. "There was a street battle. We were arm in arm. Someone fired a gun. And he was lying on the pavement."

Ramón widened his eyes. "The Fascists killed him?" Isabel nodded, tears in her eyes. "I'm so sorry," Ramón said.

Chapter Nineteen
Coatepec

The Mexican government is adding an anti-Fifth Column department to the anti-espionage department of the Secretariat of the Interior to counteract propaganda among Mexicans whose sympathies are pro-Axis.

New York Times
April 15, 1942

COFFEE HIGHLANDS, VERACRUZ, Mexico
— April 23, 1942

After cruising through a misty, mile-high forest of moss-covered beech, walnut and oak trees, Isabel and Ramòn approached the southern outskirts of Xalapa, a colonial city ringed by volcanoes of the Sierra Madre Oriental.

"I have to make one brief stop," Isabel said. "I promised our family pastor Padre Guzmán I'd deliver a book to his nephew." She pulled a musty, red book, embossed with a golden crucifix, from her bag and handed it to Ramón.

Careful not to damage the frayed binding and parchment-like pages, Ramón thumbed through the old liturgical manual.

213

"Why are some of these Latin words in red and others in black?"

"The red ones are rubrics—instructions for the mass. I think the words the priest actually says are in black."

The shambling gatekeeper of the Seminario del buen Pastor swung open the wrought iron gate, topped with fleur-de-lis, and waved them on through. At the end of a long driveway lined with red and white flowering shrubs, Isabel parked the BMW in the shade of a tall maple tree. "I'll just deliver this Missale Romanum and we'll be on our way," she said, her skirt riding high up her legs as she swiveled to exit the driver's door.

Ramón locked his gaze on her delicious thighs longer than he intended. "Okay if I come along?" He said, shifting his eyes to her face.

"Como no?" She said with a coy smile.

Padre Guzmán's nephew, a handsome young man with the same hazel-green eyes as his uncle, met them in the library of the seminary. When he leaned forward to accept the book from Isabel, the silver crucifix around his neck flashed momentarily in a beam of light streaming through a tall, stained glass window. As promised, the visit was brief and soon they were back on the road again.

Lacy limbs of trees overhanging the road to Coatepec swayed like jade-green fans in a spring breeze. Above the verdant, rolling hills, the sun rode low in the sky, brushing the tallest snow-capped peaks with the salmon strokes of twilight. As the dark-green hills transitioned to gray, limestone towers with roofs of red-ochre, appeared on the horizon. "Coatepec," Isabel said, raising her voice above the roar of the engine.

The twilight traffic in Coatepec was sparse. Laughter, shouts, honks and the distant sound of violins and guitars floated on the air above the rumble of the BMW's engine, as they cruised smoothly through town. Scattered pedestrians, ambling along the raised sidewalks, cautiously avoided cracks in the concrete or occasional twisted rods of exposed rebar. On top of wrought iron posts in the Parque Central, globular lights emitted a faint yellow glow as couples strolled, arm in arm, through the garden.

Past a Gothic church with a tall spire crowned like a minaret, a number of Baroque-style buildings and scores of adobe row houses, their conjoined walls hiding secret interior gardens, they were soon back in the rolling green countryside of the highlands.

"See those?" Isabel gestured toward rows of short, leafy trees, studded with cherry-red berries, growing in the shade of tall, thin cedars. "Arábica coffee."

Along the winding road, dense tracts of forest were interspersed with rows of coffee trees that extended up the hillsides. A waterfall, braided into three silver streams, cascaded down a stone carapace near shacks of corrugated steel and crumbling adobe. Two shirtless men shouldering heavy packs and a woman in a colorful huipil with a basket balanced upon her head, emerged from a forest trail. Close behind, a barefoot child led a burro laden with bags of coffee beans onto the roadside.

Isabel turned onto a gravel road that wound up the hillside beneath a dense canopy of leafy oak trees. In a large clearing at the top of the hill, a two-story hacienda with stone arches, wrought iron balconies and a tile roof, was surrounded by a garden of ferns and flowering plants.

An elderly, dark-skinned man in white cotton shirt and pants, scurried up to the car as Isabel cut the engine. "Bienvenida, Señorita Neumann," he said in Spanish, accented with a pleasing musical tone. "So nice to see you again."

"Buenos noches, Hedia," Isabel said. "This is my friend Ramón Morales."

Hedia greeted Ramón and insisted on carrying their luggage into the house. At the front door, Soona, a comely, gray-haired woman in a huipil embroidered with orange and red designs of the sun and moon, welcomed Isabel with a radiant smile. "Ay, Señorita Neumann. We've missed you."

Isabel turned to Ramón. "I've been coming here since I was a child. Hedia and Soona have always looked after me. In Otomi their names mean god of the wind and goddess of the moon."

Ramòn shook his head with a smile. "Fantástico. Being cared for by the wind and the moon. Who could ask for more?"

Soona led them beneath a tiled archway to a garden patio arrayed with wicker furniture. A tall man with a silver beard and receding hairline put down the book he was reading and rose from his chair to meet them. "Isabel! Mi cielito," he said kissing her on the cheek.

Julio sat them on the adjacent sofa and launched into lively conversation about Isabel's activities, how his old friend Fernando (her father) was doing and what it was like for

Ramón as a Tejano living in Mexico. Ramón liked Julio. He seemed genuinely warm and friendly and clearly loved Isabel.

Ramón picked up the book on the table—*Alma caprichos: el mal poema* by Manuel Machado. "Whims of the soul," he said to Julio. "I'm not familiar with that author, Señor. But I certainly like Antonio Machado."

"Manuel's his older brother," Julio said. "Their father was also a writer. But I like Manuel best."

"Well he wasn't in my syllabus at Texas State Teachers College," Ramón said."

Julio laughed heartily. "Claro. There are so many great Spanish authors. It's hard to cover them all in a college course."

After a stimulating hour of conversation and a few toritos, a creamy cocktail blend of rum, several fruits, peanuts and milk, they retired to a dining room with high-beamed ceilings, wrought iron candelabras and a carved oak table. The trout with black acuyo sauce and chili rellenos went well with the Jaguar Yucateca beer Isabel brought.

Sitting in a leatherback chair in the living room after dinner, Ramón looked up as the wooden cuckoo clock on the wall struck four descending notes followed by four that ascended. "That's a beautiful clock, señor. Very intricate carving."

"It's a family heirloom," Julio said. "My great-grandfather was a clockmaker who immigrated to my hometown Puebla from the Schwarzwald shortly after the Mexican Revolution."

Hedia and Soona entered the living room bearing trays of baked caramel flan and Kahlúa liqueur. Isabel took a glass and raised it toward Ramón. "Have you ever had this?" Ramón

217

shook his head no. "It's made from Arábica coffee grown right here in Julio's fields."

Ramón sipped the Kahlúa. It had a fruity aroma and smooth coffee flavor. "Excelente. How did you get into the coffee business, señor?"

"I spent many years in the Sierra Madre of Cuba as an apprentice to a coffee plantation owner. I even married his daughter." Julio sighed. "But when she died during the influenza epidemic of 1918, I came back to Mexico. The high altitude and mild climate here in Coatepec are perfect for cultivating shade-grown beans. I had a few lean years, but now business is thriving."

"Do you like living here alone in the highlands, señor?" Ramón asked.

"I do, but I must admit I miss the cultural life of Puebla. Do you like opera?"

"I really can't say. I've never seen one."

Julio stood and walked over to a tall, mahogany record player and opened its cabinet. "You don't have to see an opera," he said, removing a 78 RPM disk from its cardboard sleeve. "Just listen."

After the scratchy sound of the phonograph needle made a few revolutions on the turntable, a haunting string melody filled the room. Then a plaintive clarinet introduced a powerful tenor's clear, intensely-emotional voice. *E lucevan le stelle…*

Ramón closed his eyes, transfixed. He'd never really paid attention to music like this before. At the end of the aria, he opened his eyes and shook his head. "Wow! That was beautiful."

Isabel smiled, her eyes fixed on Ramón with loving approval.

Julio reduced the volume on the record player. "I thought you might like that. Enrico Caruso was one of the greatest tenors of all time."

It was well after midnight when Ramón finally cracked open the hinged windows in the second-floor guest bedroom and climbed into bed. What a corker of a day! Traveling with a beautiful woman in her sports car and spending a fascinating evening on a coffee plantation. Soon he was fast asleep.

Barely an hour later—Raw pa haw cha. Like a rusty engine repeatedly turning over but unable to catch, the loud cries of chachalaca birds in the garden awakened Ramón. Now, aware of a full bladder, and unable to drift back to sleep, he crept down the dark hallway toward the bathroom. Halfway there, a flashing blue-green light escaped beneath the sill of a heavy oak door. When his next footstep resulted in a loud, creaking sound, the light abruptly disappeared. What the hell was that? He stopped and stood silently for several moments. No more light escaped beneath the door sill. Was it a flickering fluorescent light? Maybe an illuminated fish tank? He sniffed the air. No smoke. No sign of flames. Probably nothing to worry about.

Chapter Twenty
Fire in the Gulf

Nazi submarines have largely abandoned the vital North Atlantic supply lines to Russia...They have arranged in packs in the Caribbean and, recently, even in the Gulf of Mexico where three ships were torpedoed in the last week. It was estimated unofficially today that 180 merchant ships have been sunk off these coasts since January 14...

New York Times
May 13, 1942

GULF OF MEXICO
— May 13, 1942

Shortly after sunrise 100 miles north of Mérida, amber stratocumulus clouds streamed high above the Gulf of Mexico like a river of molten lava, and dense patches of fog hung low over the water. Erik's voice rose above the crackling hiss of Sizzling Rita's intercom. "Looks like smoke rising from the fog, Ray. Bearing 030."

Flying at 2000 feet, Ramón squinted into the horizon at a thin column of smoke spiraling several hundred feet above the wooly, white blanket obscuring the surface of the water. With three ships sunk in the Gulf during the past week, he had to assume the worst. But a daytime attack in the Gulf would be a very bold move by a U-boat. He glanced at the v-shaped formation of four Mexican pilots, now flying with their own crews off his wingtips, and radioed the squadron.

"Yucatec five, Yucatec leader. Smoke on the horizon bearing 030. Let's drop down and check it out."

Like a synchronized flight of silver birds, the Mexican B-25 pilots and their American instructor dropped to 1000 feet above the water and flew through scattered patches of fog toward the smoke. Soon, a flaming freighter, it's bridge blown away and bow nosing deep in the water, became visible through an opening in the fog. Inky black smoke, scintillating with bursts of fiery-orange debris, billowed from the center of the ship.

"Yucatec one, Yucatec leader. Let's take a closer look, Ramiro."

While the other pilots circled above, Ramón and Ramiro dropped low and flew in tandem, in and out of drifting fog banks, directly over the sinking ship. No men or lifeboats were visible in the water. With smoke rolling over the deck, any flag or identification on the bow was obscured. However, painted on the ship's side, just above the sinking waterline, was a large flag with green, red and white bars.

Ramón was confused. Whose ship was it? Italian? No. Axis ships wouldn't be sailing in these waters. It couldn't be Mexican. There was no eagle in the center of the flag.

"Yucatec leader, Yucatec one," Ramiro broke in. "That's a Mexican ship."

"What? Where's the eagle on the flag?"

"Only military ships have an eagle, amigo."

Ramón glanced sideways at Erik. This was bonkers. Why had a neutral Mexican ship been hit?

Erik clicked in on the intercom, unheard by the squadron. "Sonofabitch, Ray. How are these guys going to take this?"

"We gotta keep things calm, Erik. Even though you and I are at war with Germany, Mexico isn't."

"Right. And we're noncombatant babysitters. What bullshit."

Ramón switched to the squadron's broadcast frequency. "Yucatec five, Yucatec leader. Tranquilo, amigos. Let's drop to 500 feet and search for survivors."

Flying low above the water, the squadron circled around the sinking ship in an ever-widening pattern, scrutinizing clearings between banks of fog. A few minutes into the search, Erik gestured urgently at the water. "Jesus, Ray! Is that a fucking U-Boat?"

For a few seconds, Ramón had a clear view of the water. Alongside a lifeboat, lay a dark-gray submarine the length of a football field. Painted on its conning tower, a ferocious wolf sprang from the stormy sea—it was the same U-boat he and Major Anderson had unsuccessfully attacked off Jacksonville.

But Ramón wasn't the only one who'd caught sight of the U-Boat. Before Ramón could decide a course of action, Diego broke formation and dropped to 100 feet over the water.

"Yucatec two, Yucatec leader. Get back in formation," Ramón shouted.

Ignoring the command, Diego headed directly toward the submarine. 1000 yards from the U-Boat, Diego's bombardier opened fire with the nose-mounted .30-caliber machine gun. A stream of bullets churned up the water and raked the bridge of the submerging U-Boat. By the time Diego circled back for another attack, the submarine was no longer visible and he rejoined the formation without a word. Ramón radioed the lifeboats' position to the Naval Air Station at Pensacola, and the squadron flew back to Mérida.

On the ground, a seething Ramón grabbed Diego by the arm. "Idiota! What the hell were you doing?"

Diego's eyes were blazing, "Those Alemanes killed my countrymen. I couldn't just let them get away." He pulled away from Ramón's grasp. "What about you *cagón*? You're the one that should have attacked."

Fists clenched and furious to be called a coward, Ramón took a step forward. "Say one more word and you'll end up in the guardhouse. You disobeyed a direct order."

"From whom? A Pan-American pilot?"

Erik stepped in between the two men. "Okay. Let's cool off."

Ramiro came scurrying down the runway and pulled Ramón aside. "Let me handle this, amigo. He's in my chain of command."

Ramón nodded silently and Ramiro led Diego away.

Erik walked closely beside Ramón back to the terminal. "Ease up, Ray. This bullshit assignment is messing with all of us. That cocky asshole Diego just did what you wanted to, right?"

Ramón's nod was grudging. "Guess so. But he sure pisses me off."

"I'm just glad you didn't pop that pinhead, Ray. Let Ramiro take care of it, okay?"

At 11 PM a faint scent, reminiscent of jasmine and cooking oil drifted in the warm air of the Plaza Grande. The rattling of light traffic, an occasional shout and a trova duet accompanied by guitars, percolated through the darkened side streets. Except for a few late-evening strollers, illuminated by the soft yellow light of the street lamps, and an occasional couple cuddling in the shadows, the square was quiet. Ramón walked to an empty courting bench with two parallel seats facing in opposite directions and sat down beneath the leafy branches of a laurel tree.

Within minutes, Manuel emerged from the shadows and sat in the opposite chair. "¿*Qué hay de nuevo?*"

Ramón looked down, his voice lowered as if talking to the cobblestones. "This morning we came across a Mexican freighter sinking in the Gulf and a U-Boat laying on the surface near some lifeboats. One of our Mexican pilots strafed the sub as it crash dived."

"The Krauts sank a Mexican ship?" Manuel paused, shaking his head. "Must've been a mistake. I doubt they'll report it."

"Why not?"

"Mexico's trying hard to stay out of this war. They don't need something like this to fan the fire we're trying to build under them. Who was the pilot?"

"Diego Bader. Excellent pilot, but quite a loner. I don't know him very well. He really pissed me off disobeying orders."

"Bader, eh? We're looking at him. Second-generation German immigrant family. Just like Fernando Neumann, your girlfriend's father."

Ramón froze. "What are you saying?"

"Even with the Mexican government's recent crackdown, there're still a lot of German agents hiding out here. Our radio intercepts suggest the U-Boats are getting inside shipping information."

"What does that have to do with Señor Neumann?"

"Maybe nothing." Manuel paused. "But he did host a Viennese singer we knew was a spy. He also travels a lot and many of his friends are Falangist sympathizers." Manuel tilted his head back and exhaled a stream of smoke into the light filtering through the laurel leaves. "What did the two of you two talk about anyway?"

Ramón felt a little lightheaded. "Nothing much with Señor Neumann. But one of his newspaper friends was grilling me about radar."

"That's right. Carlos Alvarado was at that party, wasn't he? Although he's toned down a bit, his paper still opposes Mexican entry into the war."

"What about Diego Bader?"

"Nothing obvious except his German heritage. But based on the intercepted messages, it looks like one of your Fuerza Aérea pilots is passing along information to the Krauts."

Ramón felt a tightness in his chest. "Jesus. What kind of information?"

"Pilot manuals, descriptions of armament and navigational equipment, flight plans, training exercises."

"But why would Diego attack a U boat if he's a German agent?"

"You guys weren't carrying depth charges, right? Would a few machine gun bullets do much damage?"

The knot tightened in Ramón's chest. Manuel was right. 30-caliber machine gun bullets wouldn't pierce a U-Boats hull. He looked up at the illuminated twin towers of the Cathedral. "What the fuck do I do now?"

Manuel rose. "Just keep your eyes open."

Chapter Twenty One
Engel

I believe that we all have a right to find encouragement in the fact that it was possible for us in the short space of six weeks entirely to annihilate the Anglo-French armies, to bring Holland under our power in less than a week and Belgium in a bare three weeks, and as for the British forces, to smash them, capture them, and drive them into the sea at Dunkirk.

Adolf Hitler
Reichstag Speech
April 26, 1942

140 NAUTICAL MILES NORTH OF MÉRIDA — May 13, 1942

At 0600 the first rays of the rising sun tinted the patchy fog bank surrounding the U-023 faint orange. Rainer lowered his binoculars and inhaled deeply through his nostrils. Soon he would give Jäger the order to submerge for the remaining daylight hours. But for now he was enjoying the cool morning air.

Once again Grossadmiral Dönitz had outmaneuvered the Allies. Just as the Amis were beginning to have some success off America's eastern seaboard, the old lion ordered his U-boats into the Gulf of Mexico where unescorted merchant ships were easy targets. In the past week, the U-023 had sunk an American oil tanker departing New Orleans and a Norwegian freighter carrying bauxite headed for Mobile. It appeared the second happy time would continue a bit longer.

The port lookout leaned into the bridge. "Herr Kaleun! I see a dark spot moving through the fog 30 degrees port."

Gray, smoky haze appeared above the fog as Rainer and Jäger scanned to port with their binoculars. Soon the ghostly apparition emerged from the fog as an eastbound tanker less than a mile away.

"What do you make of him, Jäger?" Rainer asked without taking his eyes off the vessel.

"Small tanker, maybe 4000 tons. Angle on the starboard bow 90."

"Increase speed to 14 knots and come right to parallel his course."

"He's probably seen us by now, Herr Kaleun."

"Ja, but what choice does he have except to run? His top speed's about 10 knots, nicht wahr? Increase to flank speed. We'll draw ahead, then close for a good shot."

At a distance of 1800 meters a large flag, painted with green, white and red vertical stripes, became visible on the side of the desperately steaming tanker.

"*Was zum Teufel*? What kind of flag is that?" Rainer said.

"Looks Italian, Herr Kaleun."

"Nein. They wouldn't be in the Gulf. Hungarian?"

Jäger paged through the Kriegsmarine recognition manual. "Nein. Hungary has horizontal stripes."

"It can't be Mexican. Their flag has an eagle in the center."

A sea wolf uncertain of his prey, Rainer pushed his cap back and ran his fingers through his hair. Verdammt! He pulled his cap back down over his forehead. Wherever it came from, this oil was certainly going to the Allies. They've used false markings in the Mediterranean. Why not here? "Sound general quarters, Jäger. Action stations torpedo."

As the U-023 closed in for the kill, Jäger manned the UZO and Vorhaltrechner to calculate the proper torpedo angle. "Forward torpedo room. Target angle 084. Enemy speed 10 knots. Range 1500 meters. Depth 3 meters. Fire one. Los!" After a few seconds, he released the second torpedo. "Fire two. Los!"

At 30 knots, the two torpedoes streamed toward the target faster than a pair of hungry barracuda. Jäger timed the runs. *Wham!* At 100 seconds, the first torpedo struck the tanker amidships. *Phwoosh.* A geyser followed by a billowing black cloud shot high into the air. At 105 seconds, the second strike was followed by a surge of yellow and red flames that swept upward, engulfing the bridge. Several crewmen, their clothing ablaze, emerged from the flames and leaped screaming into the sea. Rainer glanced at Jäger and shook his head. Scheisse. This was the part he always loathed.

A few of the tanker crew were able to launch the single lifeboat still intact. Men in the water frantically grasped at the gunwales as their crewmates in the lifeboat rowed fiercely away in a desperate attempt to escape the burning oil slicks spreading rapidly across the water around the sinking ship.

Rainer waited until the survivors in the rowboat were out of the zone of destruction, then moved in for the Fängschuss.

After a single salvo from the deck cannon, the flaming ship shuddered and rolled like a harpoon-studded whale before plunging into the emerald-green depths of the Gulf.

Sheering off from the sinking ship, the U-023 pulled alongside the lifeboat. "Where do you come from?" Rainer asked in English.

A man with a blackened face waved his arms in the air. "Tampico! Mexico no have war with Germany!"

Rainer narrowed his eyes. "Mexico?"

"Aircraft off the port side!" A lookout shouted.

Like prey caught in the open by an attacking osprey, Rainer froze and locked his gaze on a silver B-25, barely 50 meters above the water, roaring toward the U-023 with its nose gun blazing. *Ratatattat. Phlltt Pleeww.* Bullets skipped across the water and sparked off the deck. *Tzzing Twwee.* Bullets pinged around the fairwater. As the attacker swept over the bridge, Rainer recognized the distinctive red, white and green triangles painted on the fuselage—Fuerza Aérea Mexicana. "Clear the bridge!" He shouted.

Two lookouts scrambled down the hatch. The third, the silver-voiced tenor named Engel, lay folded over the fairwater railing, bright red blood spreading across his back like an angry incoming tide. Rainer draped Engel across his shoulders and carried him to the hatch where Jäger passed his limp body down the ladder into the control room. Rainer stepped onto the ladder, sealed the hatch and ordered a dive. "Alarm!"

With the U-023 inclined in a steep crash dive, Engel lay sprawled on the control room floor, a dying warrior snatched from the fray above. As the blood pooling around his body spread across the narrow space between the periscope well and the instrument panels, his stunned crewmates tried their best to maintain concentration on their gauges and dials. Funkmaat Stein knelt by Engel, applying pressure to his wounds. Although the entry point in his upper chest was only the size of a 10-Pfennig coin, the exit wound in his back left a gaping hole as large as a 5-Reichsmark piece. "He's still moving air, Herr Kaleun," Stein said. "But his pulse is rapid and thready."

"What can you do for him?"

"Not much," Stein said as he began wrapping Engel in a blanket. "I'm afraid he's lost a lot of blood."

The U-023 leveled off and proceeded for an hour further out into the Gulf. No depth charges were dropped from the air and destroyers never arrived. "Let's rest here until dark," Rainer said.

"All stop. Zero bubble. Hover at 50 meters," Jäger ordered.

Several hours later Rainer sat with Jäger in the wardroom. Neither spoke much. Rainer stretched the muscles of his neck and shoulders, trying to escape the heavy, dark weight bearing down on him. Scheisse. There was no getting around it. He'd attacked the wrong ship and been caught on the surface during daylight hours. Now one of his crew lay dying.

A seaman with downcast eyes approached. "Matrose Engel has died, Herr Kaleun."

Rainer closed his eyes briefly and released a long breath through pursed lips. He dismissed the seaman and looked at Jäger. "Where was Engel from?"

"Rostock."

"Ach. Ja," Rainer said, his voice pitched low and disconsolate. "Nice old Baltic city. I once crewed on a sailboat out of Warnemünde." He looked up as a memory swept on through. "A bit like Travemünde back home in Lübeck." He wrinkled his brow and stopped talking. Jäger politely looked down at the deck. "Of course that's all before the bombing," Rainer continued. He wiped sweat from his forehead and dabbed at his eyes. "It's getting stuffy in here, nicht wahr?"

Jäger furrowed his brow and nodded slowly, a look of mutual sorrow in his eyes. "It was about 32 degrees last time I checked," he said, running his fingers beneath his sweaty collar.

At 2100, shortly after the last light, the U-023 surfaced in the middle of the Gulf beneath a waxing gibbous moon and scattered clouds. Rainer and Jäger stood by the flak gun on the Wintergarten. A dozen crewmen waited on the deck below. Waves of silver moonlight, breaking through the cloud cover, swept across the aft deck as four seamen under the command of Leutnant zur See Wolf emerged from the hatch bearing the shrouded body of Matrose Engel. Wrapped in a red Kriegsmarine ensign, Engel was borne across the gently rolling deck to a grating above the stern torpedo room where he had so recently labored. After weighting the body, head and toe, with shells from the deck cannon, the burial team stood at attention, waiting for Rainer's command.

Rainer's voice rose like a sorrowful wind above the swells slapping against the hull. "Men. We've lost a valued comrade and the Fatherland has lost a loyal son. Mere words are inadequate to express our sorrow, so let's pray. Der Herr ist mein Hirte..."

As the ceremony continued, Rainer found himself oddly detached from the scene, as if looking down from above. The crewmen murmured the Lord's Prayer. Rainer looked up at the moon. Why had he risked surfacing at daybreak? *Es ist ein Ros' entsprungen aus einer Wurzel zart.* On the aft deck, a lone harmonica played the haunting melody Engel sang last Christmas Eve. How old was he? Maybe nineteen? A dark cloud eclipsed the moonlight and Engel's shrouded corpse slipped into the sea. Rainer saluted. His own man killed in retribution for an attack he shouldn't have made in the first place. *Ich hatt' einen Kameraden.* The crew sang the melancholic warriors' lament. Rainer's eyes went out of focus, his grief turned inward.

Chapter Twenty Two
Clouds on the Horizon

Mexico will now intensify as far as possible her protective patrols of the Gulf, following a sinking of a Mexican ship (by a U-Boat)... Because Mexico is technically neutral, as well as for local political reasons, action against Axis agents has been limited and delayed.

New York Times
May 15, 1942

MÉRIDA, Yucatán
— May 17, 1942

The deep green leaves of the plumeria trees in the courtyard of La Misión de Fray Antonio were suffused with late morning sunlight. The odors of fresh bread and nectar drifted in the air. Erik and Ramón sat at their customary table, basking in warm sunlight beside the burbling fountain. On Sunday mornings, except for clanging cathedral bells, the day usually began quietly in Mérida. Only a few businessmen and Mexican tourists sat at the other tables in the courtyard, and a single waiter stood behind the bar casually observing his customers.

Ramón washed down his pan dulce with a slug of coffee and glanced at the front page of the Revista del Sureste. "The headline says the Krauts are refusing to accept Mexico's protest over sinking the tanker."

"Anything about Diego's attack?" Erik asked.

Ramón scanned the article. "Nothing. I guess neither side wants to acknowledge it."

"So what's next?"

"It says the Mexican government will make a decision..." Ramón placed a fingertip beneath a phrase in the article. "Acorde con el honor nacional."

Erik's eyes narrowed with incomprehension.

"In line with Mexico's national honor," Ramón explained.

"Think that means war, Ray?"

"Hold it." Ramón held up a finger and cocked his head. "Hear that?"

"Sounds like drums and shouting from the plaza."

Ramón beckoned the waiter to the table. "What's that noise, Alejandro?"

"Manifestación in the Plaza Mayor, señor."

"A demonstration? Against what?"

"Against war, señor."

Ramón looked at Erik, wrinkling his forehead.

Erik pushed back his chair. "Let's go take a gander."

An aura of excitement charged the air as strolling pedestrians picked up their pace on the short walk to the Plaza Mayor. Some carried placards with handwritten antiwar phrases such as "No a la Guerra!" or simply "Paz." Others wore colorful shirts and scarves that proclaimed allegiance to a political party or trade union.

At the Plaza Mayor, the small rectangular park was packed with people surging onto the avenue in front of the cathedral. A dozen drummers dressed in paramilitary-style with gold shirts, wide belts and leather straps across their shoulders, marched down the broad avenue. Behind the drummers, hundreds of men waved red banners bearing a green image of Mexico. Following the men, women in white dresses with red and green sashes, marched silently along, many holding small crucifixes.

"Perdoneme, señor. What's that flag?" Ramón asked a balding man next to him.

"Sinarquista," the man replied.

Ramón pointed to the man's armband that bore the initials CRM. "And that?"

The man laughed. "Not Sinarquista! Confederation of Mexican Workers." He resumed watching the parade, then turned back to Ramón. "Although my union supports it," he said, tapping his armband. "I'm personally against getting into this war."

"What's going on, Ray?" Erik asked.

"The marchers are Sinarquistas. A right-wing Catholic group. Some say they're fascists."

"Then I guess it's not surprising they're against a war with Germany."

Ramón gestured toward the man next to him. "This guy's wearing a labor union armband. They're usually left-wing, even Communist. But he's also against the war."

A small group of men waving red banners emblazoned with a yellow hammer and sickle, jostled through the crowd, jeering at the marchers. "Viva la patria! No al Fascismo!" A young Communist dashed into the street and tried to seize a flag carried by a Sinarquista. The resulting scuffle rapidly turned into a fist fight between a handful of men from both sides.

Ramón found his hand inadvertently clenched into a fist. Christ. This is going to turn into a street brawl. A part of him would actually welcome some combat. But not here, not now. "This isn't our fight, Erik. Let's skedaddle."

Around midnight, beneath dim ceiling lights, a young man in a black shirt sat in a chair on the narrow wooden stage of the Café Bohemia. Isabel whispered in Ramón's ear. "Before he became famous, he used to work at a school for poor children here in Mérida."

With an open book across his knees, the young poet looked into the crowd seated at small tables around the room. "Buenos noches. My name is Octavio Paz. It's a pleasure to be back in Mérida. Tonight I'd like to read you some poems I wrote while fighting the fascists in Spain..."

Un cuerpo, un cuerpo solo, sólo un cuerpo
A body, a body alone, only a body

As the young poet continued reading to a mesmerized audience, Ramón sipped his beer and risked an occasional glance across the candlelit table at the subtle cleavage atop Isabel's open blouse. What a classy woman. Since their trip to Coatepec he'd always had her on his mind. Although she was on the road a lot, when in town they usually got together.

Except for the heat, this Mérida assignment was turning out OK. Now he was really cooking with gas.

When the poetry reading ended a guitarist quietly took the stage and began playing soft Latin melodies. Scattered conversation resumed around the room. "What did you think of him?" Isabel asked Ramón.

"I thought he was very good," Ramón said. "A bit like Neruda."

Isabel smiled, her eyes widened with affection. "I thought you'd like him. But I think he's more like Gabriela Mistral than Pablo Neruda."

Ramón tried to recall Mistral from his mother or the Spanish literature courses he took in college. He sure knew Neruda. But Gabriela Mistral? Isabel was way ahead of him. He sort of liked that in a woman.

A full moon illuminated the white mansions along the Paseo Montejo as Ramón walked Isabel home. Gazing down at the sidewalk, she remained silent.

"Did the poetry tonight revive sad feelings about your time in Spain?" Ramón asked.

Isabel stopped walking and took both of his hands in hers. "Those feelings have never left me."

Ramón stood transfixed, gazing at her sad face. Moonlight reflected off tears forming in the corners of her eyes. She radiated so much pain and sorrow that he couldn't hold back. He swept her into his arms and lifted her off the sidewalk, swaying back and forth, holding her firmly against his body. When he finally sat her down again, she gently kissed him, brushing his lips with the tip of her tongue. His fingertips trailed across the curvature of her buttocks through her cotton dress.

Isabel stood tall and gently pushed Ramón away. "It's too fast," she said. "I like you, but we need more time." She brushed a fingertip across his lips. "I just need a little more time."

A chill wave of uncertainty washed over Ramón's glowing heart. He'd never desired anyone more, but he couldn't quite read the look in her eyes.

Chapter Twenty Three
Dark Night

All signs today indicated Mexico was working up to drastic retaliation against the axis for sinking of a Mexican ship and some guesses in informed circles were that the action would be a declaration of war.

New York Times
May 19, 1942

MÉRIDA, Yucatán
— May 21, 1942

The late afternoon sun was a scintillating orange ball as Erik brought Sizzling Rita in for a smooth landing on the last day of the training program for Mexican pilots. When the checkout procedure was complete, he removed his headset and leaned back from the wheel with a stretch of satisfaction. "Guess they're on their own now, Ray."

"Yep. And they might be at war sooner than they think."

"You mean with that last sinking?"

"It's the second Mexican tanker in two weeks, Erik. And still no apology from the Krauts."

Erik and Ramón waited for Angelo to exit, then swung down to the runway through the forward hatch. The navigator Roy and radioman Vernon, exiting from the rear, joined them on the walk back to the terminal.

"Hey, Skipper," Angelo said. "Where're we going next? Back to Jacksonville?"

"I've heard rumors of Cuba, Skip," Roy said.

Ramón stopped and regarded his crew with a cryptic smile. "No orders issued yet, boys." He resumed walking. "But," he said over his shoulder. "You might want to buff up your dancing shoes."

With boisterous banter in English and Spanish, the men from the Fuerza Aérea squadron joined them halfway to the terminal. Ramón let everyone pass and waited for Ramiro.

"This was probably our last flight together, amigo," he said, extending his hand. "Me ha dado mucho gusto."

"Yo también," Ramiro said. "It's been a pleasure." He shook Ramón's hand with unusual intensity and slowly released it. "Let's get a beer, amigo."

As they ambled past a row of parked aircraft, Ramón's attention was drawn to a tall, gray tree on the edge of the airstrip. Perched up high on thick branches that reached out from its fan-tailed trunk like long fingers, were two black vultures. One sat upright, its silver-tipped wings held loosely in a V-shape against its body. The other was hunched over with wings tightly-folded, its furrowed, gray face staring down.

Ramiro followed Ramón's gaze. "That's a ceiba tree, amigo. The ancient Mayans thought its roots connected with the underworld. And those vultures in its branches could transform death into life. You can see it in their hieroglyphs."

Ramón nodded appreciatively. Ramiro was such an interesting person. It seemed there was never a topic he didn't know something about. What luck to have him on this mission —without his cheerful enthusiasm things could have been much harder. And to top it off, he'd introduced him to Isabel. Ramiro was a real stand-up guy.

Just past the last aircraft parked on the landing strip, Ramón stopped abruptly and stared toward the terminal. What the hell? His pulse quickened as he realized a squad of armed police was heading directly toward them. Before he could make sense of the situation, the police captain who'd arrested the Viennese singer at the Neumann's house, stepped forward.

"Major Ramiro Valdez?" The captain said.

Ramiro stood tall. "Sí!"

The captain nodded to the armed policemen who swiftly surrounded Ramiro. "Come with us, señor."

One man in the police unit, dressed in civilian clothes, glanced back at Ramón as he and the uniformed police officers hustled Ramiro away. Ramón looked on in confusion as Manuel silently mouthed, "tonight."

At 11 PM Ramón sat in the courting chair on the Plaza Mayor and lit a cigarette. Only a few pedestrians strolled by in the dim light. Shortly, Manuel approached and sat down in the opposite chair.

"*Tiene fuego*, señor?" Manuel asked, leaning over the back of his chair.

Ramón lit Manuel's cigarette, then turned away. "What happened?" He asked in a low voice.

"Major Valdez has been passing classified information to the Abwehr," Manuel said.

Ramon's head was spinning. "What? How do you know that?"

"For a month our Coast Guard has been intercepting radio signals from somewhere in Veracruz. Yesterday mobile Mexican direction finders pinpointed the source—a coffee plantation in Coatepec."

Ramon's breath caught in his chest. Christ! Tío Julio? "But what about Ramiro?"

"As soon as you arrived in Mérida, messages from Veracruz to the Abwehr began to include technical details about the B-25 and your antisubmarine tactics."

Ramón sat upright. "How do you know the source was Ramiro?"

"We arranged for him to see some classified information not available to the other pilots." Manuel paused. "The next transmission to the Abwehr included everything we'd planted."

Ramón shook his head in disbelief. "Why the hell would Ramiro do that?"

"Major Valdez isn't the only fascist sympathizer," Manuel said. "The Nazis have made great inroads here in Mexico. Particularly among those with pro-Falangist sympathies."

Ramón squeezed his eyes closed with great force as if he could crush the images and expel the words Manuel was saying. How could he have been such a chump? Had there been anything genuine about Ramiro's friendship?

Manuel fixed his eyes on Ramón. "But that's not the reason I wanted to meet with you tonight." He lapsed into an ominous silence.

Ramón's mouth was dry, his temples throbbing. What more could happen to the dream he'd been experiencing in Mérida? It'd even crossed his mind he might want to live here after the war. Maybe he and Isabel... Oh! It finally struck him. Isabel!

Manuel's tone was almost gentle. "I'm sorry to tell you this, but the young woman you've been involved with appears to be part of this spy ring."

Ramon's jaw went slack, his mind, whirling like a tumbleweed before a storm. Manuel's voice became a distant thrum as images rushed on by. The danzón. The alluring lips in the garden. The passionate kiss on the Paseo Montejo.

Manuel raised his voice. "Capitán. Do you understand what I'm saying?"

Like a fighter recovering from an unanticipated haymaker, Ramón shook his head and re-focused his attention. "How do you know Isabel's involved?"

"We've been tracking her for quite a while. Every time she returns from Veracruz or Tampico the radio transmissions include updated cargo manifests and destinations."

Heart racing, Ramón was grasping for some other explanation. "So you're guessing she gets information from agents in the ports?"

Manuel's cigarette glowed. "There's more to it than that, Capitán. On your trip with Señorita Neumann last month, she delivered a book to a seminarian near Xalapa."

"Yeah." Ramón recalled the red and black Latin sentences in the Missale Romanum. "What of it?"

"We've arrested the seminarian and analyzed the book. The first letter of each paragraph in red holds a microdot that can be enlarged 300 times."

Ramón slumped on the bench like a player fouled out of the game. The facts were overwhelming. "What was in the book?"

"The entire B-25 pilot manual."

"Criminy. Do you think…"

"Probably Major Valdez."

"And Isabel?"

"Where's she been this week?"

"Villahermosa."

Manuel sighed. "Last night her BMW was found on a desolate road on the coast of Tabasco."

Ramón's heart was pounding now. "Has something happened to her?"

"More likely, she's fled the country, Capitán."

Chapter Twenty Four
Burn the Boats

Enemy submarines in the Gulf of Mexico, after making their boldest show a week ago, when they struck in the very "mouth of the river," killing 27 of a merchantman's crew, have intensified their attacks off the Mississippi Delta. Seven ships have been sunk in the Gulf since May 6.

New York Times
May 20, 1942

TABASCO COAST, Mexico
— May 20, 1942

Fifteen hundred meters off a desolate beach in northern Tabasco, the U-023 rolled silently with the swells on a moonless night. Rainer adjusted the diopter setting of his Zeiss binoculars and peered into the darkness. Thirty minutes after launching the rubber raft there was no sign of their return. He turned toward Jäger whose face he could barely make out in the darkness. "Komm schon! Where the hell are they?"

"The surf may be a little rougher than it looks from here, Herr Kaleun," Jäger said. "Our boys are submariners, not fishermen. Nicht wahr?"

Rainer was in no mood for jocularity. "This isn't just dangerous, Jäger. It's a waste of time. Hunting's been good here in the Gulf. Why do we have to pick up some Mexican spy? Are we in the Kriegsmarine or the Abwehr?"

"I don't know, Herr Kaleun. Maybe he has some useful information."

Rainer scuffed the toe of his rubber-soled shoe on the deck. "Maybe so. But he'll just be in our way. The sooner we get him to the Milchkuh the better," he said, referring to the submarine tanker named after a milk cow.

"Of course our spy may see a little action on the way. We still have two torpedoes." A light flashed off and on in the darkness. "There they are, Herr Kaleun. About 500 meters astern."

"Acknowledge that."

Jäger opened and closed the shutter on the signal lamp, emitting a brief pulse of light.

Five minutes later the faint outline of four men paddling toward the U-023 emerged from the darkness. Training his binoculars on the raft, Rainer spotted a dark figure huddled between the men. "Looks like they have our guest, Jäger."

The seamen secured the raft alongside the submarine and helped their passenger onto the aft deck. Rainer squinted down from the bridge, then looked at Jäger in disbelief. "Was zum Teufel?"

Jäger shook his head. "It's a woman, Herr Kaleun."

Dressed in a black gabardine jacket and dark green slacks, Isabel followed the oarsmen toward the rear hatch. As she ducked her head to enter the U-023, her long hair fell across her shoulders.

Rainer climbed down through the conning tower and stepped onto the control room floor just as Second Warrant Officer Wolf ushered Isabel through the rear compartment door. Wolf came to attention, snapping his left foot against his right like the Prussian martinet he was. "Herr Kaleun. Allow me to introduce Fräulein Isabel Neumann."

Ignoring Wolf's irritating heel click, Rainer was acutely aware of an earthy fragrance mingling with the foul odor peculiar to a U-Boat on a long mission. As he turned his gaze fully on Isabel, he was startled by her beauty. Not since the death of Annelise had his libido been so stirred. "Guten Abend, Fräulein. Kapitänleutnant Hartmann at your service. I hope your boat ride from shore was not too stressful."

Isabel extended her hand and Rainer grasped it with a firm handshake. Her skin felt soft but very cool. "Entschuldigen Sie mich, bitte, Herr Kommandant," she said. "My fingers are not always this cold. I'm not used to being out on the water at night."

Rainer was impressed. Not only was this woman beautiful, she also spoke excellent German. The resentment he'd felt over ferrying a nameless spy was suddenly replaced with great curiosity. The twelve-day trip to the Milchkuh with Fräulein Neumann could prove interesting. "I'm sure you'll soon be warm enough, Fräulein," he said with a wry smile. "Cool air is not one of the problems we have inside our submarine."

Isabel's expression was earnest. "Vielen Dank, Herr Kommandant. I'm very sorry to cause you so much trouble."

"Kein Problem, Fräulein. It was time for us to refuel. You were on our way to a *Milchkuh* tanker in the Atlantic." He turned toward Jäger. "This is my second-in-command, Oberleutnant zur See Anton Jäger. He'll help you settle in."

"Sehr erfreut, Fräulein," Jäger said. "Nice to meet you. We're a bit crowded as you'll soon see. But one bunk is always free in the warrant officers quarters."

"Danke schön," Isabel said. "I'll try not to get in your way. Might I ask a favor? Could I go up on the bridge as we sail away from my homeland?"

Jäger glanced at Rainer who nodded. "Certainly, Fräulein. Kein problem."

STRAITS OF FLORIDA
— May 25, 1942

At 1730 the temperature of the stale air in the submerged U-023 had reached a sweltering 32 degrees Celsius and the Dräger measuring apparatus indicated an elevated carbon dioxide level of 1.5 percent. Rainer awoke briefly and shifted in the cot in his tiny quarters. With a dull headache and his grimy pillow soaked with sweat, he felt like a man, the morning after, awakening on the floor of a steaming jungle. The low-pitched hum of the electric motors soon lulled him back to sleep and a familiar dream emerged.

Komm zu mir, Liebling. Anneliese called out from somewhere above. Struggling with all his might, Rainer pulled his arms downward and kicked his feet, trying to reach a light on the surface of the water. But with each mighty stroke, the light seemed farther away and he was sinking deeper into darkness.

"Herr Kaleun," a seaman shook Rainer's shoulder. "You asked me to wake you before dinner."

Rainer pulled on his clammy uniform, ran his fingers through his greasy hair and headed for the control room. Funkmaat Stein, who was scanning the high frequency bands with headphones, nodded respectfully as Rainer passed by. In the control room Vogel was bent over a nautical chart, much like the bird his surname indicated.

"Have we cleared Key West yet?" Rainer asked.

"Ja, Herr Kaleun," Vogel said, placing a fingertip on the chart. "23 degrees, 55 minutes north. 80 degrees, 51 minutes west."

"Gut. We'll surface and slip into the Gulf Stream along the coast after sunset. Once past the Bahamas, we should be relatively in the clear."

Rainer walked forward to the wardroom where Isabel, Jäger and Wolf were seated at a table wedged between the lower berths like an ironing board in a broom closet.

"Guten Abend, Herr Kaleun," Jäger said. "Fräulein Neumann just told me she lived in Schwabing as a student. Not far from the Alstadt where I grew up."

Rainer smiled at Isabel. Although her forehead gleamed with perspiration, in a clean, linen blouse and her hair combed out, she looked somehow fresh and alluring. "Munich's a friendly city, Fräulein. Gemütlich, they say. You were fortunate to live there." He hesitated, studying her face. "Perhaps you could return there now?"

Isabel looked up with a slight tilt of her head. "Maybe one day, Kommandant. But for now, after reporting to the Abwehr in Hamburg, I'll be returning to Madrid."

Fischer the cook interrupted. "Entschuldigen Sie mich, bitte," he said, placing a steel pot on the tattered tablecloth he'd spread out in Isabel's honor. "Guten Appetit."

"What do we have from the tin cans tonight, Fischer?" Jäger asked.

"A stew, Herr Oberleutnant. Sausage, potatoes and, of course, a bit of *Bratlingspulver*."

Isabel glanced inquiringly at Jäger. "It's a soy powder," Jäger said. "It's supposed to give us a bit more protein."

Wolf grunted. "Diesel food is what the men call it."

"Don't worry," Rainer said. "It's pretty bland. You won't taste it."

"What will you do in Madrid, Fräulein?" Wolf asked.

"I'm not sure yet, but I still have some friends there," Isabel said.

"I'd like to visit Spain after we win the war," Wolf said. "Since the Führer helped the Fascists win, I imagine I'd be most welcome."

"It might depend on where you go," Isabel said with a slight pull at the corners of her mouth. "There are many wounds still unhealed."

At 2200, running with the diesels at fourteen knots, Rainer and Jäger were standing watch when Isabel requested permission to come up on the bridge.

"I'll take her onto the *Wintergarten*," Rainer said to Jäger as he led Isabel along the thin railing behind the bridge to the Flak gun platform. Lacking the solid fairwater wall of the bridge, the Wintergarten was completely open to the elements with only the railing between it and the ocean over nine meters below. Silently, the aft lookout shifted to the opposite side of the Flak gun on the rear of the platform.

As the U-023 skimmed across low swells, countless stars shimmered like sequins strewn across the fabric of a black, cloudless sky. Strange. Since the death of Anneliese and his family, nights like this had brought nothing but sorrow and a vague ache to Rainer's heart. But tonight, in the company of a beautiful woman who also knew great loss, the blazing stars brought him an almost mystical sense of the infinite.

Isabel tilted her head skyward. "There's Ursa Major," she said. "The rectangle of stars is the great bear's body. And three stars below it are his tail."

"There are a few problems with that, Fraülein," Rainer said in a gently teasing tone. "The rectangle is actually a trapezoid. And bears don't have long tails. I guess that's why we Germans call Ursa Major the big wagon."

Isabel laughed. "You Germans have a lot of funny names for things." She sighed comically. "So much for my knowledge about constellations."

Rainer chuckled. He liked a self-effacing manner in a beautiful woman. "I guess you're not an astronomer. What did you study at the university, Fräulein?"

"Mostly brewing technology and business administration. I managed a lot of business for my father."

"Why did you leave Madrid to study in Munich?"

Isabel's voice became dark and low, like a sudden fog over the ocean. "They were shooting in the streets when I left Madrid."

Rainer spoke softly. "I'm sorry, Fraülein. We don't need to talk about this." He remained silent as she leaned over the railing and stared at the water streaming along the hull.

After a while, she turned back toward him. "Actually, it would be good to talk about it. It's been so long since I could be honest with someone."

Rainer bowed his head slightly. "I'd be honored, Fräulein."

Isabel let out a long sigh into the breeze. "I was young and impressionable in Madrid, Kommandant. My professor, a handsome, charismatic man, was also my lover. He was an ardent believer in Fascism, and soon, so was I. Becoming a Fascist wasn't so difficult after seeing what happened in the Mexican revolution—unruly mobs burning churches and attacking haciendas. Gott sei dank. The army restored order. And it was no different in Spain. Franco brought order. Fascism promised stability and respect for the state, Kommandant. So I chose Fascism."

Rainer gazed at her face, faintly illuminated in the starlight, not sure what to say. He'd never met anyone like Isabel before. He was fighting for the Fatherland and his family, not some ideology. This woman believed in Fascism and was leaving her homeland and family behind. "I understand what you're saying, Fräulein. Some say Adolf Hitler also restored stability."

"I'm not so enamored of Herr Hitler, Kommandant. But Germany's been a good business partner for Mexico and the United States has never been anything but our enemy."

"So why did you decide to become a spy for Germany, Fräulein?"

Isabel looked down at her hands, slowly twisting a ring on her finger "My Spanish lover was killed by a Republican mob during a demonstration on the streets of Madrid." She paused and bit her lip. "Later, when I was studying in Munich, I met a persuasive Abwehr agent who convinced me to become an activist."

"What happened in Yucatán?"

"I met another sincere young man—an American air force pilot. Probably your nemesis. I liked him, but I did my job well. I gained his trust and passed on as much information as I could to the Abwehr."

"Why did you leave Mexico so suddenly?"

"The police arrested members of our ring and were looking for me."

"Ach, ja. It must be sad to leave your family behind."

"That's the hardest part, Kommandant. For the past few years, I've lived a double life. In order to protect my family, I've had to make sure they knew nothing. My father, who's very sympathetic to the Fascist cause, even teased me about my 'Communist' ideas."

"It must have been hard having no one to talk to."

"I did have one outlet. My abuela, who's Mayan, lives outside the culture in many ways. I've always been able to tell her everything."

"So how is it for you now, Fräulein?"

"There's a certain melancholy. Call it regret, if you will. I'm not proud of what I've done, but I'd do it again if it helped the Fascist cause." She looked up at the stars. "But I don't feel I belong in Germany. And I'd like to be free of the Abwehr. In Spain maybe I can start over again."

"You're an astounding woman, Fräulein. You make me think about my own life. I've lost most of my family in this verdammt war. But I'm fighting for my country and I have no other choice."

"Warriors are important, Kommandant. We've both had to make some hard choices."

150 NAUTICAL MILES SOUTHWEST OF BERMUDA
— May 31, 1942

The U-023 surfaced at twilight 250 miles off the coast of North Carolina. Rainer, Jäger and three lookouts manned the bridge.

Rainer blew on a binocular lens and polished it with a cloth. "Wunderbar. This fresh air at twilight. Nicht wahr, Jäger?"

"Ja wohl, Herr Kaleun. It's worth the small risk. We're pretty far offshore for any random air search by the Amis."

"Of course their new radar equipment might change the game."

"Just a matter of luck, Herr Kaleun. Still, I'm glad we have good depth here for an emergency dive."

Rainer inhaled the cool breeze and scanned the horizon with his binoculars. No obvious activity—just magnificent colors reflecting off the bellies of clouds drifting above the setting sun.

"Smoke cloud. Bearing 315," the port lookout called out.

"Looks like a steamer," Rainer said, focusing his binoculars on a thin black stream rising on the brilliant-orange western horizon.

"He's probably headed to Bermuda," Jäger said.

Rainer calculated silently for a few moments. "Course 090. Ahead one third. We'll wait for him to close, then position ourselves for a good shot."

At 2200 Isabel's voice, soft and lilting, arose from the conning tower hatch. "Permission to come up on the bridge. I 'd like to see the stars."

Rainer hastened to the hatch and laid his hand on her shoulder. "I'm sorry, Fräulein. But I must insist you stay safely below. We've begun a hunt." He abruptly returned to his vigil and Isabel descended the ladder.

"Look, Herr Kaleun!" Jäger said. "There's another smoke cloud next to the steamer."

Rainer refocused his binoculars. "Scheisse! He must have an escort."

At 2400, after following the erratic pattern of the escort destroyer, which stopped unpredictably, turned and altered its speed, the U-023 was positioned on a parallel course ahead of the target ship and its protector. Rainer ordered a dive. "Einsteigen!"

At 0030 Rainer sighted the escort with the attack periscope. "The destroyer has a flush deck and three smokestacks, Jäger."

"Probably a Wickes-class, Herr Kaleun."

Rainer then focused on the target ship. "Single smokestack. Maybe 6000 tons. Perhaps a combined transport-passenger ship."

"He must have valuable cargo to warrant his own escort, Herr Kaleun."

At 0045 the steamer lay abeam of the U-023 at a right angle to the centerline. A perfect target. Rainer released two torpedoes, then turned his attention to the destroyer that still seemed unaware of his presence.

At 0048 a bright metallic click, heard throughout the submarine, was followed by a heavy, dull explosion. Shortly thereafter, another click and explosion. Both torpedoes had hit home!

At 0050 several more explosions erupted from the steamer. Rainer maintained his focus on the destroyer as he spoke over his shoulder to Jäger. "Those were probably his boiler or munitions. Nicht wahr?" He silently scanned the surface. "Wait! The destroyer's stopped."

At 0052, after an ominous silence, where Rainer could feel his own heartbeat, he abruptly jumped back from the periscope and slapped the viewing arms back in place. "He's coming right at us! Dive to 120 meters!"

At 0055 nine depth charges, released at short intervals, passed by the diving U-023 and exploded well below the hull. Soon after, another salvo came closer, but still caused no significant damage. Then there was silence.

"He's stopped," Rainer said. "Probably calculating his next move."

At 0100 an eerie rattling was followed by heavy, crackling sounds transmitted through the depths. "The steamer's going down," Jäger said. "Congratulations, Herr Kaleun."

"Now the destroyer has to think about survivors," Rainer said. "But he'll be back for us soon enough. Maintain depth at 120 meters."

At 0115 two depth charges exploded far away. Then only silence.

At 0300 Rainer surfaced in the clear moonlight. There were no lights and no visible wreckage at the site of the sunken steamer.

"The destroyer probably picked up the survivors, Herr Kaleun," Jäger said.

Rainer only nodded. Jäger knew as well as he that most of the passengers had gone down. He stared into the empty sea, a familiar, metallic taste arising in his mouth. How many people had he killed this time? True, the large explosions were most likely munitions. And any passengers would have been military personnel. So this was a good strike. A clean strike. But Rainer felt no elation.

CHAPTER TWENTY FIVE
Milchkuh

It is true that until the Gulf of St. Lawrence was penetrated, U-boat depredation in the North Atlantic has been comparatively restricted. But south of New York, and especially in tropical waters, submarines still move with great freedom. They may have an information service in one or more supply stations somewhere in the Caribbean....

New York Times
May 31, 1942

200 NAUTICAL MILES EAST OF BERMUDA
— June 2, 1942

At 2300, Funkmaat Stein stepped out of the radio room, parted the curtain of the adjacent cubicle and roused Rainer from sleep. "Herr Kaleun. I'm receiving a weak signal on the medium frequency band."

Clad in an undershirt and gray denim trousers, Rainer sat upright on the edge of his bunk. "Homing beacon?"

"Most likely the U-491 Milchkuh, Herr Kaleun."

"Direction finding?"

"Three hundred and fifteen degrees."

"Gut. If the Enigma coordinates are accurate, we're approaching our rendezvous point."

Rainer pulled on his tunic and buttoned it up. Above his breast pocket, a golden eagle and swastika embroidered into the tan denim were the only insignia he wore.

Rainer joined Jäger, Vogel and the lookouts on the bridge. The ocean was calm with no wind. Scattered high clouds muted the light of a quarter moon.

Jäger lowered his binoculars. "*Bisher nichts*, Herr Kaleun."

Vogel turned away from the voice tube. "Funkmaat Stein says the signal is strong now."

Slicing through the rolling ocean, the U-023 hurled pale green sheets of phosphorescent water to either side of its bow. Rainer adjusted his binoculars and peered into the darkness. He'd never seen one of these new Milchkuh submarine tankers. It was about the same length as the U-023, he'd been told, but, much wider, with a hull filled with 400 tons of diesel fuel. Hidden in mid-ocean, the Milchkuh could resupply U-Boats with fuel, torpedoes and fresh, refrigerated food.

"Herr Kaleun!" The port lookout called out. "Dim flashing light. 318 degrees."

Rainer swung his binoculars and focused on a faint red light, flashing at thirty-second intervals. Soon, the signal light brightened and, like a behemoth emerging from the deep, the black conning tower of a submarine tanker came into view.

"Maintain course 318," Rainer said. "And reduce engine speed to four knots. Let's allow our Mikchkuh host to determine a parallel course."

"She's a bit chubby, nicht wahr?" Vogel joked.

Rainer smiled as he surveyed the approaching submarine tanker, now bathed in pale moonlight. Although much wider, the Milchkuh resembled his own boat with one major difference. The Milchkuh had neither torpedoes nor deck cannon. Designed only to resupply other U-Boats and defend itself, the Milchkuh had no offensive role. Despite two formidable antiaircraft Flak cannons, the Milchkuh was especially vulnerable to air attack during refueling operations. Disconnecting equipment and refueling hoses took time, and the bulky submarine tanker was a slow diver. The refueling process was also dangerous for Rainer, since the standing order was no diving before the Milchkuh had safely submerged.

Soon, the U-023 and the Milchkuh were running parallel courses, at three knots with a distance between them of 25 meters. The commander of the Milchkuh called out to Rainer from his bridge with a megaphone. "Guten Abend, Herr Kommandant. Fertig? Are you ready?"

"Fertig!" Rainer yelled back, touching the brim of his cap with a brisk salute.

What followed was like a slow-motion ballet between two whales far out to sea. With a signal from Rainer, Wolf's crew on the aft deck began hurling thin lines, weighted at the tips, toward the crew of the Milchkuh. At the same time, Milchkuh crewmen threw lines toward the U-023. After a brief, friendly competition, a cheer arose from Wolf's crew as a line they'd hurled was secured by Milchkuh deckhands. Eight seamen on the aft deck of the U-023 tended a highline between the two U-Boats, adjusting its tension as the U-Boat commanders maneuvered to maintain a safe distance between each other.

On the Milchkuh, crewmen packed rubber rafts with food and water and general supplies. The rafts were then attached to pulleys on the highline and hauled in by crew of the U-023. The transfer of seven-meter long torpedoes involved more elegant maneuvers. Four torpedoes were wrapped in life jackets and floated off the Milchkuh as the submarine submerged enough to flood the deck. The torpedoes were then pulled through the water to be corralled and stowed by the crew of the likewise flooded-down U-023.

When the transfer of supplies was complete, a rubber raft was attached to the highline to transfer Isabel to the Milchkuh. The Milchkuh commander called out: "It'll take a while to refuel, Kommandant. Why don't you join me with our mutual guest for a glass of French wine?"

Rainer looked at Jäger.

"Kein Problem, Herr Kaleun. I can manage the fuel resupply," Jäger said. "Zum wohl!"

In a rubber raft, Rainer and Isabel were pulled through the undulating water by crewmen on the Milchkuh. As they came alongside, Rainer was surprised to see the Milchkuh commander on deck to welcome them. With a weather-beaten face, crinkly eyes and a salt and pepper beard, he seemed a bit old to be commanding a U-Boat at sea. Indeed, the braided epaulets on his leather jacket indicated his senior rank of Korvettenkapitän.

The Milchkuh commander extended a hand to Isabel and pulled her up onto the deck. "*Herzliches Willkommen!* Fräulein. I am Korvettenkapitän Adler at your service."

Rainer climbed onto the deck and saluted. "Kapitänleutnant Rainer Hartmann, Herr Korvettenkapitän."

"Sehr erfreut, Hartmann. I'm Hinrich Adler." He turned to Isabel. "If you don't mind, Fräulein, I'll have a seaman take you to my stateroom while Kapitänleutnant Hartmann and I make sure the refueling hoses are connected properly."

Isabel went below. Rainer and Adler went up on the bridge.

"Do you have a good first officer, Hartmann?" Adler asked.

"Jäger is excellent, Herr Korvettenkapitän. He's been with me a long time."

Adler gestured toward his own first officer standing next to them. "Weber here is an old hand at this. Let's let the two of them manage the refueling."

The highline was taken down and a towline was fastened from the Milchkuh to the bow of the U-023. At three knots, with the U-023 trailing astern like a grown calf behind its mother, a large refueling hose was dragged through the water and attached to the foredeck of the U-023.

"Alles in Ordnung," Adler said. "Let me know when you're near completion, Weber."

When they descended into the control room, Rainer was struck by a mouth-watering aroma that overrode the usual noxious smells of a U-Boat at sea. Noticing Rainer's reaction, Adler said: "I hope you like French bread."

Astounded, Rainer could only follow in disbelief as they proceeded to Adler's stateroom where Isabel was seated at the commander's desk, perusing a book of poetry.

"May we join you, Fräulein?" Adler asked as he and Rainer sat on the edge of his cot. "Do you like German poetry?"

"Very much," Isabel said. "In my school days at the Colegio Alemán in Mexico City, we read a lot of German poets."

"Who's your favorite," Adler asked.

Isabel thought for a moment. "I think it's Friedrich Hölderlin."

"Really? He's very popular in Germany these days, you know. A spiritual forerunner of our Aryan *Volksgemeinschaft* they say."

A seaman placed a bottle of wine, three glasses and a loaf of warm French bread on the commander's table and asked. "Anything else, Herr Korvettenkapitän?"

Adler looked at his guests. "Camembert?"

Rainer and Isabel nodded enthusiastically.

"Camembert cheese bitte, Schröder," Adler said.

Rainer was impressed with the Milchkuh commander. Not only was he a seasoned sailor, but also a connoisseur of literature, cheese and wine. "If you don't mind my asking, Herr Korvettenkäpitan. How did you come to command this unique new submarine?"

"You mean since I'm not a young tiger like most U-Boat commanders?" Adler waved Rainer's embarrassed response away. "There was a time when I, like you, was on the hunt. But as I grew older, they gave me more administrative jobs and less time at sea. When these new tankers came up, I pushed for the assignment." He poured a glass of wine for Isabel, then Rainer. "Try some of the Camembert with bread."

"Do the Allies know you're here?" Rainer asked.

"We don't think so," Adler said, clinking his glass with Isabel then Rainer. "Someday this will be a dangerous mission. But for the moment, I enjoy being able to resupply you and offer some of the civilized comforts of home." He took a leather-bound book from his shelf. "And here, Fräulein, is my favorite quotation from Hölderlin."

Ich aber bin allein.
und in den Ocean schiffend
Die duftenden Inseln fragen
Wohin sie sind.

But I am alone.
and sailing on the ocean
Ask the sweetly-scented islands
where they are.

Chapter Twenty Six
Camagüey

Axis submarines have sunk 15 more ships of the United Nations, with the probable loss of 231 lives, in waters on this side of the Atlantic, it was announced yesterday by the Navy Department. This was by far the heaviest toll on our shipping that has been announced on a single day since the submarine attacks off our coast began last January.

New York Times
June 24, 1942

CAMAGÜEY, Cuba
— June 28, 1942

Erik and Ramón sat in the shaded courtyard garden of the Hotel Camino de Oro, a colonial-era building in the center of the casco histórico of Camagüey, a small city about halfway across Cuba. In a short-sleeved silk shirt and light cotton trousers he'd purchased in Mérida, Ramón found the humid Sunday morning tolerable.

During the past month at Langley Army Air Force Base in Virginia, Sizzling Rita had been equipped with an extremely accurate absolute altimeter, air to surface vessel radar (ASV), a magnetic anomaly detector (MAD) and new depth charges configured to explode within the kill-radius of a diving U-Boat.

The bombardier Angelo was trained to operate the radar equipment, while Ramón and Erik learned killer-hunt tactics from the newly-established First Sea Search Attack Group, known commonly as the Search.

After completing their training, Sizzling Rita and her crew were assigned to an airport operated by Pan American Airways in Camagüey. But unlike his last assignment as a bogus Pan Am employee, this time Ramón was a Captain in uniform at the USAAF airbase in Camagüey.

"This town's packed with Americans, Ray," Erik said. "We got into this classy place just under the wire."

"Like we always do, buddy."

Erik laughed. "Except maybe our digs last month at Langley?"

"OK, the Army's not known for its housing. But the Search training was great."

"Yup. No bullshit. Just good training."

Erik stirred his coffee slowly. "Damn! I don't know, Ray. All this new equipment and the goddam Krauts still got away yesterday."

Ramón dipped into the sugar and nudged the bowl across the table. "We came close, Erik. I think we're a hell of a lot better since joining the Search."

"Maybe our tactics. But I'm not so sure about the equipment, Ray. Spiffy new radar's fine as long as the U-Boats don't dive. And the goddam MAD equipment doesn't seem to detect shit unless we're right above the target."

"I'm not too jazzed about MAD either. We'd never have found that U-Boat yesterday on our own. We were lucky the destroyer picked them up on sonar."

"Yeah. But not for long."

Ramón grasped Erik's forearm. "Look, buddy. We're getting closer. I can feel it. It's just a matter of time."

Erik signaled the waiter for more coffee. "How's it going for you now, Ray? Gotten over Isabel yet?"

Ramón's nod was half-hearted. "More or less, I guess. But I still can't believe how she took me in. For Chrissake, I was falling in love with that woman."

"Come on, Ray. She was good at her job, that's all. And quite a knockout for a Nazi spy, I might add." He took a sip of coffee and leaned forward. "What about Violet? Seen her yet?"

"I'm not sure that's a good idea, Erik. Why don't you tell me more about this date Antonia fixed me up with."

"She's a looker, Ray. Different than Antonia, but pretty damn nice."

Ramón smiled. This was a good recommendation. He liked Erik's new girlfriend Antonia, a real doll with light-olive skin, a pretty face and shapely body. She was good for Erik. Especially since she was fluent in English.

Erik glanced at the garden gate. "Here come the ladies."

Erik and Ramón stood as two young Cuban women in light cotton dresses approached their table. Erik kissed Antonia on the cheek and she introduced her companion to Ramón. "Capitán Ramón Morales. Permítame presentarle Señorita Concepción Vargas."

"Encontado, Señorita Vargas," Ramón said with a polite bow of his head.

"Mucho gusto, Capitán," Concepción said, extending her hand.

Ramón took her hand, his pilot's eyes rapidly scanning her face and body. A beautiful, mulatto woman with hazel eyes and a warm smile. What more could he ask for in a blind date? Antonia had done well.

"Concepción works with me in the ANCRA office," Antonia said, referring to the Cuban National Academy of Civil Aviation that shared the airfield with the Americans. "But she doesn't speak much English."

"No hay problema," Ramón said, then paused with a smile. "Except maybe for Erik."

"Un momento, por favor," Erik said with a pronounced American accent. "I'm learning more Spanish each day. Correcto, Antonia?"

Antonia giggled and responded in excellent English, accented with a staccato, Cuban lilt. "Erik speaks the language of love. It's universal, you know." She took Erik by the arm. "So when do you hombres fly today?"

"Not until tonight," Erik said.

"Good. Plenty of time to show you around our town."

For the next few hours, Antonia and Concepción led Erik and Ramón through the serpentine streets, narrow alleys and irregular blocks of Camagüey. With a deliberately-irregular street plan, the 16th-century town had been designed to confuse raiders who frequently plundered the area.

Ramón hung close behind Concepción as they squeezed through dark alleys and emerged into brilliant sunlight on a square, a cathedral, a fountain or a park.

278

In front of many homes along the street, large clay pots lay half-buried next to ornamental plants. *"Te gustan?"* Concepción asked Ramón. "They're called *tinajones*. In the old days they were filled with water or wine, sometimes grain. But now they're purely ornamental."

The mid-afternoon sun was blazing in a cloudless azure sky when Concepción led them out of a dark alleyway into rows of white marble headstones, statues and crypts. Interspersed between the neoclassical columns and pilasters of the 18th-century cemetery, were newer chapels and monuments of eclectic design.

Ramón shielded his eyes from the blazing sunlight with the back of his hand and glanced at Concepción. Her caramel skin glowed deliciously in the intense white light. "It's interesting," he said. "The dead have the largest space in town."

"This *was* the edge of town in 1813," Concepción said. "When they ran out of graves in the churchyards, this cemetery was built on open land."

Ramón looked up as a shiny, black bird with blue wings fluttered loudly to rest on the marble shoulder of a young woman leaning against a cross planted in a pile of stones. With her chin resting on her hand, she gazed, unfocused, into the distance.

As Ramón studied the sorrowful monument, an unfamiliar feeling arose in his chest. Not like heartburn. Much heavier. Perhaps an awareness of death. He'd just learned about Lloyd going down on the Doolittle raid. Jesus. The goddam Japs executed him!

Ramón flew into danger every day but had yet to meet death firsthand. But he felt closer now. One of the five amigos was down. He looked up at the woman leaning on the cross with a faraway gaze. "She looks so sad," he said to Concepción.

"Waiting for someone who'll never return," Concepción said.

At half past midnight, in a starlit, moonless sky, Sizzling Rita was heading west on a routine ASW patrol. Vern clicked in on the intercom. "Pilot, radio. Got a message from Miami."

"Go ahead," Ramón said.

"Freighter attacked by U-Boat off Bahamas. Killer hunt underway. Destroyer, cutter and three B-18s dispatched from Key West. Request assistance. Latitude 24, 18, 07 north. Longitude 79, 65, 91 west."

An electric sensation surged through Ramòn's body, galvanizing his senses into action mode. "Navigator, pilot. Changing course. Get me a fix, Roy."

"Roger, nav. I'm on it."

Ramón ascended to 2,000 feet and headed north at 250 mph. He looked at Erik and spoke over the intercom. "ETA should be about 40 minutes. Hope we're in time for the party."

With Rita's roaring engines muffled by his headphones, Ramón reviewed his strategy. If the U-Boat was still on the surface, airborne radar would function until about a mile from the target. Then the signal would be lost in the unwanted echoes of sea clutter. More likely the Krauts would already be submerged. But with a maximum underwater speed of seven knots, they couldn't get far from the attack area. Ramón would have to rely on his MAD device.

Joining the Search at 0110, Sizzling Rita flew 500 feet above the ocean in tandem with the B-18 Bolos out of Key West. Like a flock of nocturnal raptors, eyes fixed on the glow of their fluorescent screens, the medium attack bombers swept back and forth over the ocean, searching for the magnetic anomalies of their steely, underwater prey. Below, sonar-equipped Coast Guard and Naval vessels trolled the sector in a parallel pattern. At 0400, running low on fuel after three hours without contact, Sizzling Rita was replaced by a B-18 from Key West and returned to base.

Erik landed Rita at the Camagüey airfield shortly before dawn. "Look at that, Ray," he said, pointing at an RAF B-24 Liberator parked along the landing strip. "The Limeys are here."

After debriefing, Erik and Ramón headed for a nearby café where a radio behind the bar played a syncopated rumba. As they ordered breakfast, Erik nudged Ramón, directing his attention to a slender man in an RAF uniform nursing a cup of coffee at a back table. "Son of a bitch, Ray. That's the Squadron Leader we met in Jacksonville. Was it Johnson?"

"No. Richardson. Wonder what he's doing here."

Squadron Leader Richardson smiled as they approached his table. "Well well. Nice to see you lads again. Jacksonville wasn't it?" He glanced around at the empty tables, then at their uniforms and flight jackets. "Just returning from a mission?" He asked, lowering his voice.

"Yes, sir. We've been out with the Search," Ramón said.

"Join me." Richardson pointed to the empty chairs at the table. "How did it go?"

"We made no contact with MAD, sir," Ramón said. "But the Search is still combing the area."

Richardson shook his head. "Damn near impossible with a submerged sub at night, isn't it, boys? The U-Boat's magnetic field falls off exponentially the deeper it dives. And, of course, you've always got echoes from the ocean floor." He leaned back in his chair. "Chin up, lads. You'll catch up with Jerry the next time out."

"If you don't mind my asking, sir," Erik said. "What brings you to Camagüey?"

"I'm on loan to the Search, flying out of Miami. Just making my rounds here."

Over the next hour Erik and Ramón, refueled with multiple cups of coffee, chatted with Squadron Leader Richardson about ASW tactics and the recent collaboration between the RAF and USAAF. Although Ramón liked him, there was something unsettling about the graying Squadron Leader. Did his affability cloak a darker reality inside?

When the discussion turned to hometowns and families, Richardson's voice became low-pitched and mournful, like a distant foghorn in uncharted darkness. "I have no home anymore, lads. Not since the Blitz."

Ramón felt a vague chill in the room. "I'm sorry, Sir. Your family?"

Richardson looked up, his nostrils widened, eyebrows knit together. "In the winter of 1940, I lost my wife and two children. Direct hit."

Chapter Twenty Seven
Phaedrus Regrets

For about 30 days Navy ships have been convoying merchant ships along the East Coast from Florida to New England...it is evident from the lessened rate of sinkings that patrols or convoys are operating quite effectively in the Gulf of Mexico and the St. Lawrence River. The net result is that the Atlantic siege lines have been pushed eastward or southward in this case without any real change in the situation of the shipping problem.

New York Times
June 28, 1942

95 NAUTICAL MILES SOUTHEAST OF MIAMI, Florida
— June 28, 1942

At 1950, with no surface activity detected by the hydrophone operator Funkmaat Stein, Rainer scanned the ocean for several minutes with the observation periscope before ordering the U-023 to surface. The sky over the Straits of Florida was a blazing orange-red tapestry, peppered with thousands of small, fleecy clouds as he and the first watch officer navigator Rolf Vogel mounted the bridge with four lookouts. A black-plumed bird with a long forked tail soared high above.

"Frigate bird," Rainer said.

"Probably looking for dinner near the surface," Vogel said.

"Look at the sky," Rainer said, looking up at the brilliant twilight. "The West is reaching for clothes of new colors."

"Goethe?" Vogel asked.

Rainer shook his head. "Nein. Rilke."

"Schade," Vogel said. "We read him in school. Now he's verboten."

"Who understands the censors? I guess it's safer to read Goethe these days."

Over the next few hours, with no maritime traffic, Rainer and Vogel spoke only briefly between long periods of silence. Although his eyes dutifully scanned the tropical horizon, Rainer's heart strayed to winter on the Baltic. Was it only four months ago he'd buried his face in her hair and brushed his fingertips across the ivory skin of her neck?

"Herr Kaleun!" The forward lookout shouted at 2300. "Green running lights 40 degrees port."

Like a predator jolted into hyper-alertness by the snap of a twig, Rainer's heartbeat accelerated and the muscles of his upper body tightened. Spinning to port, he trained his binoculars on the lights. "All ahead full. Come to course 340."

With the diesels pounding full tilt in the darkness, the U-023 soon passed within 2000 meters of the unescorted, northbound ship. Focusing the UZO lenses, Vogel surveyed the lumbering prey—a single funnel ship with paint peeling from its dingy, yellow bridge and a gray hull mottled with orange-brown rust. "I see no markings," Vogel said. "Looks like a tramp freighter. Maybe 6000 tons."

Rainer nodded. "Proceed with the attack."

Vogel relayed his commands below. "Slow engines half ahead. All compartments. Action stations torpedo. Sound general quarters."

Almost abeam, with the freighter's course unchanged, Vogel issued the attack orders. "Forward torpedo room. Target angle 090. Enemy speed seven knots. Range 2000 meters. Depth three meters. Fire one. Los!"

Rainer focused his binoculars on the target as Vogel timed the torpedo run. At 165 seconds a flash of orange light erupted from the foredeck of the freighter. Five seconds later—voompff! The deep, muffled sound of an explosion swept across the water and the freighter began to list.

"Place two torpedoes on standby, ready to fire," Rainer ordered. "Ahead one third."

At 800 meters, Rainer was able to read markings on the freighter's stern that were illuminated by flames. "The Melinda out of Galveston Texas," he said to Vogel.

"I see no unusual superstructures or windows, Herr Kaleun," Vogel said.

"Gut. Aber vorsicht! Let's approach with caution."

Funkmaat Stein reported intercepting an SSS signal sent from the burning ship: Melinda under torpedo attack. Burning forward. Require assistance.

700 meters from the burning ship, Rainer and Vogel watched from the bridge as a lifeboat was lowered into the water from the stricken freighter and a dozen crewmen clambered aboard. "They're abandoning ship," Rainer said.

"We'll wait until they're clear, then move in for a broadside shot. Come right to 020. All ahead one third. Ready deck gun for attack."

As Wolf's gun crew assembled on the foredeck, Rainer prepared for a broadside Fangschuss. At 650 meters, squinting into the darkness, he felt a vague tingling sensation in his shoulders. Why haven't they launched another lifeboat?

Bam! Heavy steel bulkheads along the side of the listing freighter flew open and slammed against the sides of the ship. *Kawuum!* A four-inch deck gun within the dark hold of the freighter fired a shell that landed 100 meters short of the U-023. *Rat-a-tat-tat.* Orange-tipped tracer bullets erupted from two Browning machine guns like yellow jackets swarming from a disrupted nest. Although the deck gun fusillade continued to fall short, the machine guns raked the deck and bridge of the U-023. One of Wolf's gun crew, mortally wounded, fell into the sea.

"Hard to starboard! All ahead full!" Rainer shouted. As the cannon fire inched closer and machine gun bullets ricocheted off the deck, the U-023 gradually pulled out of target range. "Alarm!" Rainer ordered. Vogel sounded the diving bell. Clang! Clang!

After leveling off at a safe depth of 20 fathoms, Rainer turned to Jäger. "Scheisse! A Q ship! I never thought we'd see those again." He shook his head. "Who was the crewman we lost?"

"Schröder," Jäger said. "A nineteen-year-old from Schleswig-Holstein."

"It was my own damn fault," Rainer said, clenching a fist.

"You shouldn't blame yourself, Herr Kaleun. Mein Gott. The Amis allowed themselves to be torpedoed just to try that old ruse again?"

Rainer felt his stomach turn. Why hadn't he been more vigilant? He'd been aware, of course, that in the First World War the Allies deployed seemingly unarmed merchant ships to lure U-Boats within range of their hidden weapons. But that subterfuge only worked in the early stages of the war—a time when U-Boat commanders allowed their crews to disembark before sinking their ship. Now, as in 1917, Kriegsmarine orders dictated unrestricted warfare. Rainer was no longer required to warn merchant ships before sinking them. Scheisse. Q ships made absolutely no sense.

Rainer pulled on his cap and reverted to action mode. "Bring us up to periscope depth, Jäger." At a depth of nine meters, he scanned the burning Q ship with the attack periscope. "He's settled by the bow and his propeller is out of the water. Come left 030."

At a distance of 300 meters, Rainer fired a single torpedo. A huge, dirty-gray cloud of oil and water with a brilliant orange core spiraled upward from the center of the ship. The Q ship broke in half and sank swiftly. Amid scattered debris and burning oil, the men in the lifeboat rowed furiously away.

Rainer detected no other survivors on the surface. With mixed emotions of both guilt and rage, he felt little of his normal compassion for the crew of a sinking ship. "Take her down to 200 meters, Jäger. Set course 180. We'll clear the area, then head for the Bahama Bank to rest on the bottom."

100 NAUTICAL MILES NORTHEAST OF THE BAHAMAS — July 18, 1942

Couple a jiggers of moonlight and add a star. The satin tones of Glenn Miller's popular swing tune percolated across the bridge from a Miami radio station picked up by Funkmaat Stein and broadcast throughout the boat at Rainer's request.

"Was ist das? What's a jigger?" Jäger asked.

"I'm not sure," Rainer said. "Probably some kind of measurement."

Cruising on the surface at twelve knots, the U-023 diesel engines thrummed in the warm tropical night. If all went well, Rainer calculated they'd reach their rendezvous point with the Milchkuh in less than three days. Stepping on to the Wintergarten, he lit a cigarette and pondered the recent war news. While Deutschlandsender broadcasts expressed optimism regarding both Eastern and North African Fronts, Rainer's view was more circumspect.

Against fierce resistance, over 150 Wehrmacht divisions had been slogging eastward toward Moscow for months. Finally, on the outskirts of the city, they'd been stopped by the Red Army just as winter set in. Rainer knew history. It was difficult to avoid comparing the Wehrmacht's situation with the disastrous fate of Napoleon's Grande Armée in 1812.

In Crimea, the Wehrmacht was on the brink of capturing Sevastopol. But, rebounding from Operation Barbarossa's initial Blitzkrieg thrust deep into their heartland, more than five million Russian soldiers were stubbornly resisting German advances across their country.

And after scoring a brilliant strategic victory in Libya, Rommel's Afrikorps was now deadlocked in a seesaw battle with the British.

Although the Führer was declaring victory on all fronts, Rainer knew it was too soon to predict the outcome of this terrible war. And even if Germany emerged victorious, nothing could replace all he'd lost. A heart-broken warrior with little to lose, he would fight to the end as a loyal son of the Fatherland.

"Entschuldigung, Herr Kaleun," Funkmaat Stein interrupted. "Here's an urgent dispatch from the BdU."

Holding the yellow piece of paper up to the starlight, Rainer read the message: *U-491 Milchkuh sunk by Allied aircraft at 0600 18 July. Proceed directly to Lorient.*

Dismissing Stein, Rainer gazed, unfocused, at the phosphorescent trail behind the U-023. All gone. The beautiful Mexican spy, the smell of freshly-baked French bread, the chivalrous Korvettenkapitän and the bittersweet lines by Friedrich Hölderlin. I am alone and sailing on the ocean.

Chapter Twenty Eight
Vorsicht

A major force of British bombers flew through storms and icing clouds...to attack Hamburg on Tuesday night for the second time in three nights. They bombed from low altitude under a cloud bank over Hamburg, at 1000 feet and lower, destroying trains and goods, interrupting communications and leaving tremendous fires.

New York Times
July 30, 1942

HAMBURG, Germany
— July 30, 1942

Two days after the latest RAF attack on Hamburg, scattered fires still burned along the tracks as the train from Paris rumbled into the Hauptbahnhof in mid-afternoon. Like a lucid dreamer unable to arouse himself from a vivid nightmare, Rainer stared from his compartment window as the train passed through the center of the city. Row upon row of ghostly walls, completely gutted within, remained standing above piles of twisted girders, splintered beams and broken glass. During a brief stop at the station, the locomotive's steam rose above silent passengers leaving and boarding the train, and dissipated through shattered glass panels in the semi-circular roof above the platform.

A dark wave of anger and anguish welled up deep within Rainer's chest. Such devastation. Although Hamburg had been bombed many times over the past two years, most of the damage had been confined to the docks and industrial areas of this major port city, only 60 kilometers from his hometown Lübeck. Now, over two nights, 400 RAF bombers had leveled housing and commercial districts with demolition bombs and incendiaries. First came the bombs, blowing rooftops away. Then bundles of fiery sticks rained down, igniting all the structures laid open and bare. More than 300 people perished in the raid.

Over the past year, the air war had changed dramatically. After the Luftwaffe's failed attempt to destroy the RAF during the Blitz of London and nearby targets, the invasion of Russia required massive deployment of airpower to the East. Although the Luftwaffe force remaining in northern France continued to carry out minor raids, the major air offensive against Britain was discontinued. Only the firebombing of Lübeck provoked a brief series of retaliatory raids against picturesque English towns listed in the popular travel guide published by Baedeker.

Now the RAF was purposely targeting civilian populations in the center of German cities. The smoldering embers of anger inside Rainer metamorphosed to apprehension. This air war was not going to improve. The Luftwaffe, engaged on two fronts, was being depleted while the RAF was growing stronger. With help from America, British aircraft, weaponry and navigational aids were rapidly improving. And soon the Amis would be ready to enter the European war.

A gray-white plume burst from the locomotive and the train lurched, then crawled out of the station, its iron wheels clicking and clanking every few seconds over irregularities in the track. The odor of steam mixed with oil permeated Rainer's compartment as he settled back on the upholstered seat. In less than an hour he'd be home again. He squeezed his eyes closed, trying to extrude the dark memories. Unglaublich. Six months ago the thought of losing his family would never have crossed his mind. God damn those Tommies. And damn the God that let this happen.

The muffled sound of the roaring locomotive clattering over the tracks suddenly increased as the compartment door slid open. An attractive young woman with a small child stood in the doorway with a battered leather suitcase at her feet. "Entschuldigen Sie, mein Herr, " she said in clipped high German imbued with a northern Plattdeutsch accent. "Is that seat free?"

Rainer rose with a polite smile. "Certainly, meine Dame. Please allow me to put your suitcase on the rack above."

"Danke schön. You're very kind."

Rainer hoisted her suitcase onto the rack and watched out of the corner of his eye as she and her son sat down across from him. When sunlight glinted off her golden hair as it brushed across her shoulders, he looked away and closed his eyes. Mein Gott. Anneliese. Trying to gather his emotions, he inhaled deeply through his nostrils and slowly released his breath. Settling back in his chair, he allowed the wave of emotion to subside before turning his attention to the young boy sitting across from him.

In lederhosen and a white shirt, the boy smiled at Rainer and began to roll a toy car back and forth across the rough corduroy seat cover. Rainer was impressed with the accurate detail of the toy staff car, complete with an SS driver and Adolf Hitler holding an arm aloft in salute. At the same time, he was saddened. War toys seemed to be the only childhood playthings these days.

"I'm sorry to disturb you, mein Herr," the woman said. "I promise we'll be quiet."

"Kein Problem, gnädige Frau." Rainer waved his hand to the side and turned to the boy. "Wie alt bist Du?"

The boy glanced at his mother, uncertain how to reply.

"You know how old you are. Tell the nice man."

The boy slowly extended his fingers. One, two, three, four, five.

"Ah. Ten years old," Rainer said with a straight face.

"No! I'm five."

The mother was smiling broadly.

"Oh, I'm sorry," Rainer said. "I must've counted wrong." He pointed to the toy car in the boy's hand. "Who's that in the back seat?"

"Our Führer!" The boy said.

"Of course. What's he doing?"

"He's waving to everybody. Mutti," the boy said, pointing to the Ritterkreuz Rainer wore on a black and red ribbon around his neck. "Was ist das?"

"I'm sorry, mein Herr. He just wants to know everything." She turned to her son. "That means he's a very brave man."

"Like Vati?"

The young woman's cheeks flushed. "Ja. Just like Vati."

"Where is the boy's father?" Rainer asked.

"Eastern front," the woman said, briefly biting her lip. "We've had no news for a month."

Rainer remained silent. She was vulnerable and lovely, but he wasn't going to try to reassure her.

"I'm sorry, mein Herr," the woman said, gesturing toward the gold wreath on his lapel that encircled a submarine, swastika and eagle. "I'm a Wehrmacht wife. I can see you're in the Ubootwaffe, but I can't determine your proper rank."

"Don't worry," Rainer said with a smile. "You're not the only one. My rank is Kapitänleutnant."

"Are you on a U-Boat?" the boy asked.

"Ja. What about your father?" Rainer said.

"He drives tanks."

"Ah. Panzers. He must be a very brave man."

"Vati is the bravest!"

"Is Lübeck your hometown, mein Herr?" the woman asked. Rainer nodded. "Well, I hope you have a nice visit with your family."

Rainer felt his eyes begin to water as a tide of anguish rose in his throat. But before he could respond, the woman turned to her son. "Let's let the man rest now," she said, unfolding a newspaper. The intense ache in Rainer's throat ebbed.

Silently, the boy played with his toy car while his mother began turning pages of the popular Hamburger Illustrierte. Rainer studied the color photograph of Feldmarshall Rommel on the front page. Sunglasses splayed across the top of his cap, Rommel was squinting into the desert past a row of Panzers.

A very different kind of war. But which was worse? Parched and bleeding to death beneath a scorching sun or sinking into the cold, dark abyss?

Rainer laid his head back against the seat and gazed at the rolling hills and verdant fields of Schleswig-Holstein as the train approached his childhood home. Black-and-white cows grazed or lay in the shade of maple and oak trees in fields between small farms. Orchards, wheat fields, rows of asparagus, beets, cabbage and strawberries. Chickens, horses, pigs and sheep. He turned his face and squinted into the orange light of the late afternoon sun. His homeland was still abundant. But he was bereft.

Soon familiar small towns flashed by—Lasbek, Pölitz and Meiddewadde. Rainer stood and pulled his rucksack and the woman's suitcase down from the overhead rack.

"Vielen Dank," she said. "Enjoy your time in Lübeck."

Although missing part of its the roof, the Lübeck Bahnhof was mostly intact and debarking from the train was easy. Soon Rainer was walking toward the Puppenbrücke, the bridge of statues that crossed the river to the Holstentor gate, wedged between two sagging, medieval towers. Oblivious to the summer day, he looked back toward the Bahnhof and allowed his eyes to go out of focus.

Her hair and shoulders layered with fine crystals of falling snow, Anneliese laughed, then fell into his arms on the way to their romantic getaway in Travemünde.

Rainer held his eyes tightly closed for several long moments. When he opened them again, it was a clear summer day and a gracefully-sculpted woman was gazing down at him through narrowed eyes of granite. In her left hand, she held a serpent. In her right, flexed toward her face as if to gaze into it, was the broken handle of a looking glass, the mirror blown away by demolition bombs. On a plaque at her feet was the inscription: Vorsicht.

Caution? Rainer searched the statue's face, trying to discern a meaningful message. Was it lack of caution with the Q-ship that cost the life of his crewman? The warning to proceed with caution seemed laced with irony when every day on the hunt carried the threat of instant destruction.

Although Rainer found the Holstentor remarkably intact, passing into the Innenstadt was still a shock. Familiar old buildings were now burnt-out shells, piles of rubble or had simply vanished. But signs of life were everywhere. Trucks and automobiles hummed along Holstenstrasse. A Wehrmacht squad with shouldered rifles tromped down a side street past oblivious pedestrians, bustling along the sidewalk. The sounds of hammers, shovels and machinery filled the dusty air as workmen scraped, sawed, pounded and chiseled like beavers rebuilding a breached dam. Although the faint odor of burnt wood was still detectable, it was now masked by the smells of vitality rather than destruction. Exhaust fumes, powdered masonry, industrial smoke, cooking grease, baked goods, stale beer, cigarette smoke and body odor drifted in the air.

Rainer was famished. The last thing he'd eaten was a croissant with coffee in Paris. At the Rathaus Square marketplace, he bought a Bratwurst, Semmeln roll and a beer from a rosy-cheeked, overweight man in a butchers apron. "*Senf?* Would you like mustard?" The man asked.

Rainer reached for the pigskin wallet in his jacket.

"Nein, mein lieber Herr," the man said, gesturing toward the Ritterkreuz around Rainer's neck. "You've served the Fatherland. Now allow me the honor to serve you."

Rainer was embarrassed by the attention the Ritterkreuz brought him, but since he was required to wear it whenever in uniform, all he could do was smile graciously and thank the man. He walked across the busy square and settled on a stone bench adjacent to the ruins of the Marienkirche. Since his last visit four months ago, all the rubble had been cleared away. Above the shattered windows and crumbling walls of the sanctuary, the twin towers still stood, albeit without their distinctive Gothic spires. The outer sections of the building, with its dozen elegant arches, had been destroyed, but the inner sanctum appeared intact. Although he'd intended to savor it, Rainer devoured his meal and headed for the sanctuary that held so many precious memories for him.

In the church foyer an elderly man in civilian clothes noted the Ritterkreuz and greeted Rainer with enthusiasm. "Your visit is an honor, mein Herr." He lowered his voice. "Because of the danger, please keep to the center aisle."

Rainer walked down the aisle to his family's habitual place in the fourth row and sat in the sanctuary. The aisles were now clear of debris and damaged sections of the walls, ceiling and organ had been hauled away. But the stained glass windows remained shattered, the partially-melted iron bells lay silently on the stone floor and the skeletal figure of Death in the scorched Totentanz mural still smirked as he grasped the arm of the knight in armor.

Rainer gazed upward at silvery particles drifting in a beam of blue light, filtered through the broken stained glass above the altar. Aware of a vague ache in his chest, he slowly twirled the wedding ring he still wore on his right hand. He wasn't sure what to do with the powerful emotions he was experiencing. Prayer? Although a lifelong Lutheran, he'd never been particularly religious. And recently he'd begun to doubt the very existence of God. So he simply removed his cap, closed his eyes and drifted into a reverie.

With a wave of melancholic elation, he recalled his mother, bowing rapturous notes from her cello, smiling down at him during the Sunday morning service. Then the look in his father's eyes as he rested a hand on his son's shoulder before his first U-Boat patrol. His radiant daughter Gisela, her back to the sunset, calling for him to throw her the ball. And Anneliese. A deep sigh escaped Rainer's lips as he felt her warm body pressed against his at the railroad station. *Komm sicher wieder, meine Liebe.* Come back safely, my love.

Rainer's eyes snapped open. They were all gone now. Only Joachim remained to love and protect. But how could he do that when he'd soon be off to sea again? He looked at his watch. 1830. Joachim and Horst would probably be home by now. He shouldered his rucksack and left the church.

Entering Horst's neighborhood on Kanalstrasse, Rainer noticed little to suggest the city had been firebombed a mere four months earlier. Horst's wife Ilse answered the door, grasped his hand warmly and ushered him inside. "Wilkommen, Rainer. We didn't know when you would arrive. We just finished dinner."

Horst and Joachim, in Wehrmacht and Deutsches Jungvolk uniforms, sprang up from the table when Rainer entered the dining room. Joachim seemed taller, more reserved than

Rainer recalled. Although he extended a hand in manly fashion, Rainer swept him into his arms like a small child. "Vati. Vati," Joachim murmured, tears welling in his eyes. Rainer squeezed his son against his body, savoring the embrace as long as possible. Then, with one arm still around Joachim's waist, he shook Horst's left hand firmly.

"Wilkommen, mein lieber Freund," Horst said. "We're so glad you made it home safely."

"You must be hungry," Ilse said. "Please sit down. I'll bring you a plate."

"Fish stew and crayfish pastry, mein Freund," Horst said with a wink. "Ilse did some special shopping."

"Danke schön. It sounds delicious, but I've already eaten," Rainer said. He glanced at his watch. "We still have about an hour of daylight. If you don't mind, I'd like to take a walk with Joachim along the canal."

A small boat cruised past gabled Hanseatic-style row houses along the opposite bank as Rainer and Joachim walked south on Kanalstrasse.

"I've been so worried about you, Vati," Joachim said. "You must be in a lot of dangerous situations."

Vorsicht! Rainer didn't want to lie to his twelve year-old son who certainly understood the dangers inherent in submarine warfare. "I'm very cautious," he said, looking directly into Joachim's eyes. "Of course there are risks, but I have an excellent crew and we watch out for one another."

Joachim spoke hesitantly. "How many ships did you sink this time, Vati?"

Rainer stopped walking and studied his son. "Are you keeping count now?" Joachim raised his eyebrows in expectation. "We sank six ships this time," Rainer said.

"Did anyone try to sink you, Vati?"

Rainer smiled. "Of course. They always try to sink us. It's part of the game. We're like hunters dueling each other." Joachim stiffened, his lips parted. "Don't worry," Rainer said. "We're much better hunters than the Amis. And if they get close, we just go deep."

At sunset waves generated by the wakes of passing cruisers, lapped against boulders lining the canal.

"Vati," Joachim said. "Do you ever feel bad about killing people?"

Rainer resumed walking, pondering the question he'd asked himself so many times. How much Joachim had changed in a few short months! Not long ago it was model airplanes and toy boats. Now, after surviving the bombs that killed his family and digging the dead out of the rubble of his hometown, his son had been forced to grow up fast. "I don't like to kill people," he said. "But the ships I sink are carrying war materials to England for use against our Fatherland."

Joachim looked down at the ground. "The Englanders killed our family, Vati."

"That's why I need to fight, son," Rainer said in a raspy voice that reflected the wave of raw emotion arising in his throat. "There's no other honorable choice."

Rainer and Joachim walked on in silence to the bottom of Kanalstrasse, then headed back to Horst's house.

"How are you doing in your classes?" Rainer asked.

"I'm doing all right."

"Are there any subjects you particularly like?"

"Science and math."

"What's not so interesting for you?"

"Too many lectures about inferior races and our Aryan destiny. Not just in school. Also in our DJ meetings."

"But you like the DJ group, don't you?"

"I like the target practice."

Rainer smiled. "Then I guess there're two hunters in the family. What about your interest in radio? Anything new in the DJ?"

Joachim shook his head. "Nein, Vati. Radio class is still only for Hitler Youth. I'll just have to wait until I'm fourteen, I guess."

When they reached Horst's front door, Rainer paused. "You've come through a terrible time, Joachim. But you're smart and strong." He placed both hands on Joachim's shoulders. "I am so proud of you." His voice choked. "And your mother would be too."

Chapter Twenty Nine
Martin

Things do exist that are worth standing up for without compromise. To me it seems that peace and social Justice are such things, as is Christ himself.

> *Dietrich Bonhöffer*
> *January 1935*

LÜBECK, Germany
— August 2, 1942

The cuckoo clock on the wall struck midnight as Horst, cradling a shot glass in his gloved right hand, poured another round of Korn Schnapps.

"The air bridge at Demjansk sounds like quite a feat, Horst," Rainer said, quaffing the last dregs of beer in his stein. "Sounds like you turned certain defeat into success."

As transportation officer for the 30th Wehrmacht Infantry Division, Horst had played a significant role in the dramatic break-out of 100,000 German troops encircled by the Red Army southeast of Leningrad. With limited ability to resupply their troops by ground transportation, the German situation was critical. Then an unprecedented maneuver was initiated.

Flying up to 150 missions per day, the Luftwaffe delivered desperately-needed supplies and 30,000 replacement troops, while evacuating more than 20,000 wounded. Like Hannibal's crossing of the Alps, the Demjansk airbridge operation was one of the great feats in military history.

Horst turned his cigarette between his fingertips, studying the languid smoke curling upward in the dim light. "Ja. You might call the breakout some sort of victory, Rainer. The Reds certainly poured a lot of men into attacking the pocket. Men they probably needed elsewhere." He tossed back another shot of Schnapps and chased it with a slug of beer.

"I don't understand, Horst," Rainer said. "The newspapers and radio say the breakout is evidence of continued success on the Eastern front. And the Führer just said we're about to take Stalingrad. You seem unduly morose, mein Freund."

"Ach. Der Führer," Horst snorted. "Don't believe everything you hear, Rainer. Words are cheap. The Luftwaffe lost over 250 aircraft and almost twice as many men supplying the Demjansk pocket. And on the ground?" He exhaled a doleful blast through his lips. "14,000 of our soldiers dead. 40,000 wounded." He refilled Rainer's shot glass with schnapps and opened two more beers. "Make no mistake about it, Rainer. Ivan has learned how to fight. And both Stalin and the Führer have proclaimed retreat is not an option."

Rainer felt uncomfortably warm. His mind was racing. Horst certainly knew a lot more about the Russian campaign than he did. "So you don't think were winning on the Eastern front?"

"Winning?" Horst spat out the word. "Wake up, Rainer. Our forces are vastly overextended and the Russians just keep getting stronger." He thrust his cigarette butt into the ashtray, grinding it into shreds between his fingers. "Were on the brink of disaster, mein Freund."

FUHLSBÜTTEL Police Prison
— August 7, 1942

Rainer was enjoying the breeze. With clear skies and 20 degrees Celsius, Horst had left the top down on the Mercedes staff car. Besides horse-drawn carts, bicycles and a few private vehicles, most of the traffic on the road leading to the police prison at Fuhlsbüttel was military.

Rainer took particular notice of the young men working in the fields. The last time he'd driven this road from Lübeck to Hamburg, the farmworkers had been unmistakably German. Now, with the need for more troops, most young German men were in the military. "Where are they from?" He asked Horst.

"Probably Polish *Zivilarbeiter*," Horst said.

Rainer gazed out the window as they passed a thatched-roof farmhouse and adjacent barn, shaded by towering black poplars. A verdant field, surrounded by an open-faced wooden fence, was sprinkled with yellow rapeseed flowers. This was the Fatherland he loved. But what was becoming of it now? Each time he returned from sea, he noticed dark and ominous changes. Suppression of any type of dissent from government policies. Incarceration for "defeatist" talk. Slave laborers from the conquered territories. Even murder of the disabled, Gypsies and Jews. It was hard to be proud of the Third Reich. He could see why Martin had taken a moral stand. But what would sitting in a jail cell accomplish?

Wouldn't he be more effective if he retracted his outspoken remarks and worked quietly for change?

"Do you really think they'll let us visit Martin?" Rainer said.

Horst tapped the Ritterkreuz around Rainer's neck, then his own Wehrmacht Major's insignia of a bar with two oak leaf clusters. "As long as the officer in charge is a captain or less."

Tall oak trees, their branches like supplicants reaching for the open sky, lined the sidewalk in front of the 19th-century red brick prison on the outskirts of Hamburg. At the entrance, a broad arch with iron grates was flanked by twin pyramidal towers. On the roof, two lions reared, their forepaws grasping a castle topped with a plumed Knight's helmet.

One of the sentries, in a steel helmet and gray-green uniform, stepped forward as Rainer and Horst approached the gate. "Heil Hitler!" the young sentry barked, extending his right arm in a salute.

"Heil Hitler!" Horst replied, swiftly extending and dropping his arm. "We're here to visit the prisoner Martin Ehrlichmann."

The sentry hesitated, seeming uncertain how to respond.

"Please notify your officer in charge," Horst said briskly.

"Ja wohl, Herr Major," the young man replied. "Ein moment, bitte."

The sentry, maintaining an extremely erect posture, turned and strode to a telephone at the gate. After a few minutes of muffled conversation, he returned. "*Kommen Sie bitte herein, meine Herren.*"

Passing through two locked gates, the nervous young sentry transferred the visitors to an older noncommissioned officer wearing the uniform and cap of Wachtmeister. Rainer noticed the heavy eyelids, sagging chin and age spots on his hands. This man was probably a prison guard in the last war. With a weary Heil Hitler salute and shuffling gait, the aging Wachtmeister, escorted Horst and Rainer through a musty cobblestone courtyard enclosed by towering brick walls topped with barbed wire. Rainer looked up at a billowing cloud drifting freely above, then back down toward a concrete ramp inclined into darkness. Like Orpheus, he followed the wheezing Wachtmeister as he and Horst descended into the underworld.

In the dusty administrative office of the prison, a tall, thin man rose from his desk to greet them with a Hitler salute.

"Oberleutnant Brandt, at your service, meine Herren. How can I help you?"

"We're here to visit the prisoner Martin Ehrlichmann," Horst said crisply.

"I'm sorry, Herr Major. That isn't possible. Visitation is only allowed on the first of the month."

Horst broadened his stance and fixed his eyes on the junior officer. "I'm sure you can make an exception in our case." He gestured toward Rainer with his gloved hand. "My comrade, who just received the Ritterkreuz for bravery, must go back on U-Boat patrol shortly. And I've been quite busy, I'm sure you can understand, with the Demjansk airlift."

The Oberleutnant tugged at his collar as if the room had become uncomfortably warm. "I understand, Herr Major. But

311

I'd have to clear this with my superior officer and he's not available at the moment. Perhaps you could come back..."

Horst cut him off with a brisk wave of his hand. "I'm afraid we have no more time. Perhaps I should call my commander General Stülpnagl. I'm on his staff."

Oberleutnant Brandt drew his feet together and squared his shoulders. "That won't be necessary, Herr Major. Given the circumstances, we can make an exception in this case." He turned to the Wachtmeister. "Take these officers to the prisoner Ehrlichmann."

Horst allowed a faint smile. "Very kind of you."

Horst and Rainer followed the Wachtmeister through a series of locked gates and dimly-lit corridors that exuded a pungent odor, apparently masked by frequent rinsing with an antiseptic solution. The soles of their boots clanked against the steel grating, as they ascended a narrow walkway to the second level of prison cells.

When the Wachtmeister opened the heavy iron door of Martin's cell, Rainer's jaw dropped. Somehow, he'd expected his formerly-robust friend to be relatively unchanged. Instead, a pale, stoop-shouldered man in a striped prison uniform shuffled out of the shadows.

"Visitors are allowed 30 minutes, meine Herren," the Wachtmeister said, closing the cell door.

"Mein Gott! Horst. Rainer." His eyes brimming with tears, Martin embraced each of them fiercely like brothers long separated by a distant war. "How did you...?"

Horst shrugged. "We're war heroes. Don't you know?"

Martin was too overcome with emotion to respond with the usual joviality they'd shared since childhood. "It's wonderful to see you both," he said, wiping tears from his eyes.

"How are they treating you?" Rainer asked.

"Not badly," Martin said. "Although I'm charged with sedition, most of the guards see me as a pastor, unable to compromise my beliefs. Some have even discussed their spiritual concerns with me." He gestured toward a stack of books on a small table. "And a few have even brought me books." He paused, his expression darkening. "I get an hour in the courtyard each day. But I long to be free, my friends."

"What would it take to get you out of here?" Horst asked.

"I'd have to renounce all statements I've made about the immorality of state-sponsored programs."

"What statements?" Rainer asked.

Martin's eyes flashed angrily. "*Hör auf*, Rainer! You know what I'm talking about. Euthanizing mental patients and retarded children. Deporting, or even murdering Jews."

A deafening silence filled the dimly-lit cell. Rainer bit his lip and looked down at the floor. Horst shifted his weight silently.

"Listen, Martin," Rainer finally said. "We all have to be careful what we say these days. You could do so much more as a free man."

Martin sat on his cot, his head in his hands, staring at the cold stone floor. "We've all been silent witnesses to evil deeds," he said in a low, but steady voice. He looked up, fixing his eyes on Rainer. "And God won't hold us guiltless, mein Freund."

The half-hour passed swiftly. Unable to convince Martin he had any alternative, Horst and Rainer were soon back on the road to Lübeck. Rainer lit two cigarettes and passed one to Horst. Horst inhaled deeply and blew silvery smoke against the windshield. "You know they'll probably execute him, Rainer."

Rainer simply stared out the window. Like a broken branch trapped against a boulder in a raging river, he felt powerless. Although it wasn't God's judgment he feared, he knew Martin was right. They were all silent witnesses to evil deeds.

Chapter Thirty
Concepción

A United States destroyer entered port this morning with the bodies of eight sailors who were killed when the Cuban merchant vessels Santiago de Cuba *and* Manzanillo *were torpedoed and sunk. Thousands crowded the docks and lined the streets as the coffins were unloaded and borne to the Capitol.*

New York Times
August 19, 1942

LA HABANA, Cuba
— August 19, 1942

It was midmorning when the overnight train from Camagüey rolled into Havana's central station. Ramón, feeling a tug on his shoulder, turned away from Concepción and tried to bury his face deeper between the edge of the passenger seat and the grimy window.

"*Despertarte, amor!*" Concepción said, gently tugging him into an upright position. "We're in Havana." She smiled at the silver-haired man in a dark suit and black armband sitting across from her. "Buenos días, papá."

"Buenos días, Coni," her father said with a weary smile. "It looks like we're arriving just on time."

Ramón sat up, mumbled "buenos dias," and looked at his watch. 1030. Damn! The funeral procession was scheduled to leave the harbor at eleven. But do Cubans ever start anything on time? Well maybe, if the Americans offload the bodies. He glanced at Concepción.

"Tranquilo, amor," she said, patting his knee. "Tío Miguel's going to meet us on the platform and the harbor's just a few blocks from the station."

Concepción's graying, uncle Miguel Vargas, a widower, was waiting with a burly taxista when they stepped down from the passenger car. With prominent noses and narrow lips, Ramón noticed a resemblance between the two brothers as they embraced on the platform. After the taxista took their suitcases to be delivered to Tío Miguel's apartment, Concepción, her father, uncle and Ramón set off on foot for the docks.

"*Lo siento*. I'm sorry about your son, Señor Vargas," Ramón said to Tío Miguel.

"Gracias," Miguel said, closing his eyes briefly with a nod. "Alejándro was only eighteen. He just wanted to see the world." Head slightly bowed and hands held loosely at his sides, Tío Miguel walked silently ahead of the others.

Ramón grasped Concepción's hand as they walked alongside her father on the Avenida de Bélgica. Eighteen. Alejandro was the same age as Luís when he took his fatal motorcycle ride. Had Tío Miguel and his son fought like his own father and Luís?

318

Sidewalks on the Avenida were packed with somber spectators awaiting the procession. Soon the steady, deep pounding of drums, accompanied by plaintive notes of brass instruments, arose from the wharf where the coffins of eight Cuban sailors were being unloaded from an American destroyer. Several blocks from the advancing funeral march, a policeman ushered them out of the street onto the sidewalk where a crowd, three rows deep, pent-up with sorrow and rage, silently awaited the procession.

Clip clop clip clop. Horse-drawn caissons bearing eight coffins draped with Cuban flags passed by. Ramón felt an unanticipated wave of sorrow welling up deep inside. His own missions were increasingly dangerous. What if he went down? He pulled Concepción close and brushed away the tears streaming down her cheeks. Brrumm brrumm brrumm. The drums beat a slow, mournful cadence as once-lively Mariachi horns wailed the doleful message: the Alemanes have killed our boys.

Tío Miguel stepped into the street and began walking beside the funeral procession like a guardian angel escorting his son on his last journey. When a policeman accosted him, he pointed to the coffin and his own black armband. "Soy padre del marinero," he said. The crowd began murmuring, passing the information down the line. He's the father. Let him pass. The policeman backed away and Tío Miguel continued down the avenue, apace with the caissons, gliding along the tender margins of the sympathetic crowd thronging the sidewalk.

Ramón, Concepción and her father stepped back from the curb and walked along behind the crowd, trying to keep up with Tío Miguel. When the crowd and procession turned off

319

the Avenida toward the capitol, where the coffins would lie in state, Tío Miguel stopped walking and bowed his head.

Soon Ramón and the others caught up. "Don't you want to go to the capitol building," Concepción's father asked his brother.

"I've said my goodbye," Tío Miguel said. "Let's go home."

It was well past midnight when Ramón and Concepción stood alone on Tío Miguel's balcony. The night air was muggy and tinged with the odors of oil and salt from the harbor. Dim light from the apartments lining the block faintly illuminated the narrow street where an occasional passerby was followed by an elongated shadow. *Guadalajara. Guadalajara.* A tenor voice, barely audible from the nearby plaza, sang to a cadre of strumming guitars.

Delighted that they were at last alone, Ramón placed an arm around Concepción's waist and pulled her close. Over the past few months, seeing her almost every day, he had begun to open up as he'd never before been able to do with a woman.

"It's been a sad day," he said, nestling his face against the enticingly-soft skin of her neck "I was impressed how tenderly your father treated his brother."

"We're a very close family," Concepción said.

"I wish I could say that."

"What do you mean?"

Ramón rested his forearms on the railing and looked up at the sky. "I'm okay with my mother. But my father's another story."

Concepción placed her hand on his neck. "Do you want to talk about it, *querido*?"

The love streaming from her fingertips felt like a river of sparkling light flowing into Ramón's body. What had he ever done to deserve this woman?

"Está bien, amor," she said stroking his back. "Todo bien."

Ramón straightened up and held her face in his hands, studying her smooth, caramel skin. Her curly hair. The high-bridged nose and hazel eyes that radiated loving compassion. "Te amo," he said. "I really love you."

"Yo también, querido. But you've never told me much about your father. Maybe it's time."

Ramón sighed. "When I was young my father often fought with my older brother."

"Physically?" Ramón nodded. "Did he ever fight with you?"

"No. I was the good son. My father encouraged me to study hard and be an honest person. I looked up to him." Ramón paused. Concepción waited patiently. "One day after high school, I discovered him making love with the school secretary in a storeroom. I said nothing. I don't think my mother ever knew."

"What happened after that?"

"Nothing really. We hardly talk."

"Did he keep taking care of the family?" Ramón nodded. "Did he treat your mother badly?" Ramón shook his head no. Concepción wrapped her arms around him, rocking gently back-and-forth. "Everyone makes a mistake sometime, querido. Maybe it's time to let this go."

Ramón's tears were freely flowing. "But that's not all," he said, his voice cracking. "I've done it myself. Slept with another man's wife. I'm not sure I really know how to love."

"Shh shh, querido." Concepción's whisper brushed across his cheek like a soft, summer breeze. "You just had to learn. And you have. Now it' s time to let all that go."

Ramón felt his soul scrambling to be bared to this beautiful woman. "I also have a child, Concepción," he blurted in desperation.

Eyes widened, Concepción backed away. "Que?"

"I got my high school girlfriend pregnant. She went away and they told me she gave the baby up. But now I've learned she kept the baby and got married."

Concepción bit her lip and shook her head briefly as she absorbed this startling fact. Then she stood tall and locked her eyes on his with deep compassion. "You were just a schoolboy, Ramón."

"Do you still trust me?"

"*Siempre*, amor. You made some mistakes when you were young. But you've grown and now you're the man I love."

Chapter Thirty One
Caribbean Sunset

Germany has at her disposal today more submarines than she had last year...At present, it was declared, there is no general lowering of the morale of U-Boat crews, who were found generally to be young and firm in their opinion that Germany is going to win the war. The United Nations have got to break that spirit by intensive attack, so that the U-Boat crews will know when they go to sea that they will be attacked so constantly as to make their return to their base problematic...

New York Times
September 9, 1942

180 NAUTICAL MILES NORTHEAST OF GRENADA
— September 17, 1942

At twilight, the U-023 lay on the surface refreshing its air supply and charging its batteries with the starboard diesel engine while the port engine was down undergoing repairs. Rainer stood on the bridge with Jäger watching the sun set over the western horizon. In the past week, they'd sunk two merchant ships near Barbados and Grenada, bringing the grand total for this patrol to four ships or about 20,000 GRT.

Although they had to crash dive with an approaching aircraft once, the U-023 escaped without damage. Last night the port diesel engine couldn't reach full load, but the lead engineer Rademaker assured him it was only a leaky fuel line and he would soon have it running normally again.

Rainer leaned over the fairwater wall of the bridge, rolling his shoulders and stretching the muscles of his back like a hungry wolf emerging from his lair. This patrol reminded him of his first mission along the Atlantic Coast. Avoiding the newly-constituted Caribbean convoy system, he'd found plenty of unescorted targets outside the main traffic routes. But now, as the Allies increased ASW activity in the area, the old lion Dönitz was once again changing deployment of his U-boats. With all torpedoes expended, the U-023 was heading for a mid-Atlantic rendezvous with a Milchkuh for refueling, then on to a new assignment in the North Atlantic.

Funkmaat Stein appeared on the bridge and handed Rainer a message from the BdU:

September 16 - U-156, attempting to rescue survivors of a torpedoed ship, was attacked by Allied aircraft in the South Atlantic. Henceforth, all efforts to save survivors of sunken ships, such as fishing them out of the water and putting them in lifeboats, righting their overturned lifeboats or giving them food and water, must stop. Rescue contradicts the most basic demands of the war: the destruction of hostile ships and their crews. - Dönitz.

Rainer handed the message to Jäger with a shake of his head. "U-156. That's Hartenstein's boat. I wonder if…"

"Herr Kaleun!" The port lookout called out. "Northbound ship broad on the port bow."

Rainer snapped the binoculars hanging from his neck up to his eyes and focused on a long, gray ship silhouetted against the ash-pink horizon. "He's low in the water with a raised center island."

"Probably a C2 class freighter," Jäger said. "Some of them can run pretty fast."

"I see no escort."

"Too bad we're out of torpedoes, Herr Kaleun."

Rainer narrowed his eyes, his lips slightly parted. "We still have the deck gun, Jäger. Secure the battery charge and set course 280. All ahead full with available power. And ask Rademaker how the repairs are going."

In 30 minutes, making only ten knots with the port diesel still down, the U-023 closed within 1000 meters of a lone freighter that began zigzagging like a lost buffalo pursued by a hungry predator.

"He's spotted us," Rainer said. "How soon before we have full power?"

Jäger checked with the engine room. "Rademaker says he's almost finished repairs, Herr Kaleun."

Five hundred meters astern of the freighter, Rainer ordered Wolf and his crew to ready the deck gun for a broadside attack. 100 meters astern. Rainer stiffened. Something wasn't right. Why was the green running light on the freighter's bow becoming more visible? Scheisse! He's turning to starboard! "He's trying to ram us, Jäger! Hard right! Course 340! Tell Rademaker he's got to give me more speed."

With the starboard diesel screaming full blast, the U-023 was soon making twelve knots—still not enough to outrun the rampaging freighter. Belching thick clouds of inky smoke from its funnels, the ship was looming ever closer in an attempt to split the U-023 in half.

With no stern torpedoes and a useless deck gun located forward of the conning tower, Rainer ordered the crew to man the flak guns on the Wintergarten and aft deck. *Bratatattat. Tzingg!* Most of their fire missed the narrow target or ricocheted off the bow of the charging freighter. Staring up at the freighter's bow slicing through the water only 50 meters astern of his boat, Rainer held his breath, his heart pounding in his chest. Ach so. So this it how it ends.

Vroomm! The slumbering, port diesel engine roared into full throttle and the U-023, accelerating to its maximum speed of 18 knots, began pulling away. Soon, the freighter broke off the chase and resumed its northerly course.

An hour later, under a moonlit sky with low clouds, Rainer ordered a reverse course to resume the hunt. Although it had changed its route slightly, he soon found the freighter, darkened except for dim running lights. With full power restored, the U-023 was no longer the lame wolf that was almost rammed by this lumbering freighter. Rainer felt an exhilarating surge of energy course through the muscles of his body. There would be no tricky moves this devil could make this time. Still undetected at 1000 meters, he closed in for the kill. "Deck gun, prepare to fire."

At 500 meters, Rainer nodded as Wolf's eyes met his. "Feuer!"

Kaboom! With a thunderclap, a flash of lightning leapt from the barrel of the large cannon on the foredeck.

Whamm! A fireball of splintered debris shot into the air as the 25-kilogram shell tore a hole amidships near the waterline.

"Feuer!"

The cannon roared again.

Whamm! Splooshh! A strike directly at the waterline sent a plume of fire and water skyward. After two direct hits amidships, the freighter was dead in the water. With a slow death roll, it began to sink stern first. Some of the crew managed to clamber into a lifeboat before a great explosion rocked the ship and a reddish-brown fireball, 50 meters wide, soared into the cloudy moonlight. A dozen men leapt over the sides of the rapidly-sinking ship and swam desperately toward the lifeboat that was pulling away from a pool of flaming oil spreading across the water. The muffled screams of crew trapped inside the sinking ship ceased abruptly with another loud explosion. Then it was eerily quiet as the freighter slipped beneath the water, leaving a handful of blackened survivors in a single lifeboat rowing away from the swirling debris.

Rainer observed the carnage he'd caused with mixed feelings of rage and remorse. He'd sunk the sneaky *Scheisskerl* who tried to ram him. Still, the men in the water were nothing to be proud of. He turned toward Jäger. "Ahead one third. Vorsicht! Come alongside the lifeboat."

Idling beside the lifeboat, Rainer called down from the bridge to a bedraggled officer with a blood-stained shirt and several black-faced crewmen. *"Wo kommen sie her?"*

"Aus Georgetown Guiana," the officer replied in German with a heavy British accent.

"Good evening, Tommy," Rainer said in English."Sorry for the inconvenience. Can you tell me your destination?"

"Mobile Alabama."

Rainer noted an acrid odor in the air and recalled the explosion's unusual color. Probably a shipment of bauxite to the aluminum plants. "What was your cargo?"

"I'm sorry, sir. I can't give you that information."

Rainer laughed. "Of course not. Do you have emergency provisions?"

"Nichts."

"We'll give you some basic supplies." Rainer touched the brim of his cap. "Good luck."

Jäger raised an eyebrow. "What about the latest order from the BdU, Herr Kaleun?"

Rainer shrugged. "Sometimes we have to make our own rules. Give them some water and a compass. Then all ahead full course 080."

At 0300 flashes of moonlight pierced the clouds lying low over the Caribbean. Cruising at twelve knots toward the Atlantic passage between Saint Vincent and Santa Lucia, Rainer and Jäger smoked on the Wintergarten.

"That freighter came pretty close," Jäger said. "I'm glad you decided to go back after him. It was a good kill."

The glowing tip of Rainer's cigarette partially illuminated his face as he inhaled. "We did our job. But a good kill? I'm not sure what that is. Every time I see burned men struggling in the water, I have to remind myself—if we don't sink these ships, they'll deliver the materials that kill our countrymen."

Jäger stared silently into the dark ocean for several long moments before speaking. "I'll never get used to killing ordinary seaman, Herr Kaleun. But maybe that's a good thing. Perhaps we'll come out of this war retaining some humanity."

Rainer exhaled very slowly, watching the cigarette smoke dissipate into the darkness. "If we come out of it."

Jäger stepped back from the fairwater. "Our luck's been good so far, Herr Kaleun. And the war's going pretty well for us nicht wahr?"

"If you believe our own propaganda. But to me, it looks like the Afrikakorps is struggling and we're stretched out way too far in Russia."

Jäger sighed. "And it does look like the Amis are waking up a bit. We've lost eight boats this month."

"Ja. The U-162 went down near here just a week ago." Rainer patted Jäger's shoulder. "But in a few more weeks you'll be back with your family in Lorient. I envy you."

"You still have your son, Herr Kaleun."

A shaft of moonlight pierced the clouds, unrolling a silver carpet across the water. Of course, he still had Joachim. But he could never forgive the RAF for killing his family. The moonbeam vanished in a dark cloud, and sorrow replaced the anger in his heart. How many men had he killed? 250? 300? How many families had he left crying? So many people he'd loved were gone now. But Joachim would be all right. Horst and Ilse would see to that.

"May I ask you a personal question?" Jäger said.

"Certainly."

"Are you worried about helping the survivors today?"

"Nein. It was the right thing to do."

"Don't misunderstand me, Herr Kaleun. I'm just worried about repercussions if it gets up the line."

Rainer flicked his cigarette into the ocean. "Then let's hope no one finds out."

Jäger laughed. "Maybe the Tommies will put the story on the BBC."

"The helpful U-Boat commander? That doesn't sound like good propaganda to me."

"It's been a good mission. We should be proud, Herr Kaleun."

Twee twee! A high-pitched alarm signal sounded over the intercom. An icy wave coursed through Rainer's body.

"METOX signal!" Jäger shouted over the shrill tones of the high-frequency receiver that warned of approaching enemy radar.

"Alarm!" Rainer ordered as they clambered back onto the bridge. Jäger activated the diving bell. *Clang! Clang!*

With his temporal arteries pounding, Rainer waited for his crew to scramble down the hatch. He had only a few seconds to analyze the situation. The Amis would lose their radar signal during the last mile of approach. Low clouds shrouded the U-023. If he could dive before the aircraft arrived, he had an excellent chance of escape.

An image from the Lübecker Totentanz mural flashed by. With a sinister smirk, Death promenaded with the knight on his arm.

With the foredeck of the diving U-023 awash, Rainer placed one foot on the ladder leading down to the relative safety of the conning tower. Just one. That's all he was asking. One more chance to see his son again. Maybe when this war was over...

Varroom! Rat a tat tat tat. The roar of an approaching aircraft and the staccato clacking of machine guns froze Rainer atop the hatch. Mesmerized, he stared astern as fiery crimson dashes, interspersed with white flashes, streaked toward him. *Zip Zip. Thump!* The light left his body.

Chapter Thirty Two
Blood in the Moonlight

*New methods and new devices are making life "doubly dangerous"
for Nazi submarine crews... the First Lord of the Admiralty,
declared today. Referring to heavy losses sustained in the Caribbean
and Western Atlantic, he said..."U-boats had a happy hunting
ground until our American comrades were able to mount convoy
escorts in these regions. Since then the situation over there has
improved substantially..."*

New York Times
September 4, 1942

120 NAUTICAL MILES WEST OF SAINT VINCENT
— September 18, 1942

Sizzling Rita roared 500 feet above the dark ocean, rapidly
approaching the radar target. Ramón, aware of the tension in
his body, lightened his grip on the steering yoke, and
consciously slowed his breathing. With a rare opportunity to
catch a U-Boat on the surface, he had to remain focused and
calm. Below, scattered gray clouds obscured any clear view of
the water. With a full moon, the cloud cover was good—his

approach would probably not be detected by the U-Boat until he attacked.

A hissing sound in his headphones rose above the constant roar of the engines. "Pilot, bombardier," Angelo's voice crackled over the intercom.

"Roger, pilot."

"Radar target three miles ahead."

Eyes locked on the absolute altimeter, Ramón pushed the yoke forward and dropped through the clouds, leveling off 100 feet above the ocean.

"Pilot, bombardier. Range two miles."

"Roger pilot. Open bomb bay doors."

"Bomb bay open. Depth charges set at 25 feet."

Ramón squinted into the horizon. Nothing yet. But they were homing in on the target. No time to do anything but react.

"Pilot, bombardier. Range one-mile."

"Roger, pilot. We'll drop a stick of four."

Although racing over the ocean at more than three miles a minute, Ramón had the odd sensation that time was slowing down and he was somehow watching the subtle movements of his hands and feet on the elevator and rudder controls as he maneuvered his powerful Rita into battle. He brushed his fingertips lightly across the machine gun trigger mounted on the steering yoke. After so many close calls and missed opportunities, he was finally approaching a surfaced U-Boat!

Like a nocturnal osprey, with talons extended, Ramón kept his eyes riveted on the dark water just 100 feet below. Then Jesus! 2000 feet from the radar target, a phosphorescent trail across the water led to the unmistakable shape of a conning tower. Dark and narrow, like a great blue whale, the type IX U-Boat looked longer than he'd remembered.

Ramón dropped to 50 feet and pressed the machine gun trigger. Crimson-red tracers streaked between .50-caliber bullets erupting from the machine guns mounted on Sizzling Rita's nose and fuselage. Just before they zoomed over the U-Boat, Angelo shouted: "Bombs away!" And released a stick of depth charges.

Sparks flew as Sizzling Rita's bullets ricocheted off the deck and conning tower. For an instant, something caught Ramón's eye. Was it a man on the bridge?

Ramón pulled up hard to the right in a tight chandelle turn and circled back toward the target with his mind racing. The Type IX U-Boat drew about 15 feet of water. Had the depth charges, set at 25 feet, exploded close enough to cause significant damage? Also, he knew an attack more than 25 seconds into a sub's dive was unlikely to be successful. Would the bastards be submerged before he got back there?

As he approached the target for a second run, his eyes widened. Holy mackerel! The U-Boat was dead in the water, a fire roaring on its foredeck. "Bombardier, pilot. Drop two."

Tshww! Zip Zip. 1000 feet from the U-Boat, bursts of orange-red light erupted from the platform behind the bridge. Christ! The Krauts were manning their Flak gun.

Wham! An explosion rocked the cockpit. *Flash!* Ramón was blinded by a burst of brilliant white light. *Whumpp!* A powerful, invisible force tore off his headphones and hurled him against the cockpit wall. *Screee riiippp.* Metal panels were torn away from the fuselage as Sizzling Rita slammed into the ocean at 200 miles per hour.

For several minutes, all went dark for Ramón. Then amorphous images began to flicker across the screen of his battered consciousness like an old-time movie. Gradually, a familiar voice, distant at first, then unmistakable. *Soy siempre con tigo.* His abuela had not abandoned him.

"Dammit, Ray!" Erik shouted "Wake up! I need your help."

Ramón gradually returned to his senses. First the odor of avgas, then a searing pain in his leg.

"Come on, Ray!" Erik's voice was strong and forceful. "I've unfastened your seatbelt but your left leg's pinned behind the steering column. Push down on your right leg while I try to pull you free."

Erik braced himself against the collapsed fuselage and pushed mightily against the broken steering column.

"Ayyy!" Ramón blacked out momentarily as fiery pain shot down his left leg.

Erik stopped. "Look, Ray. The water's rising. We've got to get you out of here. Hang on!" He leaned into the steering column with great force and finally pulled Ramón free.

Ramon's left pant leg was soaked with blood. Erik tore it open with his bare hands revealing a jagged piece of bone protruding from a laceration in the left thigh that was bleeding heavily. "You've got a compound fracture, Ray," Erik said, opening the first aid kit. "I'll try to straighten it out and wrap it best I can. It's going to hurt like hell, buddy. But I'll give you a shot of morphine first." He pulled the cap off a morphine syrette, plunged the needle into Ramón's right thigh and squeezed the collapsible tube.

A warm wave coursed throughout Ramón's body. Although he felt nauseous, there was a definite lightening of the pain in his leg. Nevertheless, when Erik began applying traction to straighten the fractured femur, the pain became so intense that he passed out again. He soon regained consciousness and observed Erik wrapping his thigh with a compression bandage. Scanning the scene in a dream-like state, he saw the bombardier's nose compartment was gone and the passageway into the radio room was completely submerged. Only the cockpit remained above water.

"We've got to get out of here right now, Ray!" Erik grasped Ramón's face with both hands and stared into his drowsy eyes. "The escape hatch will be underwater. Do you understand that?"

Ramón nodded hazily."What about the rest of our crew?"

Erik shook his head. "They're gone. Nothing we can do. We're sinking. Don't worry. I'll help you through the hatch."

Ramón, experiencing both pain and the mild euphoria of morphine, was having difficulty focusing. But he was able to follow Erik. Competent and brave, Erik would get him out of here. Ramón shivered. "So cold," he said faintly.

Erik put a hand on his shoulder. "Listen, Ray. I know you're not back to normal yet. But we have to go now!" He checked the bandage which was soaked with blood. "I'm going to tighten the bandage on your leg. Then we'll go under water through the hatch."

As Erik tightened the compression bandage, the pain was so severe that Ramón briefly lost consciousness again. Then slowly returning to awareness, he felt as if he were floating above the ocean, disembodied and serene. How strange. He'd never worried much about dying before. But this might be it.

"Listen up, Ray!" Erik shouted. "We're going underwater. Take a few deep breaths. Hold it. Then dive headfirst through the escape hatch. You go first. Don't worry. I'll help you through."

After the second deep breath, Ramón was light-headed. He looked down at the blood oozing from his bandages and the water rising below. Erik was pressing down on the back of his head. There was no other option. He plunged his head beneath the water.

With a strong push from Erik, Ramón made it through the narrow escape hatch. Emerging in the warm Caribbean Sea, Erik yanked the cords of their Mae Wests to inflate them with CO_2 and they both held on to Sizzling Rita's nose as she bobbed up and down with the swells. Although the water temperature was 78 degrees, Ramón's teeth were chattering and he couldn't stop shivering. Holy Mary, mother of God. The words rose silently on his lips. With all this bleeding, he knew it wouldn't be long before he slipped into shock.

Beneath the cloudy sky, patches of crimson light glinted off the water. Not 500 yards away, a fire raging on the foredeck of the U-Boat ignited a pool of oil off the port side. Then, as German seamen in two rubber life rafts paddled furiously away—*Whamm!* A powerful blast amidships. *Clank. Grrr. Groan. Shhh.* The U-023 slipped beneath the water.

A following sea brought the fleeing submariners down on the floating American aviators. From an approaching raft, a stocky, bearded officer called out to Erik and Ramón. "Sind sie in Ordnung?"

"*Mein freund ist verletz,*" Erik responded in his middling German.

"Understand," Jäger said, pointing toward Ramón, bobbing semi-consciously in the water. "This man must come out of the water, nicht wahr?"

On Jäger's order, three of the four crewmen with him clambered into the life raft drifting nearby. One crewman remained, Funkmaat Stein, the radioman who also served as the U-023 medic. With multiple groans and an occasional yelp, Erik and the two Germans managed to push and pull Ramón into the raft.

Climbing in last, Erik was addressed by Funkmaat Stein who was holding Ramón by the shoulders. "I am *Sanitätsunteroffizier,*" the young German said.

Erik shook his head. "Nicht verstanden."

"He gives medicine," Jäger said.

"Ah. A medic. Sehr gut!" Erik said.

Stein gestured toward the blood streaming down Ramón's leg. "*Wir müssen die Blutungen stoppen.*"

Blut. Although barely conscious, Ramón understood the word. Thank God. He's going to stop the bleeding.

Funkmaat Stein, Jäger and Erik twisted and shifted, allowing room for Ramón to recline. Stein splinted the fractured leg with an oar and applied a second compression bandage. With his head lower than his legs, Ramón's mind began to clear. But the pain was becoming more intense.

Stein shook Ramón's shoulder. "*Starke Schmerzen?*"

"Is the pain bad, Ray?" Erik translated.

Ramón nodded.

"*Haben Sie etwas gegeben?*" Stein asked Erik.

"Nicht verstanden," Erik said.

"You gave medicine?" Jäger said.

Erik pantomimed injecting a syrette of morphine.

"Morphium?" Stein said.

Erik nodded.

"Wie viel?"

Erik held up one finger.

"Verstanden," Stein said, selecting a tablet wrapped in brown paper from his medical kit. Ramón saw the word opium printed in capital red letters. Along with a sip of water from his canteen, he swallowed the tablet.

Erik leaned close to Ramón's face. "Hang on, buddy. The Search is probably already on the way."

As the combined effect of morphine and opium kicked in, Ramón closed his eyes and bathed in the warm sense of pain relief. Funkmaat Stein placed a Kriegsmarine blanket over him and retired to the rear of the raft, leaving Erik and Jäger flanking Ramón. Drifting in and out of awareness, Ramón heard snatches of their conversation.

Enemies, suddenly thrown together as survivors, neither man spoke for a long while. Jäger retrieved a package of French cigarettes from his leather jacket, but found nothing in his pockets to light one. When Erik pulled out his Zippo and lit his cigarette, Jäger grudgingly handed him the pack, then leaned back as far as he could in the crowded raft, gazing into the dark sky.

Moonlight danced in and out of the clouds above the Caribbean Sea. In the adjacent raft, a German seaman began playing a melancholic tune on his harmonica. Wie einst. Lili Marlene.

Neither Erik nor Jäger spoke for the next few hours. Then Erik broke the silence. "How many men did you lose?"

"Forty. Only ten left," Jäger said. "And you?"

"Only the pilot and I survived. Thanks for picking us up," Erik said.

Jäger gave a curt nod. "Kein Problem. Also, my Kommandant would do this." He paused. "But he sank with our boat."

Shortly before dawn, Sizzling Rita's shattered cockpit was riding lower in the water. Erik nudged Ramón."Looks like Rita's going down, Ray."

Ramón raised his head enough to see water swirling around the shattered windshield. Then Sizzling Rita was simply gone. "Adios, amor," he whispered.

Jäger looked at Ramón. "Long time with this airplane?"

Ramón only nodded. Erik released a sigh. "A lot of miles."

"I'm with my boat two years," Jäger said.

"How many patrols did you make off our coast?" Erik said.

"Patrouillen?" Jäger said. "Three. Every time, more south."

Ramón perked up. "Where were you last March?"

"Cape Hatteras to Florida Strait."

"Florida," Ramón said, sinking back into the blanket.

Jäger looked puzzled.

"Did you see any Ferris wheels?" Erik asked.

"I don't understand."

Erik groped for the German word. "Ein grosser Kreis," he suggested. A large circle.

Jäger shook his head. "Nicht verstanden."

"*Mit kleine,*" Erik hesitated, then came up with the word. "*Wagen*. With little cars."

"Ach Ja! *Ein Riesenrad,*" Jäger said. "My Kommandant changed course not to shoot into Freizeitpark."

Erik, his brow furrowed, began breaking down the compound German word. *Frei* is free. *Zeit* is time. A free time park. "Amusement park is what we call it." He pointed at Ramón. "He was on that Ferris wheel. Thanks for not shooting him down."

Jäger sat upright and cocked an ear to a subtle rumbling arising in the west. Then, as the sunrise tinted the sky shades of orange and red, a faint silhouette appeared on the horizon. A droning engine transformed into a whine, and finally a rumble, as an A-29 Hudson bomber emerged from a cloud bank, waggling its wings.

"Looks like this war is over for you," Erik said. "Unless you intend to resist, of course."

Jäger half-smiled. "I'm sailor not SS. Better chance to go home alive."

Author's Note

Although based upon actual events of 1942, this history-inspired novel is purely fictional. My intention is to elucidate the desperate Allied struggle that year against German U-boat attempts to sever the vital artery of war supplies to a besieged Great Britain. Additionally, with protagonists on each side of the conflict, I attempt to explore the conscious experiences of enemies in wartime.

German submariners, already at war for two years in the North Atlantic against Great Britain and her allies, were quite skilled at their craft. In 1940 U-boats sank nearly 300 ships in the British Isles. The Germans called it die glückliche Zeit—the happy time. When the British naval and air forces finally resolved enough inter-service conflict to fashion a coordinated anti-submarine warfare (ASW) effort using updated technology and tactics, U-boat losses increased and fewer Allied ships were sunk.

Shortly after the attack on Pearl Harbor in December 1941, five long-range U-boats were dispatched to the east coast of North America with orders to sink any merchant ship they encountered. Emerging reluctantly from a period of isolation after World War I, the United States of America was woefully unprepared for modern warfare. America's small military force lacked modern equipment and had virtually no experience in current ASW techniques. The age-old "turf" battle between the Army and the Navy (seemingly common in all warring nations) also hindered early American efforts to develop a coordinated strategy against the U-boat attacks.

In addition, the behavior of civilian and commercial interests along the East coast during the first half of 1942 is hard to fathom. Shoreline blackout requests were routinely ignored and fully-lit ships travelled up and down the East coast on their usual routes. U-boat captains were incredulous —enemy ships were silhouetted against the shore like ducks in a shooting gallery! It was the second happy time.

The first six months of 1942 were dark for the United States. Imperial Japanese forces ran amok in the Pacific. German forces had swept through Europe to the English Channel. And now U-boats were sinking ships right off the east coast of the homeland. Wartime industry went into high gear. Millions of civilians were inducted into the military. The learning curve for American fighting men against battle-seasoned Axis forces was steep.

I chose a young Mexican-American from Southwest Texas as one of the protagonists in this novel to highlight some of the social problems of America at the time. Although not numerous, there are a number of Mexican-Americans who rose above the marked prejudice and discrimination of the era to achieve high levels of success in the United States military during World War II. As a young man passing through the normal stages of development, in addition to the art of warfare, Ramón is gaining emotional maturity.

In contrast, my German protagonist is an older, career naval officer from a medieval city in northern Germany. After growing up in a cultured household with loving parents, Rainer lives happily with his wife and two children. A sincere patriot and skilled submarine captain, he puts his life on the line for the Fatherland. He is not, however, a Nazi and worries greatly about the safety of his family and the effect of the crudely-evolving social order on his children.

The sequence of events in this novel follows the 1942 patrols of the infamous type IX U-boat known as the U-123 down the east coast of America. The captain of the U-123, Reinhard Hardegen, famous in U-boat lore, has just turned 105 at the time of this writing. I wish to emphasize, despite the use of Hardegen's logbooks and other resource materials regarding the patrols of the U-123, my character Rainer Hartmann and the U-023 (there were no initial zeros in U-boat names) is purely fictional. Any resemblance to Reinhard Hardegen of the U-123 is purely unintended and coincidental.

Finally, I would like to clarify that the actual chronology of important ASW developments in 1942 is not always exactly in synch with the narrative of this work of fiction. For example, although B-25 bombers were used in some ASW tactical groups in 1942, radar was not installed on them until several months later than indicated in this novel.

Several factors seemed to turn things around for the Allies in the Battle of the Atlantic during 1942. First, the rivalry between the army and navy had to be cooled down before effective, coordinated ASW searches could be performed. The next task involved acquiring skill in ASW tactics. Flying about in a blind search for a U-boat that had submerged after a nocturnal surface attack against a merchant ship, proved futile. Resistance to well-intentioned British efforts to impart knowledge gained during their equally-steep learning curve earlier in the war had to be overcome. While Americans usually remained on the scene for only a few hours before returning to base, the British stayed longer, sometimes for days, in a coordinated air-sea search pattern. Finally, and probably most important, came technological advances with the ultimate ASW weapon—radar.

Writing this novel has been a fascinating endeavor. No trained expert in the field, I have relied on many valuable resources listed below. My ultimate desire, as expressed in my website enemyinmirror.com, is to impart to the reader some understanding of America and her enemies in wartime.

Acknowledgments

Since I am neither an historian nor a military expert, my research for this book has relied on many resources in addition to my own extensive web searches and books listed in the bibliography.

Public library staff in Tacoma Washington, Jacksonville Florida, Mérida Yucatán and Lübeck Germany assisted me in review of historical newspaper articles. Institutional assistance was obtained from the Department of the United States Air Force Public Affairs and National Media Outreach Division, the American Radio Relay League and the Musée du Louvre.

Websites and forums that provided significant technical information include: armyairforces.com, axishistory.com, history.army.mil, uboataces.com, uboatarchive.net, uboat.net, warfarehistorynetwork.com, ww2db.com, ww2f.com, ww2talk.com, and several closed groups on Facebook including: German U-boats of WWII, The Battle Of The Atlantic Group and U-boats.

Motion pictures with useful footage of U-Boats include: Das Letzte U Boot, In Enemy Hands, The Enemy Below, U-571 and the gold-standard—Das Boot. Movies with footage of North American B-25 Mitchell bombers include: Catch 22 and Thirty Seconds Over Tokyo.

Individuals who were particularly helpful throughout my research and writing of this book included: Dr. Robert W. Allen, U.S. Army Fort Lewis, Washington historian who provided historical information about the McChord Army Air Field during WWII, Bob and Sherry Denham who researched Imeson Air Field in Jacksonville, Florida and Captain Jerry

Mason and Charles Wendt who provided invaluable technical information regarding the operation of German U-boats.

Museum exhibits I found particularly interesting were at the Evergreen Aviation and Space Museum in McMinnville, Oregon, the Tillamook, Oregon Air Museum and, best of all, touring the actual Type IX submarine U505 at the Museum of Science & Industry in Chicago.

On-site research for this book was carried out in Tacoma Washington, Crystal City Texas, Jacksonville Florida, Veracruz Mexico, Mérida Yucatán, Camagüey Cuba, Hamburg Germany and Lübeck Germany.

This book could not have been accurately written without the extensive technical support of my ever-patient and reliable military consultants: Colonel (ret) Karl Polifka, a former United States Air Force bomber pilot and Lieutenant Commander (ret) Lee Walker, who served in the United States Navy Submarine Division.

I wish to give special recognition to my honored teacher and the editor of an early draft of this book, Jessica Morrell. My transition from academic medical writing into creative literature has been challenging and I thank Ms. Morrell for her help every step of the way. In particular, the editorial feedback I received from my first draft of this book shaped all subsequent drafts.

Individual reviewers who provided me with valuable feedback regarding my early drafts include: John Anderson, Angela Angelini, Tom Engel, Doug Fenton, Margo Glenn, Bob LeRoy, Ted McMahon, Finn Nielsen, Jann Smith and Trevor Smith.

My Hoffman Center writing critique group of Katja Biesanz, Marcia Silver and Kay Stolz have been with me all the way in this endeavor. Their in-depth critical reviews of my ongoing drafts have been outstanding and I am grateful for their astute support.

Valuable assistance with the cover design and illustrations was provided by Daisha Kissel of elementsofevolution.com and Steven Cannoodt of stevencannoodt.com.

To my wife of 34 years Holly, I can only say ~ Without you, this book would have been a mere shadow of itself. Your perceptiveness, intuition and ability to understand the characters and see the big picture has opened new avenues of creativity for me. Gracias, mi amor.

Selected Bibliography

Ayçoberry, Pierre. The Social History of the Third Reich - 1933-1945. New York: The New Press, 1999.

Bessel, Richard. Life in the Third Reich. New York: Oxford University Press, 1986.

Blair, Clair. Hitler's U-Boat War-The Hunters : 1939-1942. New York: Random House, 1996.

Buderi, Robert. The Invention that Changed the World (radar). New York: Simon & Schuster, 1996.

Cooke, Alistair. The American Home Front: 1941-42. New York: Atlantic Monthly Press, 2006.

Jonathan Dimbleby. The Battle of the Atlantic. Oxford: University Press, 2016.

Dönitz, Karl. Memoirs—Ten Years and Twenty Days (English translation). London: Greenville Books, 1990.

Gannon, Michael. Operation Drumbeat. Annapolis: Naval Institute Press, 1990.

Grover, Roy.L. Incidents in the Life of a B-25 Pilot. Bloomington: Author House, 2006.

Erenberg Lewis A. and Hirsch, Susan E. The War in American Culture. Chicago: University of Chicago Press, 1996.

Higham, Robin. Flying American Combat Aircraft of WWII. Mechanicsburg: Stackpole Books, 2004.

Offley, Ed. The Burning Shore. New York: Basic Books, 2014.

Orozco, Cynthia E. No Mexicans, Women or Dogs Allowed. Austin: University of Texas Press, 2009.

Pine, Lisa. Life and Times in Nazi Germany. New York: Bloomsbury Academic, 2016.

Rivas-Rodriguez, Maggie. Mexican Americans and World War
II.   Austin: University of Texas Press, 2005.

Stargardt, Nicholas. The German War.
New York: Basic Books, 2015.

U.S. Army Air Force. B-25 Mitchell Bomber Pilot's Flight
Operating Instructions.   Dayton: The Otterbein Press,
1944.

About the author

After a satisfying career in academic medicine, I moved to the Oregon coast to write historical fiction aimed at understanding America and her enemies during wartime. My first novel Enemy in the Mirror: Love and Fury in the Pacific War was inspired by Japanese submarine attacks on the Oregon coast during World War Two. Told from the points of view of Japanese and American protagonists, the novel relates the tragic consequences of war in the Pacific and its effect on the home fronts of America and Imperial Japan. With completion of this current novel about the Battle of the Atlantic off America's shores in 1942, I have begun research in preparation for my next novel which will take place during the Korean War. My website about understanding America and her enemies in wartime can be found at enemyinmirror.com

Made in the USA
Columbia, SC
20 August 2018